GUNMAN'S PASS

GUNMAN'S PASS

RALPH COTTON

THORNDIKE PRESS
A part of Gale, a Cengage Company

LIBRARY OF CONGRESS CIP DATA ON FILE.
CATALOGUING IN PUBLICATION FOR THIS BOOK
IS AVAILABLE FROM THE LIBRARY OF CONGRESS.

ISBN-13: 978-1-4328-9967-7 (hardcover alk. paper)

Published in 2022 by arrangement with Berkley, an imprint of Penguin Publishing Group, a division of Penguin Random House, LLC.

Printed in Mexico
Print Number : 1   Print Year : 2022

For Mary Lynn, of course

PART 1

PART 1

CHAPTER 1

Eagles, Indian Territory

The horse trader Will Summers straightened only slightly at the bar when two shotgun-wielding lawmen walked in through the batwing doors. One of them called out his name. These two were about the same height, and both of them, Summers noted, were tall, big-boned, wide across the shoulders.

"We're looking for Summers! Will Summers!" the one on his left called out.

Summers raised his face an inch and looked at them by way of reflection in the smoke-stained mirror on the wall behind the bar. They were also dressed in similar fashion, whether by coincidence or design. Each wore tall faded black hats with dusty bandannas around their necks, one black, one red. Each wore a long faded black duster, the bottom edge of which reached down past their scuffed boot tops. They

9

wore U.S. federal deputy marshal badges on black vests, partially hidden by their dusters. *Judge Parker's deputies out of Fort Smith,* Summers decided right away.

He saw no tension in how they held their shotguns, not tight, just firm and ready. In the mirror he could see they were staring straight at him when the one started to say his name again.

"I'm Will Summers," Summers cut in, calmly. "Who's looking for me?" He turned quarter-wise to face them across the near-empty saloon. He let them see him look them up and down, taking close note of their shotguns.

"I'm Federal Deputy Claude Parks," said the one wearing the black bandanna. He turned a thumb toward the man beside him wearing the red bandanna. "This is Deputy Hughes."

"*Edmond* Hughes," the other man added in a corrective tone.

Under the circumstances, Summers saw nothing out of the ordinary in laying his hand on his Winchester lying across the bar top. His other hand drifted easily to the tied-down Colt standing holstered on his hip.

"Deputies," he said with a nod, "*why* are you looking for me?"

"We've got the outlaw Dolan Coyle in chains outside," Parks said. "You've heard of Dolan Coyle?"

"I have," said Summers. Not only had he heard of Dolan Coyle, he knew him. Maybe he wouldn't mention knowing him right now. Maybe he shouldn't mention it at all. He'd wait and see.

"We captured him and killed some of his gang yesterday down near Brayton Siding —"

"The rest of his saddle tramps have been dogging us ever since," Hughes cut in. "Sniping at us every chance they get, trying to get us to give him up."

"Are you going to do the talking now, Deputy?" Parks asked Hughes in a brassy tone.

"No," said Hughes, "I'm just saying —"

Parks gave him a look that shut him up. To Summers, Parks said, "You might have heard, Coyle's gang sprung him from Hangman's Row in Fort Smith near two weeks ago."

Summers just stared at the two, but he let his hand move away from his rifle.

"I heard," he said. He was ready to ask what any of it had to do with why they were looking for him, but he decided to wait. It would come.

11

"He's gone hog wild ever since," said Parks. "Killed and robbed his way all through Indian Territory. Some bandidos and Indian lawmen finally banded together and run him and his bunch off." He gestured at Hughes and nodded toward the posse men outside. "We're Judge Isaac Parker's federal posse from Fort Smith, sent out to bring Coyle in. And, by thunder, we've got him."

"Good work," Summers said, watching, listening.

"Yeah. We trimmed his gang down, too. Trouble is," Parks continued, "we've lost four good men ourselves. Mostly to his brother, Axel. He's a killing *dog.* Said he'll keep killing till we let Dolan go." He stopped and looked closely at Summers.

Summers gave him a questioning gaze.

"Truth is," Parks said, "I've found myself about half-willing to shuck the whole deal, shoot Dolan in the head and send him to his brother strapped over his saddle."

Okay, that's enough, Summers thought.

"*Why* is it you're looking for *me*?" he asked again.

"Like I said," Parks went on, "we've lost four men to these bastards. I'm short on men, and our horses are worn out." As he spoke, he and Hughes each held a batwing door open for Summers to look outside. "I was told by a fella back there that you're a horse trader. That you can help us out with some fresh horses."

"I am a horse trader," Summers said. "I run the town corral, and I have a few horses . . ." He saw a line of exhausted horses, their muzzles stuck into a water trough beside the hitch rail. Posse men had lifted hats full of water from the trough, poured most of it on their heads and gulped the rest. "Looks like you need more than horses."

Parks fell silent for a moment as Summers took in the bloody, bandaged, battered men and their half-dead horses.

"It's a fact we're beat to hell. We need to lay up and rest, get back in fighting shape." In a lowered voice, he continued, "In case you're wondering I've got a half-dozen more men out there, scouting, keeping an eye on us, but if I don't get us some help, real quick, these sonsabitches dogging our trail are going to kill us every damned one."

Summers saw the town doctor hurrying along from across the dirt street toward the wounded posse men, while onlookers gathered from every direction.

"Let's get these horses over to the corral while the doctor looks at your men," he said to both deputies. "We'll get them fed and watered, then swap them out for you. Coyle's gang won't try hitting this town."

"Not with you here, they won't," said Parks. "I know your reputation. I need to tell you, Summers," he added, "I'm authorized to pay thirty dollars to any men who'll serve on this posse until we escort Dolan Coyle into federal custody. Are you interested?"

"No! Not at all," said Summers.

"I heard you do some bounty work," Parks said. "Did I hear wrong?"

"You didn't hear wrong, but you heard about two years too late," said Summers. "I'm not in that line of work any longer. I'm strictly in the horse business."

"I hate asking for help," Parks said. "But I have no choice. I'll go as high as fifty dollars."

"I can't help you," Summers said. "But as soon as we get your men and horses taken care of, I'll spread the word you're looking for posse men. If you need to stay here a couple of days, the men of this town will keep the Coyles out while your men rest and heal up some."

"Fair enough. My scouts will be helping, too," said Parks, realizing this was all he was going to get from Summers.

14

Parks gestured for Summers to follow him and Hughes as they turned and walked out through the batwing doors. Summers stepped over and picked up his rifle from atop the bar. Before following the two deputies he gave an undetectable nod at the door behind the bar, which led into the darkened stockroom. On the other side of the door, his young Cherokee business partner, Johnny Two Red Wolves, watched through a door crack.

On the dusty boardwalk lay Dolan Coyle, flat on his back, his arms stretched out above his head, his cuffed hands relaxed, a foot of chain between them. He'd given a crooked battered little smile to the two passing deputies, now another one to Summers.

"*Hola,* horse trader," he said with a dry chuckle as Summers passed by. Summers only glanced down and kept moving along.

"You boys know what I'd love right now?" Coyle said in a rasping voice. "I'd love a big piece of *sweet cherry pie. Lord,* how I surely would!"

"Why don't you *die*! You lousy son of a — !" A dusty boot reached out and gave Coyle a hard sharp jab. Coyle grunted, then gave a dry, crazy cackling laugh.

"Leave the fool alone, Hank," another

15

posse man said. "You know he's just tormenting you!"

"Yeah, *Hank,*" Coyle said in a strained voice. "Try to be a *sport.* Who knows, you might be begging me to kill you one of these days. Can I get some water now?"

"Keep it up," a posse man named Dowd said. "You won't live long enough to —"

"Shut up, Dowd!" Parks snapped. To the townsmen who stood watching, he said, "A couple of you men watch the trail coming in. We might be getting company anytime." Two local men moved away toward their horses. They looked at Summers, who gave them a nod of approval.

"Yeah, shut the hell up, Dowd," said Coyle. "Get me some water!"

"One of you get the prisoner some water," Parks said, turning away.

Summers noted that the outlaw hadn't addressed him by name, only as *horse trader,* which anybody in or around this part of the territory might do.

Good, he thought, catching up with the two deputies. This wasn't the time to have to stop and explain anything about him knowing Dolan Coyle, or Coyle knowing him. If he knew any of the men riding with Dolan Coyle, and he was certain he did — maybe even *all* of them — they would

16

already know what this posse needed most here in Eagles. They needed rest and they needed horses. He had ten horses here in the public corral, and his personal buckskin, Moby, stood in a stall behind the barn.

"Here's my stock, deputies," he said, the three of them stopping half in, half out of the open barn door. "All ten of them. The two cream-colored mares over by the far rail belong to a fella named Lowes Bratcher. He bought them to breed, but he might let them go."

"We'll leave our wounded men here when we leave," said Parks, ignoring the two mares. "That makes six men, counting us, unless you change your mind and go. I've also got five scouts up there already —"

"No," said Summers. "I'm still not interested." To change the subject, he mentioned Lowes Bratcher's two mares again.

"To hell with breeding mares," said Hughes, looking back through the barn to where Summers' big dapple buckskin stood watching across rows of empty stalls. "What about that one back there staring a hole through us?"

"That's *my* horse," Summers said. "He wouldn't be the best on a hard ride. He's more of a town horse. He gets me around, on weekend ride-arounds mostly."

"Yeah, I bet," Parks said, knowing the practice of a shrewd horse trader to downplay his best horse and keep it for himself. He eyed Summers, then said, "All right. I'll take all ten of these after we check them over good."

"Take your time. Check all you want," said Summers. He glanced around the rolling hillsides, cliffs and sparse woodlands in distant sight. "But let's round these cayuses into the barn while you look them over."

"You think Coyle's men won't launch an attack, but they will lay out there and shoot anything that moves on the street?" said Hughes.

"Unless you tell me why they *won't,* I'm going to figure they *will,*" said Summers. "I've got extra stalls. Use them until you're ready to ride out. No charge," he added.

"That's being a little too cautious for my style," Hughes said.

Before Summers could answer, Parks cut in.

"Let's get them all indoors," he said. "Breeding mares, too. If Coyle's men start shooting, their bullets won't know brood mares from geldings. We don't want to get the man's breeding mares shot." He looked closely at Summers. "I'll check all ten over myself, quick-like. If anything shows up

18

wrong on them along the trail, I expect you'll take them back?"

"No!" Summers shook his head, figuring the deputy was just testing him.

"Why not?" Parks asked.

"I saw how bad your horses look." Summers nodded in the direction of the hitch rail out front of the saloon. "Not blaming you, knowing how tough it can get on a manhunt. But these horses are leaving here as is. Cash today."

"What about the horses we're swapping?" Parks asked.

"Leave them here," Summers said. "I'll feed them, water and rest them. If they recover, I'll make an offer on them." He nodded at the ten horses walking toward the open barn door, a young man in buckskin guiding them with a rifle in his hand.

"Same with these ten," Summers added. "Bring them back worth saving, and I'll give you the same deal. Right now, I want thirty-five dollars a head, three hundred and fifty dollars — all cash in hand before you leave with them."

"Done," said Parks as the horses began filing past him into the barn. A young Cherokee walked behind them, guiding them in with his hands spread.

"Just one minute!" Hughes said, looking

confused by everything that had just been said.

"Don't start talking now, Deputy Hughes," Parks said in a firm tone. "We're done here."

Hughes fell silent.

Summers saw how both deputies had given the young Cherokee in buckskins a curious look.

"Deputies Parks and Hughes," Summers said, "meet Johnny Two Red Wolves. Johnny Two is my business partner. Any questions about these horses, ask him.

"Johnny Two," he said to the young man, "meet Deputy Claude Parks and Deputy Edmond Hughes."

Johnny Two Red Wolves nodded respectfully.

"Pleased to meet you," he said in clear reservation-school English. The two lawmen returned his nod with equal respect.

Summers stood and watched as Johnny Two and the deputies walked the horses to a place inside the barn where the afternoon sunlight slanted in across the straw-covered floor. As Parks quickly began checking the horses, Summers thought about what Dolan Coyle had said on the boardwalk moments ago, about sweet cherry pie.

What was that? Had Coyle come up with

it out of the blue? Yeah, maybe. But Summers couldn't let it go. It kept coming back to him. He'd never known Dolan Coyle to spout off something like that for no reason. Was it Coyle's way of letting him know he recognized him, but wasn't going to mention it for the posse and the two deputies to hear? Well, he had nothing to be ashamed of. He was no outlaw. He might have started out a wild kid, but he'd become an upright businessman.

He and Dolan Coyle had never had any trouble between them. They had not been the best of friends, nor had they been enemies. Okay, Coyle had chosen a wild reckless outlaw trail for himself, the same as Summers and many others had done in their early years. Summers could not say exactly what had directed him off that sharp fast trail before it managed to get too deep and settle into his blood. Whatever it was that saved him, he was grateful.

Obliged, he found himself thinking, to nothing or no one in particular.

Now, out of a clear blue sky came someone he'd known from his dark lawless days. Dolan Coyle, a captured outlaw, a killer and thief headed for Fort Smith to hang, like as not. If his gang didn't stop it.

What had Dolan meant, lying there on the

21

dusty boardwalk in the footsteps of thousands of others? *I'd love a big piece of sweet cherry pie.*

Turning in the open barn door while the deputies and Johnny Two Red Wolves inspected the horses, Will gazed out into the distance, to the line of low hills mantled by that same perfect, clear blue sky. *Sweet cherry pie,* Summers heard him say again. But this time, he heard Coyle's words end as a rope snapped taut, followed by the gasp of a crowd and the creaking sound that followed.

Wouldn't we all, Dolan Coyle, he said to that wide-open sky.

Moments later, finished with the deputies and checking the horses, Johnny Two walked to the front barn door and stood beside Summers, looking out at the now-empty corral. Beyond the barn, they both saw that the main street lay empty.

"Looks like word made its way around town real quick," said Johnny Two. He took out a short cigar from a pocket tin and offered Summers one. They both lit up and stood checking out the empty street. An aging saloon dove named Silk Polly ran from a small weather-beaten clapboard hotel to the saloon, a colorful scarf raised and spread

22

with both hands above her head.

Johnny Two smiled behind a puff of smoke.

"Does Polly think waving a frilly scarf like that will stop a rifle bullet?" he asked Summers, sidelong.

Summers chuffed and shook his head a little.

"Who knows what Silk Polly thinks," he said quietly. Changing the subject, he said, "Parks has a few scouts out along the back trails already. I might take a couple of townsmen and scout out ahead of them, make sure the back trail looks clear."

"You're going out the back trail, down across Little Springs?" asked Johnny Two. "Who are you taking with you?"

"I figure on asking Yancy Reed and Scotty," said Summers.

"That's my plan, why?" he continued.

"Just wondering," said Johnny Two. "It'll likely be dark before you get under way. There's a quarter moon on the wane tonight — likely some cloud cover. If everybody here keeps their lights off, Coyle's gunmen will have nothing to shoot at." He drew on his cigar and let out a puff.

"Why are you quoting me the weather?" said Summers.

"So you'll know I'm up to the job, taking

them out the back way," Johnny Two said, studying a low encroaching sky.

"I know you're up to it," Summers said. "But if something comes up, one of us ought to be here."

"But it doesn't have to be you," Johnny Two said. "I know every inch of the back trail out of here, even a couple of cutoffs I've never mentioned."

Summers looked at him, considering. There was no way to refuse without it looking as if his confidence in Johnny Two might be less than it should be. He had to admit, the young man was levelheaded, smart, and his trail savvy was as keen and sharp as anyone Summers knew. *So, what's your objection?* he asked himself. He took a resolving breath.

None, he decided. None at all. The longer it took him to answer, the more he knew it looked like he was stalling.

"All right, Johnny," he said. "You want to be up most of the night, go ahead. I'll take a look at these posse horses after they've settled in here awhile, maybe give them some extra hay, check their hooves."

"All right." Johnny Two nodded. "I'll go round up Reed and Scotty and tell them to bring their bedrolls." Before hurrying away, he stopped and said, "Obliged, Will. I'll

24

come tell you when the three of us leave."

"Be sure you do," said Summers. He nodded and touched his hat brim, then watched Johnny Two walk away in the declining evening light.

From the livery barn, Parks came up, wiping his hands on a wrinkled bandanna.

"I hate second-guessing myself," Parks said, "but I wonder if I should go ahead and get some fresh horses for my scouts, too, while I'm at it." He took a fold of cash from his shirt pocket and tapped it on his palm while he contemplated the idea.

"From *where*?" Summers asked.

Parks gave him a curious look.

"Fresh horses *from where*?" Summers repeated. "You've bought all my trading stock. I haven't heard of anybody wanting to sell their horses. If there were I'd have already bought them."

"Oh yes, I see," Parks said. "I was just speculating out loud." He handed Summers the money. Summers counted it at a glance, folded it and pocketed it. Parks smiled. "I must have been thinking that being a trader, maybe you had held back some horses, waiting for a better price, later on?"

Summers' first thought was not to even answer such a question, with men's lives on the line. But finally, he did.

25

"No, Deputy Parks," he said. "I brought out everything I have. If there were more around here for sale, I would have already told you about them. Your posse men and my townsmen's lives are more important than a few dollars I would make *holding back.*"

"Yes, of course," Parks said. "I didn't mean to imply otherwise. No offense, Will Summers!" He extended a hand, as if a handshake was the instant remedy for bad manners. Summers ignored the offered hand and looked off along Eagles' main street.

"It'll be dark in another half hour," he said quietly. "If your scouts haven't watered their horses already, there's two creeks around here. Or, if they want to ride in and feed themselves and their animals, they're free to do that, too."

"Much obliged, Summers," Parks said. "I know they'll appreciate coming in, eating, feeding their cayuses."

Summers looked at him as if in second thought.

"Let me ask you, Deputy," he said. "These extra *scouts* you hired. Are you paying them more than posse wages, like you intended to pay me?"

"Ordinarily I don't say what I pay other

posse men, but in this case, yes, I am paying them a little more —"

"These are all good men, out of Fort Smith?" Summers asked.

"Four of them are," Parks said. "Two of them I hired along the way. But the other four said they knew them, vouched for them and so forth."

"But you had no time to check them for yourself?" Summers asked.

"No time at all," said Parks. "I figured I was lucky they came along when they did."

"I see," said Summers, careful not to reveal any doubts he might be considering.

"Why do you ask, Summers?" said Parks. "Have I raised suspicion about how I came to hire my men?"

"No, Deputy," said Summers. "But it never hurts to look at every hand on the table."

"I couldn't agree more," Parks said. "I admit I hired them on the fly. But the fact is, how many men want to hire their gun out against the Coyle brothers? We both know that gunfighters can be an ornery, shiftless bunch anyway."

"I understand," Summers said. "Send one of your men out and bring your scouts in. Let everybody know to watch for my friend Johnny Two and a couple of townsmen I

27

sent out to scout the back trails."

Parks gave him a troubled look. "Is something wrong, Summers?" he asked.

Summers kept his suspicions in check. "Your scouts are hungry and their horses are tired. Bring them in. Get them fed and rested. We've plenty of guns out there watching for the Coyles. We don't want so many of our men out there, they start shooting each other."

"I should say not," said Parks. "I'll send a rider right away."

Summers watched him walk away toward the doctor's office in the purple evening light.

Good thinking, he told himself, letting out a breath of relief. He had no idea who Parks' new scouts were, or where they'd come from. Now that he'd talked to Deputy Parks, he realized Parks didn't know, either.

CHAPTER 2

Seven of Dolan Coyle's crack riflemen lay spread out in an uneven line of cutbank and low rock shelves mantling a dry creek bed a half mile west of Eagles. They had lain there most of the afternoon. More men had spread out farther back away from town. These seven were the ones with rifles and reputations best suited for *long* shooting.

Earlier that day, Axel Coyle, leading his brother's gang, had swung the outlaws wide of Eagles when they saw the posse headed there with his brother, Dolan, hatless, cuffed and beaten half to hell.

"We've got them in a fix," Axel had said to Prince Drako, the two of them forcing their horses down onto their sides in the thin shade of an ancient live oak. "Give them a chance to settle down. Come nightfall we'll shoot the living hell out of them."

"Ready when you are, Axel," Prince Drako replied, patting his downed horse on its damp neck. "Can't be soon enough to suit me."

"I told you, *come nightfall,* damn it," said Axel Coyle, sounding touchy. "We still got some waiting to do."

Sparse broken shade slanted down through the twisted boughs and branches of the huge but nearly leafless live oak. On its side, the horse had managed to shift its head around on the ground enough to get its right eye into a strip of shade.

"That's all I've got for you, Chico," Drako said quietly between the two of them. "Here, pal." He held out his hat and dropped it back down lightly over his horse's eyes.

They had flanked the little town and slipped in, one and two at a time. They had taken positions while the blazing morning sun rode higher and hotter in the sky. By midafternoon the land lay baking, veiled in a harsh glare of wavering white sunlight. A Kansas gunman named Eddie Moon had scouted forward and found a small ranch two miles farther up along a hill trail. When he returned and told Axel about it, Axel grinned.

"Good work, Moon," he crowed. To Prince Drako he said, "Have the men go up there in turns, get the horses watered and come on back here. We've got a busy night ahead of us."

In afterthought, Axel called out to Eddie Moon.

"Moon, what have they got walking around there fit to butcher?"

Eddie Moon, who had already started walking in a crouch downhill to where he'd left his horse standing below the line of vision, stopped and gave a shrug.

"I only saw from a tree line. But it looked like lots of chickens, ducks and such. They're not hurting," he called back to Axel Coyle. "There's a mud pond there. I'd say lots of frogs. Maybe a turtle or two."

"Damn it!" Axel made an ugly face. "I mean *real food,*" he said. He spit on the ground. "Damn a bunch of chickens, ducks, frogs and turtles! I'd sooner eat a live rattlesnake!"

"They've got some milk goats running loose," Moon said. "I saw a young steer whose hindquarters would look good turning over a fire nice and slow."

"Take a few men with you," said Axel. "Ask about the steer, but don't push for it. Show them some gold coin. Tell them to roast us up a hundred dollars' worth of duck, goat and whatever else is walking around and not coughing its head off. Tell

31

them we'll pay something extra for any kind of alcohol! I'm talking *any kind* at all!"

Prince Drako laughed.

"If we have to, we'll put the town of Eagles in a siege situation. I don't plan on going hungry, here or nowheres else," he said. "Ain't that right, Drako?"

"Right as rain," said Prince Drako. "My money's on these deputies making a run of it. We've beat the blue living hell out of them!"

"All right," said Axel. "If they make a run for it again, we'll chase them down *again,* but this time we'll do it with a full belly under us." As he spoke, he raised a dusty telescope to his eye, one hand rubbing his horse's neck, keeping it settled where it lay on the ground beside him.

"What do you know about Eagles," Prince Drako asked, watching him scan the small town in the distance, "and this horse trader Summers?"

Axel gave a little smile without lowering his long telescope. "One thing at a time, Prince," he said. "Has this Summers jake got you nervous?"

"Ain't no jake ever had me nervous," said Drako. "I just like to know what's going on around me. Who to shoot, who not to shoot, things like that."

Seeing through his telescope that the posse's horses had been led away and the wounded posse men carried off the boardwalk, Axel lowered the lens and rubbed his eye.

"Summers is known as a man you'd best not crowd," he said to Drako.

"You're saying he's a killer?" said Prince Drako.

Axel looked at him squint-eyed.

"Yes! I would say that he's a killer!" he said. "Him and Dolan rode with the same bunch for a while, even rode just the two of them a couple of times, robbing some stagecoaches. He's one of them boys came back from the war with a mad-on that took him a while to get rid of. Living on the trail made him faster than a rattlesnake with a gun. He learned horse trading right along, from his pa and his grandpa. He's known to be good at it. Same as they were." He raised a hand. "That's all I can tell you about the man."

"A killer," said Drako.

Axel just stared at him.

"Faster than a rattlesnake," said Prince Drako. He spit and looked out through a shroud of wavering deep afternoon heat.

"Just to be clear, Drako," Axel said with a twist of sarcasm, "he is a killer, and he is

33

faster than a rattlesnake, gun-wise, that is to say." He eyed Prince Drako closely. "Does that sate your curiosity?" he asked.

"I don't need sating," said Drako. "My curiosity is my business. Every time I turn around, I find I might have to shoot a sumbitch, so I like to know what I can about a sumbitch I might have to shoot."

"What makes you think you'll be called upon to shoot Summers?" Axel asked.

"Just a feeling I got riding in here," Prince Drako said.

"I hope I've helped to set your feeling straight," Axel said, and grinned. "Anything else I can tell you?"

Prince Drako thought about it.

"Yeah. What's a heavy shooter like Summers doing in a pissant of a town like Eagles?" he asked.

"I hear it's home for Summers," said Axel Coyle. "Eagles just happens to be the closest place these deputies could run to. Their horses are spent to death."

"You ask me, Eagles is a pissant of a town," said Prince Drako.

"Yeah, I heard you the first time," said Axel. "That's my thoughts on the place, too. Eagles started as a rail workers' depot, back in the Indian Wars," he continued. "Used it for tools, equipment and such while they built a rail spur from Brayton Siding to here. It served supplies to Fort Glory till Geronimo's bunch burnt the fort to the ground."

"Fort Glory, *burnt to the ground,*" Prince Drako mimicked. He gave a dark chuckle.

"Yep," said Axel, not sharing the humor of it. "Eagles dried up and staggered along near dead for the longest time. Will Summers started bringing good horses here, half a dozen at a time, resting them, feeding them good, watering them. Then he'd take them on the Brayton Siding. Sell them to the army, maybe take in a trade or two. Word got around that he had good horses priced fairly. Folks come from all around."

"So, the deputies figured it a good place to get fresh horses," Drako put it. He looked back and forth in the distance, at the small town and not much else in either direction. He shook his head.

"*Eagles,* huh?" he grumbled. "Pissant, I say."

Axel considered it, and said, "Army named everything out this way after their war generals. They mighta run out of generals and had to name it something else. So, Eagles it was?" Again, a shrug. "And Eagles it is," he added. "Hell, I don't know. I'm just what they call, conjecturing."

"You're what?" said Drako.

"I'm *guessing, damn it!*" said Axel Coyle. "Look around you, Prince," he said. "There ain't fifty people living in a fifty-mile circle of this town. So, why'd they name the place Eagles? I'm damned if I know! Had you been here to teach them better they might have called it Pissant."

"It would be more fitting if they had," Prince Drako said. The two looked off through the wavering evening heat. After a moment Drako said, "So, you're saying folks come here now because they are so fond of swapping horses with this Summers *jake?*"

"Listen to me, Prince Drako!" said Axel. A sudden hardness set into his eyes. "You don't want to make light of what I say. The *posse* came here needing horses! We came here dogging them, so's to kill them! We don't know who the hell else might show up next, now *do we*? I mean, *gawl-damn it!* Do we?"

Prince Drako saw he'd gone as far as Axel's temper would allow. For his own safety he said, "No, we don't." He gazed off again at the small town as Axel spit and raised the telescope back up to his eye.

Zetra Wilson watched from her kitchen window as the five horsemen appeared into

36

sight. They set their horses forty yards away and stared toward the house from the edge of a sloping oak-covered hillside. She looked down at the older children she'd trusted to churning butter from goat milk.

"Little Bob," she said, "take Baby Greta and go back to the creek and get your sister and brothers."

"What about this butter, ma'am?" eight-year-old Little Bob asked.

"Quickly now," the woman said, seeing the four hounds racing across the front yard, growling, their hackles up. "Tell them I said to get on back here, but stay out of sight till it's dark out."

As Little Bob and his toddler sister, Baby Greta, hurried out the back door, Zetra yanked her apron off, grabbed her slouch hat from a peg and the long ten-gauge goose gun from its spot beside the front door. Checking the gun as she hurried out, she jumped atop the mule standing asleep at a hitch pole, and hammered her bare heels to its sides. Caught by sudden surprise, the shaken animal bucked once, high and wild-eyed. He hollered out like he'd been stung by a hornet and ran braying loudly toward the horsemen. The woman held on, gathered the mule beneath her and raced on. She saw one of the riders point a gun at the threatening hounds.

"Shoot one of my dogs, I'll cut you in half, *mister!*" Zetra shouted above the barking, growling, threatening hounds, raising the goose gun one-handed, already cocked.

"The hell's this?" said Eddie Moon to the four other gunmen who had gathered closer together facing the hounds' imminent assault. He saw that two of his men had drawn their holstered sidearms and held them aimed at the four hounds.

"Put your guns away, Cruz, Yates!" he shouted. "If she lets go with that goose gun, they'll be picking you out of the trees the next *six months!*"

"I'll not be eaten alive, *gawl-damn it!*" shouted Arvin Yates. "Call these dogs off, *woman!*"

"Holster your irons, both of you!" Eddie Moon shouted at Yates and Cruz. In a more even tone he called out to the woman above the hounds, "Ma'am, I'm obliged if you'll call these dogs back! They're spooking the horses."

The woman called out *"Neeche kutte"* in native Cherokee, and the hounds fell silent instantly.

Eddie Moon and his four gunmen looked amazed.

"I'll be an ass-kicked ape," Yates said

38

under his breath.

"What's your business here?" the woman asked Moon, as the hounds circled slowly and settled even more. One sat down and scratched himself on the neck.

"Ma'am," said Eddie Moon, "I'm going to be as honest as I know how to be."

The woman gave him a suspicious look.

"We're rail hands," JW Bendigo put in.

Eddie Moon gave Bendigo a sharp look.

"Ma'am, my pal here is telling you a black lie," said Eddie Moon. "What we are is, we are outlaws on the run. There, I said it, and that's the truth of it. There is a posse and two of hanging Judge Parker's federal deputies over there in Eagles right now. They are fitting up and getting fresh horses, so's they can come after us and kill us every one, or take us to Fort Smith and hang us till our eyes squirt out. Picture our poor mothers' faces when they hear what become of us!"

"I have never thought highly of Judge Parker," the woman said. "Lots of folks around here feel the same way." She let the long ten-gauge goose gun slump in her hand. "What is it you come looking for?"

"We are in sore need of food and drink," said Eddie Moon.

"We don't have much," the woman said. "Just enough to keep our five little ones from starvation. If we had it, we're the kind who helps anybody —"

"Ma'am," said Eddie Moon, cutting in, "begging your pardon." He didn't want to tell her he had been by there earlier and saw what they had, the young steer, the goats. "We are in sore need, and we have money to pay for whatever you're willing to sell us."

"Well, all right, then," the woman said. "In that case, how many are there of you, and what does everybody like to eat?"

"There are some twenty-three of us, ma'am." Eddie Moon grinned. It was only a guess. He had no clear idea. "Can I impose on you to fix us up a hundred dollars' worth of goat, beef, duck and chicken, or anything else you feel like cooking up?"

"You sure can!" the woman said.

"Is that a young steer I see up in the corral?" he asked, craning his neck to get a better look.

"Yes, and it's all yours if you fellows want it," said the woman. "I'll get it dressed out and skewered over a fire." She smiled. "By the way, we are the Wilsons. My husband is Reuben Stallard Wilson and I'm Mrs. Zetra Hattamire Wilson. My husband is on his way home from some business affairs. I

40

don't know how long he's apt to be. But my young ones and I are going to fix you outlaw boys some food fit for kings —"

"God bless you, Mrs. Wilson!" Moon said, cutting her off. "And if you'd be so kind, some of us are in sore need of *medicinal* alcohol, should you happen to have any on hand."

"No, we have no *medicinal* alcohol," she said, "but we do have a few gallons of copper kettle sipping whiskey we made last year, if that would help any?"

"A few *gallons*?" said Moon. He slipped a look around to the others and grinned.

"Yes," she said. "A dozen or so, I think. My husband's people are Tennesseans. They make whiskey that he says will melt your belt buckle."

"Yes! That would help us more than you could know," Moon said. He looked around at the others again. "Says her husband cooks whiskey that will melt your belt buckle."

"We heard her!" said Dan Hurley. "If it's going to take a little while cooking, maybe we could trouble Mrs. Wilson for some of that belt buckle–melting whiskey whilst we wait?"

41

CHAPTER 3

In the Eagles jail office, Summers found
Deputy Hughes sitting at a battered oaken
desk cleaning one of the repeating rifles he'd
taken down from a wall rack. He glanced
up as Summers walked in and closed the
door behind himself.

"Evening, Will Summers," said Hughes,
working in the light of an oil lantern standing on the corner of the desk. "Just trying
to make something of this mess here." He
motioned a hand around the dusty cluttered
jail.

Without asking permission, Summers
stepped over to the front window, closed
the wooden shutters and latched them in
place. He slid a wooden cover plate over
two cross-shaped gunports facing out on
the street. He stepped over to the desk and
trimmed the lantern down to a pale shadowy glow. Hughes watched in silence for a
moment.

"Not that it happens to matter to you," he said to Summers, "but I'm using this lantern to see what I'm doing here." He started to reach out and turn the lantern back up, but Summers gave him a look that stopped him.

"Maybe nobody told you, Deputy," Summers said low and even, "but we've got all the lights off in town tonight, to keep the Coyles from sniping at us from out there."

"Dang it," Hughes sighed, embarrassed. "I was told, I just plumb forgot." He stood up as he spoke and leaned on his palms atop the desk. "The place is such a mess, I just —" He stopped and revised his excuse down to saying, "It won't happen again, I promise you."

"Obliged, Deputy," said Summers. "You've got five men out there coming in, and I've got three. We don't want them riding into a barrage of rifle fire because we failed to protect them."

"No, we for sure don't," said Hughes.

"This jail gets overlooked sometimes, because we have no sheriff and there's no ordinances here to speak of," Summers offered.

"No law in Eagles," Hughes said. "You can bet there's cities and towns all over this nation who envy a town with no law to speak of."

43

Summers corrected him. "Not a town with no laws," he said, "a town with no *need* for laws. Everybody living here knows what Eagles expects of them, so they all walk straight and like they've got some sense."

From the large single cell came a peal of laughter. Summers and Hughes looked around as Dolan Coyle stood up, wiped his long hair back from his eyes and wrapped both hands around the bars.

"Ain't this place just a sweet ripe plum on the road to paradise," he said, the laughter falling away. In the grainy darkness, he appeared as some dark apparition spewed up from a bottomless pit.

He looked Summers up and down in the dim light.

"So, you are what Will Summers turned out to be," he said with a dark grin. "Your shirt looks clean and pressed, I'll give you that." He stared at Summers.

Summers stared right back.

"You would not believe the rotten *sonofabitch* I've heard you are, Sheriff."

"I'm not a sheriff," said Summers.

"And you watch your mouth, Coyle!" Hughes warned. "I'll cuff you to the bars in there and let him take you apart and put you back together all wrong!" He looked at Summers. "I've got a hickory head-buster under the desk. Let me get the keys. You take all the time you need to —"

"Stay where you are, Deputy," said Summers, keeping Hughes from standing up. "The man is locked up, waiting to go back to Fort Smith and hang. Leave him be." He looked at Dolan Coyle, his hands still wrapped around the bars. "You might want to keep your mouth shut while you're here, Coyle. I told you I'm not a sheriff. I'm just a horse trader living here in Eagles. This posse has taken some hard losses from you and your bunch. Walk softer."

"Walk *softer*?" Coyle laughed a little and shook his lowered head. He looked back at Summers through the bars. "Either you don't remember me at all, or you think it's better you act like you don't. Which is it, Not-a-sheriff?"

"When you change your mind," Hughes said to Summers, "it's right under the desk." He gave Coyle a look of contempt and added, "I'd beat him plumb to death with it, if I could square it with Judge Parker."

"We won't have any of that here in Eagles, Deputy," Summers said.

"Begging your pardon," said Hughes, "but you wouldn't say that if you saw how they shot our men down like dogs!"

Coyle chuffed, staring through the bars.

"Yeah, Not-a-sheriff," he goaded Summers, "what about them poor men we killed, the grieving folks they leave behind? Wouldn't a good head-busting make up for some of it *a little*? I don't recall you being so squeamish back in our outlawing days."

"I'll get it for you," Hughes said, seeing Summers take a step toward the cell door. "Nobody will ever know."

"Hold it," said Summers, stopping him from getting the hickory club. He stepped close to the bars. "I've seen more than one prisoner act this way." He looked down at the thin worn-out moccasins the posse had replaced Coyle's boots with when they'd caught him.

"Take your moccasins off, Coyle," Summers said.

"What?" Coyle said. "You're razzing me."

"I don't razz. Take them off, right now!" said Summers, leaving no room for dispute.

Coyle stalled; again he gave the dark laugh, the lowered head shaking.

"Here's an idea, Not-a-sheriff," he said. "Why don't you spring in here, hero-like, and take them off me?" He looked past Summers at Hughes. "Hell, bring your friendly side of sowbelly with you. *I'm* not taking them off."

"Just what I've been waiting for," said Hughes. Again, he stepped toward the club under the desk. Again, Summers stopped him.

"Hand me the shotgun," Summers said to the deputy, motioning him toward a short double-barreled shotgun leaning against the wall beside the desk. Hughes grabbed it and handed it to Summers.

"You don't want me to get the club?" he said, sounding excited.

"No," Summers said quietly, staring straight at Coyle. "Get a bucket and a mop." He stepped closer to the bars, raised the shotgun and stuck it through the bars. Coyle stepped backward, toward the bunk against the wall.

"Oh, I get it," he said to Summers. "Now you're going to count to three, give me a chance to rethink —"

"I already counted," Summers said. He lifted his thumb over both hammers and cocked them, slow and distinctly.

"You're going to shoot an unarmed man?" Coyle said.

"You're *armed*," Summers said with certainty. He raised the shotgun butt to the hollow of his right shoulder and aimed it along the short barrels at Coyle's face.

"I am downright *unarmed*!" Coyle said.

"Wait just a *damned minute!*"

"Adios, Dolan Coyle," said Summers in a somber tone.

"Holy God," Hughes said under his breath.

"Wait, damn it, wait!" shouted Coyle. "Look! Look here!" He threw off his moccasins. A small penknife with a closed three-inch blade fell out and clattered on the stone floor.

"There, you call that *being armed?*"

"Not anymore," said Summers. "Kick it over here."

"Damn it to hell, Will Summers!" said Coyle. Summers noted that this was the first time Coyle had called him by name since he'd been in Eagles. "I wasn't going to pull that little nose-picker out here, against the two of you! I'm not a fool."

"Liar!" Hughes exclaimed bitterly. "You tried to lure us both in there and backstab us, you sumbitch! I've still got a good mind to grab —"

"That's enough, Deputy," said Summers. "I don't want to hear any more about the head buster, or I'll feed it to the woodstove."

Coyle stifled a short laugh, seeing that the goading and razzing were over. The look on Summers' face told him that his ol' trail pal had evidently picked up a lot of good, hard

48

learning back then, living by the gun. He wondered at what point Summers had seen through his jailhouse game of pushing to get him and this Deputy Hughes in the cell with him, where he could carve the life out of them.

"Hey, no hard feelings, Summers," said Dolan Coyle. "I found the knife and shoved it in my moccasin, in case I needed it later on. Judge Parker runs a tough place." He gave a shrug as Summers picked up the knife and pitched it to Hughes.

"You said yesterday that you're never going back to Fort Smith, desperado," said Hughes, now the one doing all the goading. "Something has changed your mind quick-like —"

"Deputy, *out front!*" Summers butted in, gesturing toward the dark street.

As soon as Deputy Hughes and Will Summers stepped out onto the boardwalk and closed the jail door behind them, Hughes took on an apologetic tone. Around them the streets and alleyways lay in darkness beneath a starless cloud-covered night.

"I don't know what it is about this murdering skunk Dolan Coyle," Hughes said. "But every time he opens his lousy mouth, I think of all the good men he's killed and want to blow his damn brains out!"

"He knows it, Deputy," said Summers. "He's using it to keep you rattled and off-balance. As long as you fall for it, he's got you playing right into his hands. Keep it up and you'll get yourself killed. Can't you see that?"

"I see it, and I know you're right," Hughes said. "It's not going to happen again. From now on when he runs his mouth, I'll remind myself why he's doing it."

From the dark street a slight clink of a water bucket caught their attention. Turning toward the sound they saw the dove Silk Polly walking out of the greater darkness toward them.

"Will Summers, it's just me, Polly," she said, keeping her voice almost to a whisper. All around, the town of Eagles lay quieter than Summers could ever recall.

"Let me give you a hand, Polly." Summers stepped off the boardwalk, met her and took the water bucket from her hand. He lifted the dipper and carried it in his other hand, keeping it from clinking against the bucket rim.

"Bless your heart, Will," Silk Polly said. "I'm near give out carrying it from the town well." She gave a sharp little giggle that caused Summers to shush her.

50

"We're trying to keep the noise down tonight, Polly," he said. "There's riflemen out there wanting to shoot us."

"I know," Polly whispered. "I'm sorry, Will. I'll be real quiet now."

"That's okay, Polly," he said. "I want you to go back indoors and stay in until we say it's safe to be out here."

"Oh, I will, don't you worry," she said. While they were talking, a series of rifle shots resounded from the low hills behind the town. *"Uh-oh!"* Polly said. She started to turn and run back up the street. But Summers, not wanting her running in the darkness, took her by the arm and walked her across the boardwalk to the front door of the jail. Hughes took the water bucket in hand and held the door open for her.

"Whatever that's about, it's not good!" he said in a wary voice.

Summers helped Polly inside and shut the door behind the three of them. Hughes dropped a latch in place.

"I want you to stay here and visit with us for a few minutes, Polly," Summers said. "Maybe we'll boil up some good strong coffee and pour you a nice cup."

"That's fine, Will," she said. "But what about the shooting?"

"It'll stop any minute," Summers said to

51

keep her calm. "It's a long ways up behind us. Anyway, that's not the gunfire that's got us laying low here. We're watching for gunfire from the *other* direction."

"Oh, okay," she said with a puzzled look. "You sure have lots of people shooting at you tonight."

"We sure do." Summers smiled. He gave her shaky hand a squeeze. "We'll be all right."

"Oh, hush now, I know we will be. I'll just boil that coffee for us you were talking about," said the aging dove. "It'll give me something to do." She returned the hand squeeze. "Anytime there's shootings going on, this ol' gal likes to stay busy."

"I feel much the same way," Summers said.

A hard sudden pounding on the door almost caused Summers and Hughes to draw their sidearms.

"Let me in, Hughes! Damn it to hell, man, let me in!" Parks shouted above the sound of rifle and pistol fire still going strong up along the low hill trails behind Eagles. Summers thought about Johnny Two Red Wolves and the townsmen, Yancy Reed and Scotty White, with him on those dark dangerous trails.

More hard pounding ensued. Before

unlatching the thick door, Hughes looked to Summers for approval.

"Let him in, Deputy, before he stirs up every gunman in the territory," Summers said.

Hughes lifted the big wooden latch, let Parks inside and closed and relocked the front door.

"Great *jumping Jesuits*!" said Parks, his rifle hanging in his hand. "It sounds like two whole army regiments are going at it head-to-head up there!"

"The hills make gunfire sound worse than it is," said Summers. "But it's bad enough. I'm going to ride up and see about the men I sent up there."

"I hope to God my scouts and your three men aren't shooting each other," Parks said.

"Not a chance," said Summers. "Even if it started out that way, they would have figured it out before now." He looked over at Dolan Coyle, who was watching them from between the bars. "How many men do you suppose your brother sent up there?"

"Don't ask me," said Coyle. He gave a sly little grin. "I'm just a prisoner, remember? As long as I'm in this cell, I don't know *nothing* about *nothing*."

"See how the sumbitch does?" Hughes said to Summers. "Every time he opens his mouth, I want to grind my boot heel in his teeth!"

"What the hell's got into you, Deputy?" Parks said to Hughes.

"Nothing," said Hughes, grudgingly. "I was telling Summers how Coyle gets under my skin, makes me want to kill him. But I've got it *under control* now." He shot Coyle a hard look. Coyle chuckled and turned away from the bars.

"You sent a rider up to bring your scouts in?" Summers asked Parks.

"Of course I did, just like I said I would," Parks replied. "I hope the shooting didn't run him off." From the hills, the gunfire had slowed almost to a stop.

At the door another knock resounded, this one quiet.

"It's Leonard!" a raspy voice called out from the boardwalk. "Let me in, before I get winged, Summers. I've got some news for you!"

Summers gave Hughes a nod. "Let him in, Deputy. It's our telegraph operator, Leonard Spires."

When Hughes unlatched the door, the elderly telegraph operator hurried inside and stood away from the door and window.

"Why's it so dark in here?" Spires asked, looking around in the dim lantern light. But he caught himself before anyone could answer, and said, "Never mind, I know. You don't want to highlight yourselves here."

"That's right, Spires," said Summers. "What's the news you've got for us?"

"My lines are down twixt here and Brayton Siding," he said. "With all the goings-on here, I started sending a test ever' so often. Brayton didn't answer the last one I sent, over half an hour ago." He gave Summers a concerned look. "They always answer a test right away."

"I'm heading that way, Leonard," Summers said. "As far up as the high pass if I have to go. I'll watch for any broken lines while I'm there."

"The high pass?" The old man looked confused for a moment, but then understood. "Oh, Gunman's Pass, you mean?"

"All right, Leonard," Summers said patiently. "I know some of you still call it that."

"Owing to our respect for *you,* Will Summers." Leonard Spires shook a long-weathered finger. "But I've gotta say, don't go looking for broken lines tonight. I've got a lineman. He'll go checking lines as soon as he can. But you stay out of Gunman's Pass, Will Summers."

Gunman's Pass? The two deputies looked to Summers for further clarity.

55

"Suit yourself, Leonard. I've got to get going," Summers said. "I've got three good men somewhere up there. I need to go find them."

"Aren't they trained to get home on their own?" said Deputy Parks, restraining a little smile.

Without reply, Summers swung the rope handle of a wooden ammunition crate over his shoulder.

One thousand rounds of mixed rifle and pistol ammunition, he reminded himself, hoping it wouldn't all be needed.

He stepped over, reached his rifle barrel out and raised the front door latch. Hughes swung the door open. Summers prepared to head to the livery barn to gather his horse.

"Will?" Silk Polly asked, closing in on him at the threshold. "May I get you to escort me home? It's right on your way."

Hughes looked ready to guide her away but Summers blocked him.

"You certainly may, Polly," Summers said, offering her his free arm. "I'd be honored."

Dolan Coyle watched closely as Summers and Polly walked out the front door. He grinned and muttered, "Someone still likes the ladies."

CHAPTER 4

Summers walked Silk Polly back to the darkened Eagles Saloon, bid her good evening at the door and waited until she was inside. The front of the saloon revealed no light in the direction of Axel Coyle's and his brother Dolan's gang.

Summers walked on to the livery barn, knowing it was unlikely that the gang would make a flat-out assault on Eagles with Dolan sitting inside the jail. They would lie back out of sight and take whatever target they were offered on the dark street. For now the town was in a standoff until Axel or Dolan signaled otherwise.

Inside the livery barn, under the dim light of a candle on a shiny tin reflecting stand, Summers hefted his saddle and blanket from a rack and set it atop his shoulder. Moby stepped across his stall to the stall gate, his ears perked with anticipation, but he grumbled as Summers walked past his stall to the big paint horse on the other side.

"Not this time, Moby. I'm giving you the night off," he said. "Use it wisely." Moby nickered and sawed his head in discontent.

As Summers saddled the paint, drew the cinch and slid his rifle down into the empty saddle boot, he heard the sound of horses walking toward the barn from an alleyway out back, then hushed voices. He looked through a crack in the rear doors and saw three riders leading two horses with lifeless bodies draped over the saddles.

Summers quietly backed away from the doors and led the paint horse to an out-of-sight stall toward the front of the barn. He ducked down just as the rear doors swung open and the three men led the five horses inside.

"Stick them in here for now," one of the men said. Summers snuck a gaze along the top of the stall rails and saw men and horses in shadowy silhouette. He barely made out the men leading the animals into an indoor corral.

"For now?" said another man with a dark chuckle. "These poor sumbitches won't complain if we leave them here from now *on.*"

"I meant the horses," the first man said. "Leave them here for now and water them.

Drag those two unlucky jakes outside. Let the town bury them." He cursed the darkness. "Suppose this place can't afford oil for their lanterns?"

"It looks like they can't," said one of his companions.

"Damn, Red," said the third man. "We ought to do something for them. Don't you think so, Waco?"

"Like what, Charlie?" the one called Waco asked. "You went through his pockets, took all his money, didn't you?"

"I did," the man he called Charlie said quietly. "Can't say I'm real *proud* of it."

"If you're ashamed of these men's money, give all of it to me and Red!" said Waco. "Our mommas didn't raise no fools."

"All right, that's enough bull plop from the two of you," Red said, raising his voice. "Let's get squared up and see where they're hiding Dolan Coyle."

"Yeah, let's grab him and get out of town," said Waco, "before other bounty men hear about the ten thousand bucks Judge Parker has stuck on his head. I don't want to shoot it out with all the bounty hunting trash west of the Missouri!"

Red looked around the blackness surrounding them. "What the hell is wrong with people here? I just now bumped my head on my own damn horse."

"Like I said, let's get Dolan and get out," said Waco. He fumbled with a lantern hanging on a post until he got it lit and raised the wick. Light spilled in every direction.

"This is more like it," Waco said, admiring the light in the barn. "Now that we can find the jail without breaking our danged necks, we'll be done here before you know it. Don't forget, if Will Summers is in that jailhouse, kill him!"

"Consider it done," said Charlie.

Summers let the three of them get out the front door using the lantern to guide them. He stayed back twenty feet in case Axel and his outlaws started shooting from a long distance away.

As he followed, he considered the names he'd heard them calling one another. There was Red, whom he'd quickly decided was Red Zorn. Waco, whose voice he'd recognized, was Waco Bud Clifton. The name *Charlie* hadn't come to him, not yet. But it would. Meanwhile, he stayed back a safe distance and followed them to the darkened jail.

The sound of knocking on the front door so soon after Summers and Silk Polly left made Hughes think it was Summers returning.

Inside his cell, Dolan Coyle watched expectantly as Hughes stood at the door with a hand on the latch and grinned at Parks.

"Watch this," he said under his breath. "Who *is it*?" he asked in an exaggerated tone.

"You *know* who it is," said the voice on the other side of the door. "Open the damned door, man! Don't get us shot out here!"

It dawned on Parks that the shooting had ceased in the past few minutes. He gave a quick glance at Dolan Coyle and saw the look on his face as a dark warning.

"Don't open that door!" he shouted at Hughes, but his words were too late. Hughes had already started raising the latch. The impact of the door flying open sent him staggering backward as the three bounty hunters rushed in, Red Zorn's Colt firing a streak of fire in the dim light. Hughes fell backward to the floor, a bloody hole in his chest.

Parks grabbed for his big Colt, but never got it out of his holster. A bullet streaked from Waco's Remington and hit him in the right shoulder, keeping him from any further resistance. Waco held his Remington at arm's length.

"Tough break, Deputy," he said to Parks.

"Kill them both!" Coyle shouted from his cell.

"My *scouts*?" Parks stared at Waco in disbelief. "I trusted you! You double-crossing . . ." His voice trailed off.

"*Another* tough break, Deputy," Waco chuffed. He took careful aim at Parks' forehead. The deputy saw his hand jerk on the trigger. He heard the blast, saw a streak of fire explode from the barrel, yet he didn't feel the bullet hit him. Instead, he heard it whistle past his ear as Waco's forehead, hat and all, flew away in a blast of blood, bone and brain matter.

Summers stood in the open door, his Colt smoking in his hand, as Red Zorn tried hurriedly to unlock Dolan Coyle's cell.

"Hurry up, Zorn!" Coyle shouted. "Get me out of here!" Then his eyes raised and locked on Summers in the doorway. "Damn it!" he said, backing away toward the other wall of his cell. His hands went up, showing his handcuffs and the foot-long chain between them. Red Zorn turned around to face Summers. Knowing he was too late to make a move, he let the ring of keys fall from his hand.

"Oh hell!" Zorn whispered. He raised his hands in surrender.

"You saw it, Summers," Coyle said. "I had

nothing to do with this. They come busting in —"

"Shut up, Coyle," said Summers. "Whatever it was, it didn't work." To Red Zorn, he said, "Reach your left hand down, loosen your gun belt and let it fall."

"You know something, Summers?" said Zorn. "I can't help but think this is all just one big mistake. I should never have come here tonight."

"I agree," said Summers. "Yet here you are."

Parks stood with a wadded-up bandanna pressed to his bleeding shoulder wound. From under the desk, Leonard Spires stood up, visibly shaken, but looking excited at having been there through it all.

"Are you all right, Leonard?" Summers asked.

"Never better," Spires said in a shaky voice. "I wish I had a shot of whiskey, though. Something to calm my belly down."

"Bottom drawer," Parks said, nodding at the desk. "Hughes bought it earlier. Poor bastard." He looked at Hughes lying dead in a puddle of blood. "I'll take a shot, too," he said to Spires. "Hughes would want me to." He looked at Summers.

"No, thanks, maybe later," said Summers. He looked around as he stepped forward, stuck his gun against Red Zorn's belly and picked up his fallen gun belt. He stepped back, unloaded the pistol and stuck it down behind his gun belt. He wrapped the belt around the holster and laid it all on the desk. "Who's Charlie?" he asked Zorn. As he asked, he stepped back in close, turned Zorn around and shoved him against the bars.

"Charlie . . . ?" Zorn said with what appeared to be a sudden lapse of memory. He felt the tip of a gun against the back of his head, a hard nudge. "All right, don't get violent," he said over his shoulder. "That's young Charlie Ross. I'm glad he got away."

"He didn't get away," said Summers.

"Could've fooled me," said Zorn. "I don't see him around here anywhere."

"He'll never make it out of Eagles," said Summers. He yanked Zorn's shirttail up, lifted a .36 caliber Navy Colt and handed it to Leonard Spires, who laid it on the desk.

"I forgot that little Navy was back there," Zorn said.

"Your memory has gone bad, Red," said Summers. "I bet you don't remember telling Waco and Charlie Ross to kill me if I was here in the jail."

Zorn fell silent, but only for a second.

"You were in the barn, listening, when I

said that?" Zorn asked. "Hell, I didn't mean nothing by it."

"I understand," said Summers. "But hearing it made me want to crack your head like a walnut. So, I'm going to ask you one time to explain who you're working for. If I think you're waltzing me around, I'll see how long it takes me to bend your gun barrel on your head."

Johnny Two Red Wolves and the town gambler, Yancy Reed, rode into Eagles leading Scotty White's horse, with Scotty's body draped over the saddle. A ringing silence followed the last of the gunfire from the low hills. A black overcast sky had turned to steely rain under a still-invisible quarter moon.

"I hate that we couldn't do something to save ol' Scotty," Johnny Two said quietly.

"There was nothing to do," said Yancy Reed. "He was dead before he hit the ground. When dying has to happen, be glad it happens that way."

"Yes —" said Johnny Two, his thought cut off upon hearing the sound of boots running straight at him in the darkness. Instinctively, he jerked his horse away, but not in time to keep the young outlaw Charlie Ross from running headlong into his horse's side.

"Whoa!" he shouted, feeling the impact, hearing the loud *smack.* His horse neighed loudly. Charlie Ross tried to shout, but his breath had exploded from his lungs. He could only roll back and forth on the ground.

Reed and Johnny Two both jumped down from their saddles and grabbed the young man while he was still struggling to catch his breath. Johnny found Ross's gun belt, felt the butt of his gun sticking up and pulled it from his holster. Ross lay rolled into a tight ball, like a man having a fit.

"Let's get him on his feet," said Johnny Two, "see if we can get him to walk it off some."

"As dark as it is, this was bound to happen," said Yancy Reed. "There's not a doubt in my mind, he's one of the ones who killed Scotty."

With Charlie Ross between them the two walked in deep darkness, leading the horses toward the thinnest candle glow from the jail's open doorway.

"Am . . . I . . . *all right?*" Ross managed to ask in a badly strained voice, wobbling along on rubber legs, his arms over their shoulders.

"You're coming around," said Reed. "Why were you running so fast in this dark wretched night?"

"Getting . . . away," said Ross. "Five of us . . . were scouting for Judge Parker's posse."

"Hello, the street," Summers called out in a low cautious voice from the boardwalk out front of the jail. "Who's out there?"

"It's Johnny Two and Yancy Reed, Will," Johnny called back.

"Oh hell . . . not Summers," Ross said. "He just . . . tried to kill us."

"Was that the shooting we heard a while ago?" Johnny Two asked.

"I'd say it was," said Ross. "Are you the ones . . . we fought with up there? You followed our trail . . . down to here?"

"We started out following the sound of your horses," Johnny Two said, helping the winded man along. "But when we lost your sound, we were just trying to get down and get home."

"Lucky we didn't . . . all break our necks . . . getting here," said Ross, coming around.

"Look out there," said Reed. "One of Coyle's men just struck a match."

In the distance, an orange-blue flame flared up, then fell away. A heartbeat later came the sound of a bullet striking a building.

"It's not a match!" shouted Johnny Two. "They're shooting at us!" Even as he said it, the sound of the rifle caught up with the bullet and resounded across the western horizon.

"Shut the door," Johnny called out to Summers, "we'll make a run for the barn, get out of this line of fire!"

"Watch yourselves!" Summers called back to him. "I'll get there when I can."

"Bring some coffee, Will," Reed shouted at the jail. In the distance, other orange-blue flashes rose and fell in the night.

"Let's move out of here before the rain gets worse," Johnny Two said. They moved along as quickly as they dared, leading the horses, Ross and Scotty White's body through the darkest night any of them could ever recall. Bullets thumped with increasing frequency against buildings and on the street, followed by the sound of the shots a moment later.

Inside the livery barn, the sound of rain intensified. Larger drops pecked like hungry crows on the metal roof. The sound of horses neighing at the door brought Johnny Two over to investigate. He opened the door a crack and a horse's big nose pushed it open farther. A dead man lay over the horse's saddle.

"God almighty!" said Yancy Reed, who'd lit a low-trimmed lantern in spite of the rifles facing Eagles from open land.

"Don't worry, he's one of ours," said Ross, holding a bandanna to his broken nose, which had bled worse as soon as he tried to twist it straight.

The horse stepped in and walked briskly to the horses gathered at the indoor corral where Zorn, Waco, and Ross had left them.

"There's more," said Ross through his broken nose. "We lost two scouts . . . up there." He looked at Johnny Two.

"We didn't shoot them," Johnny said. "Must be Coyle had some men up there."

Before Johnny could close the door, another horse with a body draped over it pushed inside and walked to the corral.

Johnny Two pushed the door shut and dropped a large latch in place.

"That should do it," said Charlie Ross. But a scraping sound on the other side of the door caused Johnny to open it another crack. This time a nervous horse stepped inside, shook a limp body from its saddle and raced back to a far corner of the corral as a heavy streak of lightning twisted and curled in the black-purple sky. A hard clap of thunder followed the lightning.

The storm raged. In a moment between sharp stabs of lightning and thunder roaring like cannon fire, a series of hard knocks sounded at the door, accompanied by Will Summers' voice.

"It's me, *Will*," he shouted through the heavy rain and thunder. "Let me in! I've got coffee!"

"If he's got coffee, let him in with it!" said Yancy Reed in a loud voice, as if Summers might otherwise be turned away.

"Watch it, it's hot, Johnny," Summers said as the door creaked open. He stepped inside the barely opened door and right past Johnny Two. He set the pot of steaming coffee down atop the lid of an oaken barrel and stepped back from it. From under his rain slicker, he took out three thick coffee mugs and two stained tin cups and set them all down beside the coffeepot.

"That's a terrible thing, losing Scotty White that way," he said. "I was headed up to bring the three of you ammunition when these three *scouts* slipped into the barn, hauling two of their dead over their saddles. I heard them talking about breaking Dolan Coyle loose from our jail. Coyle thought they were working for him, but all they wanted was the ten-thousand-dollar bounty Judge Parker had placed on his head."

70

"For breaking out of Parker's jail?" Johnny Two asked.

"That's right, Johnny," said Summers. "I heard it, and I knew I had to stay here and stop them. With the shooting stopped I figured you'd be riding down before long anyway." As he talked, he filled a coffee mug for Johnny Two, and another one for Yancy Reed.

The smell of coffee brought Reed walking over from the corral, where he'd removed his saddle from his horse's back and swung it over a corral rail.

"So," said Johnny, "the five men hired on as scouts with the deputies looking to return Coyle to custody in exchange for thirty-dollars-a-day wages, but one whiff of Judge Parker's reward money turned everything in another direction."

"Yeah," said Reed, as he walked in close and picked up his steaming mug of coffee. "They're not a real loyal bunch, these border outlaws. Some of the wounded deputies might not be, either, once they're up and around. Ten thousand dollars is a great changer of mind and direction." He grinned, blew on his coffee and sipped it.

"It's already started changing my mind and direction," said Summers. He poured a tin cup of hot coffee and looked at Charlie

71

Ross leaning against a barn pole with his bandanna up against his busted nose. "What did you hit him with, to mess him up so bad, Johnny?" he asked.

"My horse," Johnny Two said flatly. The three shared a short quiet laugh, then Summers carried the hot coffee back to Ross and handed it to him and motioned him to the far rear of the barn.

"Here's some hot coffee until the rain quits, and you go see if the doctor can make the bleeding stop."

The young outlaw nodded and kept his bandanna close at hand as he sipped the coffee.

"I want you sitting back there by the wall, where I can see you," Summers said. "Listen to the rain. If you hear anybody riding through it, come tell me right away. Can you do that?"

Ross nodded slightly, keeping his head tilted back.

"What's that about?" Reed asked as Summers walked back to the cooperage barrel.

"He's listening to the rain for us, while we talk about what we've got to do," Summers said. "He's one of the scouts for the posse. He gets feeling better, he can leave, as far as I'm concerned."

"If he waits long enough, he might get

72

himself a pine overcoat and a nice burial, compliments of the town of Eagles."

CHAPTER 5

In the hour before dawn, the storm passed and rumbled off among the hills. The streets and alleyways running throughout Eagles lay under stretches of groundwater and mud. Dawn arrived calmly, under a sunless gray sky. Summers, Johnny Two and Yancy Reed left the bodies laid out in the barn for townsmen to attend to, except for that of Scotty White. They wiped Scotty's face as best they could and wrapped him in a dry sheet of canvas by the indoor corral. The three rode their horses abreast to the jail, avoiding the mud.

"We lost a townsman and a federal deputy," Reed said. "With all respect for Scotty White, as gunfights go, this could have been worse."

"Yes, it could have been worse," Summers agreed quietly, a thin sliver of steam rising from his mouth and the horse's nostrils. "If it keeps on, it *will* be worse."

"I'm surprised they're not shooting right now, just for the hell of it," Reed added.

"As soon as they see something to shoot at, they'll shoot at it," Johnny Two put in. "They're counting their bullets."

"As long as they're watching their ammunition, we better do the same," said Yancy Reed. "Sounds like they're in this till the devil shows his horns."

Ahead of them they saw Deputy Parks standing on the muddy boardwalk out front of the jail. He wore his right arm in a sling beneath his shoulder wound. He took a step forward as he watched them ride in closer, as if he couldn't wait to talk to them.

"Is it just me," said Yancy Reed, "or does it seem like every time the law comes to town, they always stir something up and get people killed?"

"I think it's because law and trouble always travel close together," Summers said. "One might arrive ahead of the other, but they always catch up with each other in time to tear a roof off."

"See there, Johnny," said Reed to Johnny Two. "Will works all this out in his head. Everybody says he ought to be a lawman. I never know if it's his friends wanting him to get a job, or his enemies wanting to get him killed."

"I'm a horse trader, Yancy," Summers said. "It'll have to do for me." He nodded toward Parks. "He looks like a whipped cur this morning. Wonder what kind of *bad news* he's got for us now."

"We already know Deputy Hughes is dead. It'll have to be bad enough to top that," said Reed.

"Holy Mother! I'm glad to see you men!" said Parks as the three stopped their horses at the hitch rail and stepped down into the mud.

"We were just at the barn, sitting out the storm," said Summers. The three stepped onto the muddy boardwalk and stamped and scraped their boots.

"I know," said Parks, keeping his voice down, guarded. "I couldn't leave this place unattended, not even long enough to go to the barn!"

"What is it, Deputy?" Summers said, stepping to the door with him.

"I'll have to show you," Parks said, barely above a whisper. "This couldn't be any worse." He held the door open just enough for the three to step inside. He stepped in behind them, closed the door and dropped the latch in place.

The three looked around; the office was still a bloody scene from the night before.

76

Furniture lay jumbled and overturned. Bootheel marks streaked bloodily across the floor from where Deputy Hughes's body had been dragged into a small room near the rear door. He'd been left there until after last night's storm had passed through and moved on.

The place was such a bloody mess that it took more than one quick look across to the cell to see Dolan Coyle sitting on the floor leaning back against his bunk. A twisted stream of dried black blood reached down from a bullet hole above his right eye. His face, chalk white, pale blue around his eyes, stared at the four men with a half-gaping grin. The men stared back, except for Parks, who had seen all he cared to of the dead outlaw. Parks backed away from the cell and plopped down in a wooden chair.

"I know this looks awfully bad on me," Parks said. "I was the only one here with him."

Reed scoffed and said, "We were just talking about how every time *law* comes to town —"

"Let it go, Yancy," Summers said under his breath.

"I hope none of you think I killed him," said Parks. He looked at Summers.

Summers thought about what Parks had

said, about putting a bullet in Dolan Coyle's head and sending him to his brother, Axel, strapped down over a saddle. *Who knows,* he thought, glancing down at Coyle's body on the cell floor. But he wasn't going to bring it up right now.

"How did it happen?" Summers asked Parks.

"I know this sounds bad, too," said Parks. "But I have *no idea*! I left him sitting there so you could see him for yourself. I haven't moved him, didn't touch him, sure as hell didn't *shoot him*!"

"Yep," said Yancy Reed with a dark chuckle, "the *law* has arrived in Eagles."

"Stop it, Yancy," said Summers.

"What's *that* supposed to mean?" Parks snapped.

Summers cut in. "He doesn't mean anything, Deputy. Unlock the cell. I want to look at the bars on the window."

"Wha— What are we looking for?" Parks asked, picking up the key off the desk. He stepped over to the cell door, opened it and sat back down.

"A ricochet, Deputy," said Summers, stepping inside and up onto the bunk. He looked at Johnny Two and Reed. "Take a look around out there, too. If he was sitting here just like this, a bullet could've hit him from the front."

"He was sitting right there, just like that, I swear he was!" Parks shouted.

"All right, take it easy, Deputy," said Summers. "How long do you think he might have sat there dead before you knew about it?"

"After you left here with the coffeepot," Parks said, "it might have been ten, fifteen minutes? There were a few rifle shots that came from west of town, out where Coyle's men are. Front door was closed, window shutters were closed. A few minutes after the rifle fire, I said something to him. He never answered. I looked in at him and saw that same strange look on his face — and I knew he was deader than hell!"

Summers, Reed and Johnny Two moved away without another word. Each of them began inspecting the door and frame, window shutters and walls and bars, for any sign of a stray bullet.

"What the *hell*?" said Parks. "Do any of you believe a word I've said?"

No one answered. Instead, Summers rose from under the desk with a hand closed around part of a misshapen bullet he'd picked up from the dusty floor. "This was stuck back under a desk leg. Let's hope it's what we're looking for." He opened his palm for the others to see.

"All right," said Yancy Reed. "Half a bullet found, half a bullet still missing."

"Don't look too hard for the rest of it," Summers said.

"Why not?" Reed asked.

"Tell him, Johnny," said Summers.

"The rest of it is likely inside Dolan's head," Johnny Two answered matter-of-factly. "A ricochet splits like that, it loses lots of its power, but it can still do some terrible damage before it stops."

"Yes, as we can all see," said Reed, looking at Dolan's body with his eyes staring blankly back at them.

"What is this?" Summers suddenly looked in surprise at a tiny sliver of fresh blood seeping from the dried black hole on Coyle's face.

Reed and Johnny Two moved into the cell behind Summers, who crouched down beside Coyle and lifted his wrist between his fingers and thumb.

"He's checking his pulse?" Reed said to anyone listening.

"He's what?" asked Parks, half standing from his chair for a better view.

"Checking his pulse, Deputy," Reed answered in a louder voice. "Dead men don't bleed."

"He can't be *alive,* can he?" Parks asked in a shaky voice, standing all the way up.

"That's why he's checking," said Reed. "But if he is alive, you *don't* get to shoot him again —"

"I did not shoot him, *damn you!*"

"Both of you *shut up,*" Summers shouted over his shoulder. A silence fell heavily about the jail, the three men staring intently at Summers' determined face.

"I can't tell," Summers whispered. Seconds passed. Summers laid Dolan's hand back in his lap and half turned to the others.

"Johnny!" he said. "Get the doctor over here right away! Tell him to keep quiet! Hurry, Johnny!"

Prince Drako stood looking down at Eddie Moon, who lay stretched out naked on the big feather bed in Zetra Wilson's bedroom. He allowed a surprised Zetra, who lay as naked as Eddie Moon, to get up and grab her dress on her way out the door. Once outside the door, she looked back.

"Some coffee for you, Prince Drako?" she asked cordially, having met him when he'd ridden in two days earlier to pick up more bourbon and tell Moon that Axel wanted him back right away.

81

Drako stifled a laugh.

"Yes. Obliged, Miss Zetra," he said. "If you will, pour it into a canteen." Their eyes met, and Drako took a pouch of gold coins from inside his shirt and handed it to her. "For the food and whiskey, and something extra," he said.

"Ah, many thanks, Prince Drako!" she said, hefting the pouch, feeling the weight of it.

He heard her bare feet plop away along the plank floor. He looked back down at Eddie Moon, who rolled his red eyes up through an unseen swirl of sour-smelling bourbon.

"Wake up, you drunken sot," Prince Drako said. He reached down, thumb and finger, and flipped Moon mercilessly on his ear.

Moon shrieked and clamped a hand down over the side of his head.

"My God, Drako! Why'd you do something like *that*? That hurt like hell!"

Drako grinned.

"I knew it would," he said. "I flip *hard*! This next one is going to hurt worse, if you don't get your pale ass up from there."

Moon's free hand protectively cupped his privates even as he rolled up onto the side of the bed and looked around bleary-eyed.

"Where're my drawers, my trousers?" he said.

"Under your feet," said Drako. "Pick them up yourself," he added sourly. He nodded down at the trousers and long johns on the floor beside the bed.

"Aw, hell," Moon groaned, moving his hand from his stinging ear to his forehead. "Where's my gun? My boots? Where the hell is Zetra?" He looked up, red-eyed and slightly asway, at Prince Drako. "I am too damn drunk, to do any damn thing!" he declared with drunken resolve. "Don't even ask me to."

"I'm not asking you to do nothing," said Drako. "You ain't been at camp since Axel sent you here. Our men have come and gone, watering their horses, picking up more food. They said every time they've been here, you and the woman have either been in this bed, or outside staggering around, naked as a couple of spring deer!"

"Watch your mouth, Drako," Moon warned. "I did what I was told to do. I even sent along gallons of bourbon as an added treat!" He picked up his long johns and looked them over, deciding the best way to put them on.

Drako watched, his gun still hanging from his hand.

"All I know is, Axel said bring you back this time dead or alive," he said.

"*This time?*" said Moon. "What the hell does that mean?" He bent forward and pulled on his long johns up to his knees. He stood up shakily and raised them the rest of the way.

"It *means,* he's sent three different gunmen to bring you in, but you haven't come back yet." He stepped in closer and looked Moon in the eyes.

"What do you want, Drako?" Moon asked, getting edgy.

"You don't remember a damn thing that's gone on here, do you, Eddie Moon?"

Noting the gun in Drako's hand, and knowing how skillful the man was at drawing it and shooting a man full of holes, Moon took the question seriously.

"I — I remember there was a bad storm?" he offered, as if he were still uncertain.

"Where's the woman's young ones?" Drako asked.

"I have no idea," said Moon.

"She sent them all five to a neighbor's house," said Drako. "I expect by now the neighbor is starting to wonder what's happening here."

"Damn it, you're right," said Moon, looking around. "Where's my gun? Where is Zetra?"

Drako sighed.

"Your gun is in your saddlebag," he said. "I unloaded it and put it there. Your rifle is in the saddle boot. It's unloaded, too."

"Oh? So that's how it is?" said Eddie Moon, with a cold sobering look.

"Yeah, that's how it is," said Drako. "I've been trying to tell you. I'm here to take you back, one way or the other. Axel wants you back, or he wants you dead. *Comprende?*" He jiggled the gun in his hand.

"Where is Zetra?" Moon asked again.

"She went to boil coffee."

"Ha!" said Moon. "It's going to take more than hot coffee to get me straightened out." He paused, then said, "So, Axel is killing mad at me?"

"How many times do I have to say it?" said Drako. "He's offering you a chance to get sober and come on in. We're riding into Eagles today, see about getting Dolan out of jail."

"Bust him out, or buy him out?" said Moon, his words still a little slurred.

"Whatever it takes," said Drako. "Axel says he'll be reasonable if they'll let him. But either way Dolan is coming out." He looked Moon up and down. "Maybe if you

85

show up for all this, he'll have a lot on his mind and ease up on your drunken spree."

Moon thought about it as he picked up his trousers and stepped into them.

"You think so, really?" he said, buttoning his trousers. He looked at his boots and socks lying scattered on the floor.

"No! *Hell no!*" said Drako. "If I knew Axel Coyle was wanting me dead, I'd go anywhere except where he is."

Moon thought about it.

"What if I took him a couple more gallons of bourbon?" he said. "You know her and her husband make some of the stuff right here! His people are from Tennessee." He gave a crafty grin.

"I can't say it will help," said Drako. "But it sure can't hurt."

Once dressed, Eddie Moon followed Drako through the house. When Zetra met them at the front door and handed Moon the canteen full of hot coffee, he looked surprised.

"I had her pour it in the canteen for us," said Drako.

Moon nodded and turned back to Zetra.

"I'll send you what we owe you as soon as our boss gives it to me —" Seeing Zetra smile at Drako, Moon stopped.

"I paid her," Drako said. "Axel gave me

the money this morning. So, we're all done here."

"What about the bourbon?" he asked.

"It's in tins, hanging from my saddle horn," said Drako. "Zetra has thought of everything."

"I don't know if I like you paying her," said Moon. "I wanted to do it *myself.*"

"I saw you did," said Drako, "but now it's one more thing you don't have to worry about."

"Are the hounds locked up?" Moon asked.

"Yes," said Zetra. She turned and walked away, the pouch of gold tucked down between her breasts.

"This is not how I like doing business," Moon said, headed out the front door. "I had plans for that money."

"I know," said Drako. "Take it up with Axel. Just be glad I didn't kill you."

CHAPTER 6

Dr. Otto Adams straightened up beside the jail bunk where the men had placed Dolan Coyle and held a bloody palm out sidelong. Gathered close around Summers and the doctor stood Yancy Reed, Deputy Parks, and Johnny Two Red Wolves. The three had watched intently as the portly doctor broke a black lump of dried blood off Dolan's forehead.

The dried blood was the size of the doctor's fingertip. He examined it closely, dropped it onto a saucer and set it aside.

"Pour a few drops of alcohol over it and leave it a few minutes," he said to Summers, who uncorked a small bottle and poured a few drops on the lump of blood.

"Now then, let's see what we've got here," the doctor said. He crouched slightly again and blotted a tiny pool of fresh blood from the small wound in Coyle's forehead. He stared, absorbed for a second, at the raw, bloodless wound. As fresh blood seeped back in and filled the small cavity, he sighed, blotted it and stared again.

"Well?" Summers said quietly. "What do you see there?"

"Let's start with *Is he dead or alive?*" the doctor said. As he spoke, he fished a small mirror from his open medical bag on the bunk beside the unresponsive outlaw. He held the mirror down close, an inch from Dolan's face. After laying the blotting cloth on the wound, he reached his free hand down and checked Dolan's wrist for a pulse.

"He's *breathing,*" he said, as a haze of breath on the mirror appeared and disappeared. "He has a *pulse,* such as it is," he added. "For those two reasons I have to declare him alive. If we call this living."

"His *death,* or I should say, *wounding,* was caused by a ricocheted bullet going into his brain?" Deputy Parks asked.

"Well, well," Yancy Reed scoffed with a sly grin before the doctor could reply. "Sounds like the law is going straight to the point."

"Stop it, Reed," said Summers. "You can't blame the deputy for worrying about Coyle's men blaming him."

"I apologize, Deputy," said Reed. "Sometimes irony overwhelms me."

"Here's the thing," the doctor said, ignoring any other issues at hand. "It's unlikely there's a bullet inside this man's brain. When I blot the wound, before it fills with blood again, I see an object protruding from his skull."

The three men stared at him in rapt attention.

"It is a ricochet, but it's not from a bullet," the doctor went on. "The bullet hit a solid object of some sort and sent it into this man's forehead."

"My God," Deputy Parks whispered.

"How deep do you suppose it is?" Johnny Two asked.

"We're about to find out," Dr. Adams said. Washing his hands in a pan of clean water, he went on, "I have to remove it, whatever it is. Once it's out, if all goes well, we'll know more about this man's condition, and whether or not he'll recover."

"And if he doesn't recover, we'll all take the blame for killing him," Summers said.

Yancy Reed cut in.

"I say yank it out, whatever it is. Let the chips fall where they fly."

"Easy for you to say, *gambler,*" said Parks. "It sounds like no matter how this turns out, I'm the one who's going to catch hell for it."

"Don't you two start," said Summers. He

looked at the wound on Dolan's forehead. It had filled with blood again. The doctor reached out with the cloth and blotted the blood. "Can you show me, Doctor?" Summers asked.

"Lean down here with me," the doctor said. "I'll clean it up. You be ready to look quick, before it fills back up again."

Summers stared into the open wound as Dr. Adams touched the cloth to it and drew it momentarily free of any fresh blood.

"See it?" the doctor asked.

"I saw something that looked like the point of a splinter sticking up from the center."

"That's the object," said the doctor. "But I doubt it's a wooden splinter. With all the blood, I think it would have gotten soaked and broken off before now, which would have been even worse."

"Yeah?" said Summers, glancing around the jail.

"I'm going to try to get a clamp on it and remove it real slow, if it will come out."

"If it won't come out?" Summers asked.

"Then I would have to open his forehead enough to get inside and remove it."

The others leaned in, listening.

"Have you ever done something like that, Doctor?" Summers asked.

91

"No, I haven't," the doctor said. "But these are our only two choices." He sighed. "And I'm afraid we have to do it now. The longer we wait, the worse I think it will become. If it has inserted itself in the frontal cranium the bone will quickly start healing around it." He turned to Yancy Reed. "I need you to go get Silk Polly and bring her here."

"What if she's too drunk to come?"

"Then *carry* her if you have to, damn it," the doctor said. "I'm going to need her help, drunk or sober. Unless you feel like being nursemaid to a man with a sliver of steel stuck in his brain."

"No, I'll get Silk Polly over here right away, Doc, you bet!" Reed said hurriedly.

"Doctor, you mean whatever this object is, it could be stuck in deep enough to be inside his brain?" Summers asked.

"I have to be prepared for that possibility," said Dr. Adams. "While we hope and pray it's not. What I know about milled steel is that it fractures lengthwise, usually in short segments less than an inch, but possibly longer."

"What can I do to help?" Summers asked.

"It would help me greatly if you and Johnny would examine the round wall bars and the flat crossbars for any sign of a bullet striking them."

"Tell me where to start looking," said Johnny Two.

"Good," said Adams. "I'll start getting things in order. I'll need a small table on which to lay out my surgical instruments."

"I'll go find a small table for you and bring it here straightaway," said Deputy Parks.

The front door opened. Leonard Spires walked in, looked around, and without stopping came up to Will Summers, who was examining the iron crossbars of the cell.

"The bartender sent me, Will," said Spires. "There's three of Coyle's men there. Came in drunker than skunks, one carrying a white pocket kerchief tied to a rifle barrel. Said they want to see you under an honest flag of truce." Behind Spires, Reed walked in, escorting a sober and alert Silk Polly on his forearm.

"A white kerchief tied to a rifle," Summers said. "Sure sounds like an honest bid for peace to me." He looked at Reed, who he knew had heard Spires. "What do you say, Yancy?"

"Anytime I go looking for *peace,* I go into a saloon dog drunk, carrying a rifle with a white kerchief tied to it," Yancy said. He stepped over to the gun cabinet. "I saw their horses at the saloon hitch rail. Even the *horses* looked drunk." He took out a sawed-off double-barreled shotgun, checked it and snapped it shut. "Ready when you are," he said.

"One second," said Summers. "How do you know they're Coyle's men, Spires?"

"The bartender said they keep asking him about Dolan Coyle," Spires replied. "That's all I know."

"Let's go, Will," said Reed. "We don't want *peace* to break out and us not be there to see it."

Summers looked at Dr. Adams.

"Are you all right with me going with Reed, Doctor?"

"I'll wait for you as long as I can," said the doctor. "I want someone to witness that I've done what I can to save this man's life."

"I understand," said Summers. He started to leave, but he saw Johnny Two watching him expectantly.

"What's the holdup, Johnny?" Summers said. "Are you going with me or what?"

"I am absolutely going, Will," said Johnny Two, taking a rifle down from the rack and levering a bullet up into the chamber on his way to the front door.

Inside the Eagles Saloon, three of the Coyle gunmen had caused most of the other

94

morning drinkers to leave. Berle Kamps, a rangy Texan from El Paso City, stood leaning with one arm on the bar. A bottle of whiskey stood beside his cocked .45 atop the bar, next to a shot glass and half a mug of beer. He wore a battered slouch hat with a red hawk feather pinning the front of the brim up to the crown. He stood steady, relatively sober for the time being.

At a table less than ten feet away sat two hardened paid killers, gunman Lee Ozine and former Montana stock detective JW Bendigo. Both men were boiling drunk, had been for three days and nights on the Tennessee whiskey from the Wilson ranch. Ozine weaved in his chair, his cocked Smith & Wesson in hand. He waved his rifle back and forth slowly, the white kerchief tied to its barrel.

"I'm not going to ask you again, *barkeep,*" he said to Mort Javins. "You're going to go to the jail and tell the sheriff we're here to talk with him under a flag of truce."

"I told you already, there is no sheriff in Eagles," said the bartender.

"I think this bar swamper is sassing you, Ozine," said Bendigo. "Say the word and I will box his jaws for him."

"I'm not sassing anybody," said Javins. "We've got no elected lawman running

95

things here. That's one reason I live here. Will Summers is our unofficial town spokesman. If you're wanting to see him, I expect you'll get your wish most any minute now."

Berle Kamps stood quarter-wise to the front door, able to keep an eye on any comings and goings from the street.

"I'm tired of jawing," said Lee Ozine. He stood up, steadier on his feet than he was in the chair. "See this, you slack-jawed idiot?" He stepped closer to the bar, still waving the white flag on his rifle barrel slowly, closer to the bartender's face every measured step. "We're here under a truce. No man better step through them doors saying otherwise. We'll kill him deader than hell!"

"Watch yourself, Ozine!" Kamps said with urgency. He tried to quietly nod Ozine's attention to the doors, where two tall hats were stepping inside. But Ozine would have none of it. Seeing the two hats, he let out a bloodcurdling yell. "Kill these sumbitches!"

He swung his rifle up and started firing. The white kerchief stood straight out from the tip of his barrel on an orange-blue flame. Bendigo jumped up, joining him, firing round after round from his pistol.

A stray bullet came through the open space above the doors and thumped loudly into the side of a passing freight wagon. The teamster in the wagon seat quickly brought the horses under control, but grabbed his shotgun, jumped down and came running toward the saloon.

"I bet I kill *me* a sumbitch," the teamster shouted.

Before he got there, Summers stepped into the doorway and shot Lee Ozine in the high right side of his chest.

Ozine went down hard atop the long brass footrail running along the floor at the bottom of the bar. A spittoon flew up and emptied itself midair.

Berle Kamps, caught off guard by Ozine's drunken panic, had jumped over the bar and took aim at Summers in the open doorway. Behind Summers the teamster came running toward the doors; but Reed grabbed him by his coat collar, yanked his rifle from him and shook him roughly.

"The hell you think you're going?" Reed asked.

"I want to see the turd who shoots a man's animals for no reason!" said the teamster.

Holding the man by his collar, Reed shoved him close to the batwing doors where they could both see over the doors' top edges.

Summers had stepped inside the saloon

and walked toward the bar, where the bartender had first dropped down for cover, but then rose up with a wooden mallet, beat Kamps senseless, and left him lying face-down over the bar top.

"Holy Joe and Mary," the teamster whispered, watching in amazement as Bendigo made a run for the rear door, only to have Johnny Two stand up from behind a beer barrel and smack the unsuspecting outlaw with the hickory shotgun butt.

"Seen enough yet?" said Reed to the teamster. A mumbling Ozine writhed in a dark pool of blood and tobacco spittle.

"All this over a bullet hitting my wagon?" said the teamster, stepping back.

"There was a little more to it," said Reed. He turned loose of the man's coat collar and straightened it back into place. "Get out of here before I charge you with *aggravation.*"

With the sawed-off shotgun in hand Reed turned and walked inside the saloon. Johnny Two was dragging the knocked-out JW Bendigo to the front by his shoulder, so Reed gave him a hand. When he turned Bendigo loose, he helped the bartender pull Kamps limply across the bar and drop him on the floor beside Lee Ozine.

"Anybody going to help me?" asked Ozine

in a timid voice. "I'm bleeding something awful."

"First, let me ask you something," said Summers, nudging the wounded outlaw with his boot toe. "Did Axel Coyle send you three here, or did you get drunk and decide to come on your own?"

"I ain't telling you damn law dogs a thing —" His words ended in a short groan of pain as Summers nudged him again, this time a little harder.

"All right," Summers said. He drew his boot back, this time farther. "Maybe I'll give you a good solid kick!"

"Let me kick him some," said Reed.

"Me, too," said Johnny.

"Us three came on our own," Ozine mumbled. "Axel didn't send us."

"What did you say?" said Summers. He pulled the outlaw to his feet. "Say it loud enough that these two can hear. It might keep them from kicking the hell out of you."

Ozine let out a sigh and said, "Axel Coyle didn't send us here. We got drunk and decided to cut Dolan loose on our own. Axel is coming here today to get Dolan out. We thought we might beat him to it."

"There we have it," Summers said, giving Lee Ozine a shove toward the front door.

"Take him to the barn and find a place for him."

"The *barn*?" said Ozine, looking over his shoulder.

"That's right," said Summers. "We've run out of room in the jail. You three are going to the livery barn, if these two ever wake up." He nodded at the two outlaws sprawled on the plank floor amid sour tobacco juice, spit and soggy cigar stubs.

"I'll stay here with them," Reed said, shotgun in hand.

Mort Javins had already started wiping the bar with a wet towel when Summers said, "Mort, I'm going to leave Yancy here with you until Johnny gets back."

"Where am I going?" asked Johnny Two.

"I want you to go to the jail, get Polly and bring her to the barn."

"I've got it," said Johnny Two.

Turning back to the bartender and Reed he said, "Keep your shotguns on these scarecrows until I come back for them."

"Sure thing," said Reed.

"I'd be honored to help, Will," said Mort, laying down the bar towel and taking a shotgun from under the bar.

"Try not to shoot them," Summers said, giving Ozine another shove toward the door. Johnny Two slipped out ahead to get Silk

Polly from the jail.

Outside, Summers saw Deputy Parks walking toward them.

"Dr. Adams says to tell you he's *ready when you are,* Summers."

"As soon as I take this one to the barn and cuff him," Summers answered.

"I'm bleeding to beat hell," said Lee Ozine.

"I'm sending a woman over to patch your shoulder," Summers said.

"A woman?" whined Ozine. "What about a doctor?"

"The doctor's too busy right now."

Parks walked alongside Summers behind the wounded outlaw.

"I know this might not be the best time to talk, Summers. But I need to clear up some *business* with you, in case I have to leave town."

"Leave *town?*" Summers laid a hand on Ozine's good shoulder, stopping him.

"I know it's a bad time to leave," said Parks. "I know you've got a mess here, and I'd like for me and my men to stay and clean this up for you."

"Are we talking about the mess you brought here and dropped in our laps?" Summers asked.

"We could argue all day about how it got

101

started," said Parks. "Fact is, I'm needed back in Fort Smith."

"How do you know?" Summers asked. "Has our telegraph line been repaired?"

"No," said Parks. "I mean, not that I know of. But I always get a sense of when I'm needed back there —"

"Hold on, Deputy," said Summers. "Walk with me to the barn. We don't want to talk out here in the street."

"I agree," said Parks, extending a hand forward, ushering them on toward the livery barn. "This is no place to talk *business.*"

PART 2

PART 2

CHAPTER 7

Inside the barn, Summers handcuffed Ozine to a stall rail and brought him a wooden saddle rack to sit on. Ozine looked at his bloody shoulder and shook his head. He opened and closed his fist a few times and winced.

"A *woman,* huh?" he said cynically. "How does she know anything about treating a gunshot wound? I might be better off treating myself."

"Keep running your mouth and you *might* be treating yourself," Summers said. "The woman is an experienced battlefield nurse, Ozine. She knows how to do anything we might need her to do."

"Yeah? Like *what?*" Lee Ozine insisted with sarcasm, rattling his handcuff on the stall rail.

"Like sewing your tongue to your shoulder," Summers said, "after I tell her what a bastard you're being about her nursing you!"

A startled look of recollection came over Ozine's face.

"Wait a minute," he said. "This woman's not Silky Pearl, is she?"

"No," said Summers. He saw relief come over the outlaw's face. But it went away a second later when he continued, "Her name is Silk Polly. She's been in these parts a long while."

"Oh hell," said Ozine. "I had the woman's name wrong. It is Silk Polly, not Silky Pearl."

"I'm sure Polly will understand."

"No, no," said Ozine. "You see, I know her! For some reason, she thinks I owe her money!"

"Oh?" said Summers. "Why would she think that?"

"We spent an afternoon together. She thought I didn't pay her for her time. We argued on the street, one thing led to another. She started shooting at me with a little hideaway she carried. I got away and rode out, but just barely."

"Maybe this will be a good time to settle your differences," Summers said.

"No, it won't," said Ozine. "We'll never get it settled between us. She won't listen to reason. I don't want her near me!"

"Too bad," said Summers. "You sit there and keep quiet. The deputy and I need to talk." He and Parks walked a few feet away to have some privacy.

"I've got to get over to the jail," Summers said. "But go ahead and tell me what's on your mind, Deputy."

"Like I said outside, my four men and I have to get back to Fort Smith. I think they would be better off riding the stage to Brayton Siding and taking the train home from there. Call me a worrier, but I take their health most seriously."

"Sounds to me you're wanting your money back for the ten horses I sold you," Summers said.

"That's one way of putting it," Parks replied.

"What's another way?" Summers said bluntly.

"Here's the thing," said Parks. "We didn't even use *one* of the ten horses I bought from you."

"That's true," said Summers, "but you've kept them in my livery barn, safe from the storm, and safe out of any gunfire."

"Yes, but —"

Summers cut him off.

"They've eaten every meal here, been watered daily, saddled and tacked and unsaddled and untacked. My stable boys have rubbed them down, looked after them and kept them ready to go at a moment's notice."

"I know all that, but —"

"The horses your men wore out coming here have been fed, watered, rested and kept in a clean dry stall every day and night. What amount do you think you are owed?"

"I haven't finalized a number yet. I was confident that under the circumstances you might simply refund me the amount I paid you for the horses."

"I see," said Summers. "You'd like me to refund you the money for the ten horses, and charge you per day for feed and care of the ten worn-out horses I've been boarding here?"

"Whoa now," said Parks. "That comes to a lot of money."

"Then you tell me what part of it is not a fair and legitimate fee," said Summers.

"I'll have to take a pencil to it and see how it looks," said Parks. "I'll get back with you before my men and I leave."

"You do that, Deputy," said Summers, glancing at the barn door as it eased open enough for Silk Polly and Johnny Two to enter. "I'll be here."

"I'll just get out of your way for now —

go check on my wounded men. We might have to leave here anytime."

"If you leave, I'll wire Judge Parker's office and tell him where we stand on the horses and livery," said Summers.

Wordlessly, Parks gave him a sour look and left. Summers had a feeling that was the last he'd see of him.

Yancy Reed watched through the Eagles Saloon's dusty front window as three strangers rode their horses into town at a walk. They reined up across the street, but Reed had a nagging feeling they would be coming to the saloon any minute. For the time being they stayed in their saddles long enough to look all around the peaceful little frontier community.

Before the three men swung down from their saddles, Reed hurried to the bar. One of the gunmen had come to and managed to crawl to the bar and pull himself up. Now he stood struggling to get his hat on. His empty holster hung low on his hip.

"Let's go, Mort!" Reed said to the bartender. "We've got company coming."

"Company?" said the bartender, grabbing a big Colt he'd kept close at hand.

"Yeah, it looks like bad company!" said Reed. "Might be Coyle men, might not.

Let's get these two out of sight, just in case."

"What *two*?" slurred Berle Kamps, swaying against the bar. His hat fell back off his head onto his shoulders, and hung there by a wet hat string.

Reed swung Kamps' arm over his shoulder and hurried him to the back stockroom. Mort Javins jumped over the bar like an athlete, then stooped and pulled JW Bendigo up and over his shoulder like a limp bag of grain.

"Damn, what a smell," the bartender said, hurrying back to the stockroom.

"Hey, I know you," Bendigo said in the same slurred voice as Kamps'. "You're Mortimer Javins the —"

"Shut up!" said the bartender.

In the stockroom, the bartender and Reed shoved the gunmen down onto a large pile of straw where a she-hound lay nursing three pups whose eyes were yet to open. The hound growled, showing her teeth, and stood up and walked away stiff-legged, two of the three pups hanging from her teats.

"Sorry, Mama," the bartender murmured, hearing boots on the boardwalk that stopped at the swinging doors.

Scooping up the third pup in his hands, he followed the mother hound to a pile of bar towels in a corner. The hound lay down

110

with her two sucklings still attached under her belly. The bartender laid the third pup down with its littermates.

"They're at the bar!" Reed whispered, his Colt out, cocked and ready.

"I've got it," said the bartender. The Colt he'd kept close was now shoved down in his bar apron, his shirttails hanging down over it.

Mortimer Javins the . . . what? Reed asked himself, having heard the gunman say he knew the bartender. *Knew him from where?* Reed wondered as Mort reached over and grabbed a mop and bucket on his way to the bar.

"Be right with you, cowboys," he called out to the three at the bar.

"Cow*boys*?" one man said.

"In a pig's eye," another said. "Not a *cow* in sight, and not a boy in our bunch."

"No offense intended," said Mort Javins, mop and bucket in hand. "I've had a terrible morning."

"I bet you have," one laughed.

"Place smells like an overfull privy," said another.

"I apologize for the smell," said Javins. "We just had a hell of a fight here."

"Yeah," said one man. He nodded at all the blood on the floor. "I don't smell no

111

pistol smoke. Somebody must've took a sticking or two."

"Yeah, it was a knife fight," said the bartender, standing a bottle of whiskey and three shot glasses on the bar. As he drew three tall frothy mugs of beer, one man nudged the man next to him and said, "Who said we wanted whiskey and mugs of beer?"

Mort Javins stood the three mugs on the bar in front of them and grinned.

"I read your minds," Javins replied. He picked up the whiskey bottle and filled the three shot glasses. "Every one of you was saying, *shots of whiskey and frothy beers.*"

"Like hell," said one. "I don't like nobody meddling with what I want, or don't want."

"Shut up, Matthew," said another man. "You know damn well this is what we came here for." He threw back the shot of whiskey and sucked down a long swig of beer. "When a bartender reads your mind, think of all the time he's saving you."

"That's true," the other two agreed, raising glasses, laughing, slapping dust from their shirts.

When their laughter waned, the one named Matthew Stiles said to the bartender, "We came here to drink, sure enough. But we're also here looking for three men who rode in earlier this morning." He glanced at the blood on the floor.

"I hope they weren't a part of all that went on here," Mort Javins said. He looked past the three drinkers, out the window, at Yancy Reed carrying Berle Kamps over his shoulder and shoving JW Bendigo ahead of him across the empty street toward the barn. Javins hoped none of these three looked around and saw them out there.

As Matthew Stiles turned to a position that would give him a perfect view of the two gunmen outside, a wagon rolled along the street at just the right speed to block his view until Reed and the two gunmen had vanished inside the barn.

Close call, thought Javins.

Grinning, he filled the three shot glasses. As he poured, he noted to himself how calm and steady his hands remained.

"This one's on the house," he said.

"Obliged, barkeep!" the men said, raising their glasses.

"I'm Grady Cooper," said one. He motioned at the man next to him. "This is Bobby Conners. We call him the Rattler."

"And I'm Matthew Stiles," said the man he'd been talking to. "Say," Stiles added, "you sure look familiar, if I might say so."

"You *can* say so," said Javins, "but I'm

113

not from around here. I'm Mortimer Javins, from Oregon."

"Your *name* even sounds familiar," said Stiles.

"Leave him alone, Matthew," said Conners. "Maybe he don't want to be familiar."

"That's all right," said Javins. "I get that a lot, tending bar. Folks think they've seen me somewhere before. I'm used to hearing it."

He glanced out the window. The street was clear. He smiled and poured the men another round of beers.

Inside the livery barn, Yancy Reed rolled Kamps off his shoulder onto the dirt floor. He let Bendigo slump against the corral railing.

"What's going on over there, Yancy?" Johnny Two asked, watching Reed struggle through the doors with the two outlaws.

"Three riders came in," Reed said. "They're Coyle men unless I miss my guess. I got these two out and got them over here, to tell Summers before any of their gang sees them. This situation is growing worse by the minute, Johnny." He looked around and asked, "Where is Summers?"

"Him and Silk Polly went to the jail to help the doctor with you-know-who," said

Johnny, careful what he said.

"Both of them had to go to the jail?" Reed asked. "Couldn't one of them have helped the good doctor?"

"I believe it would have only taken one of them, but Will Summers didn't want to leave Silk Polly here with Lee Ozine too long. Seems there's been some bad blood between them a couple years back. So, as soon as she got Lee Ozine's bleeding to stop, Will swept her up and got her out of here quick-like. Back to the jail. I believe he thought Polly might kill Ozine if he left the two of them together for long."

Reed shook his head, looking from one whipped outlaw to the next, each of them coming back to their senses slowly.

"I don't care which one of us does it, Johnny," he said. "But one of us needs to watch this bunch while the other goes to the jail and tells Summers there's other gunmen showing up, and they look like Coyle men to me."

Inside the Eagles Saloon, Mort Javins stood behind the shiny bar with a boot hiked up, resting on the top edge of a metal insulated cooler box. He relaxed and shared laugh after laugh with his three new friends, keeping them busy, drinking with them, getting them drunk.

Then the *tap-tapping* sound of the she-hound's nails came clacking along out of the stockroom and across the wooden floor. Matthew Stiles was the first to look at the hound walking toward them with a slouch hat wadded up and clamped between her teeth.

What the — ? Javins froze and stared at the hound and the slouch hat for a second, then suddenly realized what was going on. *Oh hell, here it goes.*

"Come here, girl," he called out to the rangy hound. But the hound paid no attention and walked on. She walked past him, past Conners and turned and walked between Cooper and Stiles to the exact place at the bar where Berle Kamps had stood earlier with the same hat atop his head.

"Here, come on, girl, come to me," Javins said. But the mother dog would have none of it. She appeared to stick to a plan she had in mind. She stopped and looked up at Matthew Stiles.

"Well now, pals," Stiles said to the others, "she's handing me a hat!" He laughed. "I believe we're being asked *to leave*!" He laughed again; the others laughed, too. Javins laughed with them, but his heart wasn't in it. The hound opened her mouth

116

and dropped the slouch hat at Stiles' feet. She stood for a moment as the men fell silent. Then, she turned around and walked back to the stockroom, her nails clacking every step of the way.

Javins started over to Stiles and reached out for the hat.

"Here," he said, "I'll take it. She's got pups back there, so she's acting crazy lately."

Stiles held the wadded-up hat out to Javins, who took it and started to walk away.

"Wait a damn minute! Come back here!" said Stiles. Javins stopped but didn't turn around. Instead, he looked back over his shoulder, his free hand slipping up under his shirt, down behind his apron. He wrapped his palm around the gun butt, cocked it.

"What is it?" he asked, pitching the hat over onto the bar.

"See this?" Stiles said. He held up a red hawk feather that had fallen from the hat.

"Yeah, we see it," Bobby Conners said.

"Damned right we see it," said Grady Cooper. "That's Kamps' hawk feather! He beat a red hawk dead into the ground with his pistol barrel to get it! He *always* wore it in *his* slouch hat."

"Well now, I agree," said Stiles. "I believe that's Kamps' hat, *and* his hawk feather."

He took a step closer behind Javins. "What do you say, bartender?"

But Javins was through talking . . .

He'd already decided on the fastest, most risky move a gunman could make. *Risky?* Yet, with three-against-one odds, it was a move that would level those odds in a heartbeat. He would draw the big Colt faster than lightning, fan the hammer once, twice, three times, *four,* so fast the four shots would sound almost like *one. Four rapid stings of a mad hornet,* he called it.

He saw himself making the move in his mind, a steely move he had made many times before, too many times to remember. A move made only by an expert gunman — *or a straight-up fool,* he thought to himself. He felt a familiar cool calmness come over him.

Without looking back, he stood relaxed, his feet planted shoulder-width apart, steady, listening to three pairs of boots spreading out slowly around him. Without changing his stance, he glanced sidelong into the mirror behind the bar and sorted it all out in his mind.

"All right, Javins, where's Kamps?" said Stiles. "If Javins really is your name."

Javins didn't reply.

"Either answer me, you son of a bitch,"

Stiles shouted, "or turn around and face what's coming to you!"

Javins turned as his Colt streaked out, his finger already pressed back on the trigger, his left hand striking back across the hammer, fanning it fast and steadily. Not one of the three gunmen's sidearms cleared the top of their holsters. They fell in turn, one, two, three, dead on the floor, while four shots resounded in a rising gray cloud of smoke. Javins walked from one gunman to the next, surveying the familiar damage.

He nudged Stiles in his side with the toe of his boot. Stiles' gun barrel lay half out of its holster. *Close, but no cigar . . .* Bullet number one had bored through his heart, leaving a trail of thick blood strung out on the floor behind him.

He walked on to Grady Cooper, lying flat on his back, his gun having fallen back down into its holster as bullet number two killed him quick, in the same manner as Stiles. *Dead and gone . . .*

He stepped around Cooper and stood over Bobby Conners. Bloody holes in Conners' chest belonged to bullets three and four. The *extra* shot was something he always did instinctively.

No matter how many shots he fanned, he always fired that extra shot rather than give up that split second it would cost to stop all at once. He'd learned that move the hard way.

He dropped four warm shells from his smoking Colt and replaced them with fresh rounds. With six rounds in the Colt, instead of the usual five that some men carried, he swung the chamber shut, spun it, and set his hammer for further use. Pulling off his bar apron, he rolled the big main door shut in front of the batwings, but left it unlocked. He turned the open sign in the front window to closed and walked back to the stockroom, where he found the she-hound trembling, her pups pulled in close around her.

"Aw, don't worry, Mama," he said quietly, rubbing her nervous bony head. "Nobody's going to hurt you or your babies."

The hound continued to shake, but not quite as bad. She managed to venture a careful tongue up to lick the back of his hand.

CHAPTER 8

The gunshots from the Eagles Saloon registered loud and clear. Dr. Otto Adams and Will Summers faced each other across Dolan Coyle, who lay on the bunk in the jail cell. They each stood leaning in, Summers with one hand firmly atop Coyle's head, and the other resting on the outlaw's chin. Neither of them moved a muscle or twitched a nerve when the gunfire thundered along the empty street.

"Good work," the doctor whispered to Summers across the outlaw's motionless chest. They knew what could have happened when the explosions erupted, had it not been for someone holding Coyle in place. That's if Dolan Coyle was even alive, Summers thought.

"I'll have to go check on the gunfire, Doctor," Summers said calmly, quietly.

"I know, Will," said the doctor. "Just one second." He took a breath and leaned in close to Coyle's forehead with his right finger in the handle of a long pair of tweezers. What seemed to be only seconds later, the doctor straightened up with an exhale and laid the now-bloody tweezers on a tray atop the small table beside the bunk.

"There," said the doctor, "that's that. You can turn loose." He stood looking down at the tweezers.

Summers removed his hands from the wounded outlaw and straightened up. He was surprised at the doctor's words. He had not seen anything, heard anything, or felt anything. Yet, looking down now at the tweezers, not only were they bloody, they held in their small jaws a sliver of iron over an inch long, a quarter of an inch wide, one end of its sharp point glistening.

"You just pulled that out of his forehead, Doctor?" Summers said. "I never felt you doing a thing."

"Thank you, Will. That's what I wanted." He smiled wearily. "Now, we'll wait and see if anything changes." He nodded at the door. "Go see about the saloon. If you need me, send someone to stay here with this man, and I'll be right there."

Out front of the jail, Summers looked down the street and saw Johnny Two and Yancy Reed closing in slowly on the Eagles

Saloon. Reed stood in the street. Johnny Two had taken a position at the corner of an alley beside the big plank-covered building. Summers hurried as Reed waved him in closer.

"What was it, Yancy?" Summers asked when he stopped beside Reed and they both looked at the quiet saloon.

"It was some fast, slick shooting, I think," said Yancy Reed. "There were three gunmen coming into town when I took the first three to the barn." He shook his head. "Three down, three up, Will. We're a *real* busy place here."

"I know," said Summers, staring at the saloon. "It was some quick *fanning*. Then nothing after it. See anybody leave?"

"No," said Reed. "We can check it."

"Did Parks come back? Is he watching the three in the barn?"

"No, he never came back," said Reed. "I put a double-barrel in Silk Polly's hands and sat her in a chair. The three gunmen are cuffed to a rail. They look scared to death to even *breathe* with her there."

"Good enough," said Summers. He looked over at Johnny Two and motioned him toward the end of the alley at the rear of the saloon. Johnny slipped down the alley and disappeared like smoke. "I hope the bartender's not dead."

"I don't think he is," said Reed. They both looked at the three gunmen's horses hitched to the rail out front.

Summers heard a clear certainty in his voice. "I hope you're right," he said.

"I recognized something about the bartender's name right before the shooting started," said Reed. "Mortimer Javins?" He paused, then said, "You ever hear of the Rebel Kid? Rode guerilla with Bloody Bill Anderson before he'd even turned sixteen?"

"I heard of him, years ago," said Summers. "You think Javins is him, the Rebel Kid?" They walked forward slowly.

"We're fixing to find out," Reed said.

The two spread farther apart as they drew closer to the boardwalk. Then Reed with his shotgun took a position beside the main door. Summers grasped the handle of the big rolling door. Seeing it was unlocked he gave a strong pull on it and stepped back as it rolled open wide.

The two looked around at the three bodies strewn on the floor, then, hearing a sound from the direction of the stockroom, Summers raised his Colt.

"Are you back there, Johnny Two?" he called out.

"Yes, it's only me, Will," Johnny Two

replied. "Nobody back here except me and a dog with her pups. I think the bartender has been looking after her."

"Come on out," Summers said. "We've got three dead men laying out here."

Johnny Two stepped out of the stockroom. The she-hound stood at knee level, peeping around the doorframe into the bloody saloon. Johnny rubbed her head, his rifle in his other hand.

"But no dead bartender?" he said.

"No," said Summers. "He managed to take these three down pretty quick and got himself out of here. Even left the door unlocked so we can get in and feed his animals." He nodded at the hound whose head Johnny Two was now scratching.

"I'm not surprised he killed them," said Reed, "knowing who he is."

"Who is he?" Johnny Two asked.

"The Rebel Kid, I'm thinking," said Reed. "Ever heard of him?"

"Heard the name," said Johnny Two, "but he's before my time."

"I might have a poster on him over at the jail," said Summers. "Let's drag these bodies out and cover them up, and we'll go see."

A loud knock came at the front door.

"Summers!" a loud voice called out from

the front boardwalk. "Is that you in there?"

"Who is it?" Summers replied.

"It's Arnold Mason, from Brayton Siding. Can I come in there?"

"You can, Arnold," said Summers, "but watch where you step."

The big man stepped inside. "Watch where I step?" he said, grinning, then his eyes went across all the blood and three dead faces on the floor. *Whoa!* he said, turning away quickly toward the street. "I just come to tell you there's a dozen or more riders coming here about an hour out. I spotted them from a higher trail and remembered the deputy said you might have trouble coming. So, I rode like hell to tell you."

"Obliged, Arnold," said Summers. "It's good you told us. Trouble has started already."

"Can I help?" Arnold Mason asked. "I don't mind the blood after I see it. I was caught off guard, but I'm good now."

Summers thought for a second, then said, "You tended bar at the old Roi Tan, didn't you?"

"I did," said Mason. He looked around. "You need a bartender here? What happened to the new man, Javins?"

"Javins left us in a hurry this morning,"

126

Summers said. He gestured at the floor.

"Damn," said Arnold. "They must've pissed him off bad, from the looks of it."

"I'll tell you sometime," said Summers. "Right now, if you'll help us clean up and get these jakes over to the barn, I'd like you to open this place up."

"Same man still owns the place?" Arnold asked.

"Yes, Angus Smith," said Summers. "He's up north right now, will be the next few months. But he gave me the say-so on what goes on here. You're hired, if it suits you."

"It suits me," said Arnold. He took off his long trail duster coat and laid it over a clean part of the bar. "I suppose if we don't open this saloon those riders coming here will tear it to the ground?"

"You've read my mind, Arnold Mason," said Summers.

Inside the livery barn, Silk Polly sat in a wooden chair with a shotgun over her crossed legs. She stared intently at the two prisoners, Berle Kamps and JW Bendigo, standing handcuffed to the corral rail, not even turning when Summers and Reed walked into the building. The third man, Lee Ozine, sat in a chair beside the corral, handcuffed to the rail, one arm in a sling owing to his shoulder wound.

"Everything all right here, Polly?" Summers asked softly, not wanting to surprise her and cause her to start shooting.

"It's fine here, Will," Polly said. She nodded toward Ozine. "As you can see, I have not blown his head all over the barn, as I feel strongly compelled to do." Ozine wisely kept his head bowed.

"I'm grateful and obliged, Polly," said Summers.

Silk Polly gave him a firm look.

"You can't be grateful *and* obliged," she said. "They both mean the same thing."

"You're right," Summers said. "I'm obliged for all your help. I'm grateful being able to depend on you."

"I should say so," she replied with a faint smile. "It was hard, not shooting his brains all across the corral."

"I bet it was," said Summers, stepping forward and gently taking the shotgun from her hands. "Eagles owes you a debt of gratitude."

"Anytime, Will." She took his forearm to steady herself as she stood. "I should tell you Judge Parker's deputy came by here wanting to take a lot of horses from the stables and corral."

"Really?" said Summers. He and Yancy

Reed exchanged a *not too surprised* look. "What did you tell him?"

Silk Polly winced a little.

"I hope I didn't say anything I shouldn't," she said. "I told him to get out of here and go to hell or I'd open his guts for him."

"He didn't take any horses?" Summers asked.

"Not even his *own,*" Polly said, "not after I held the shotgun in his face and cocked both hammers."

Reed stifled a dark laugh.

"You didn't say the wrong thing, Polly. Not under the circumstances," Summers said. "If he wants the horses, or his own, he can come talk to me."

"I suppose I could have just said that," said Polly.

"What you said was good," Summers reassured her.

"Where is Johnny Two Red Wolves?" she asked, looking off in the direction of the saloon. "I hope he is all right."

"Johnny's fine, Polly," said Summers. "He's at the saloon, helping our new bartender get the place opened up."

"New bartender?" asked Polly. "I heard that terrible string of gunfire. I hoped it wasn't . . . ."

"Yes. We had some trouble, but it's settled

129

now," said Summers.

"And my old friend Mortimer?" she asked. "Oh, of course Mort Javins is all right — he always is."

"You and Mort Javins are old friends?" Summers asked, surprised.

"Oh my goodness, yes," said Polly. "We've been friends longer than either of us like to admit." She smiled. "When I heard that strange-sounding gunfire, I knew it was him. He wanted so much for things to work out for him here. Are things all right for him?"

"I'm sorry, he left," said Summers. "He shot three gunmen, which was likely in self-defense, but he didn't stick around to see if he'd be all right."

"Polly," Reed cut in, "how well do you know him?"

She gave a weak little shrug.

"I don't know," she said. "Well enough, I suppose. We knew each other during the civil conflict."

"Did you know him by another name?" Reed asked.

Polly's expression turned cagey.

"Several, over the years," she said. "After the war, lots of men took different names for many reasons. Mortimer was like that. He had worked almost as a spy, and spying was a hanging offense."

130

"I understand, Polly," said Reed. "But I'm thinking of one name in particular. Way back years ago."

"Yes," Polly said quietly, "I think I know the name you mean." She beckoned the two closer.

Her eyes darted back and forth furtively. Her voice, already quiet, dropped to a whisper.

"You mean the Rebel Kid?" she said, oh so softly.

"I knew it," said Reed, also softly.

Polly looked at Summers, her eyes pleading.

"Mortimer is a good man, Will," she said, almost tearfully. "He even reminds me of you, some." She clutched his forearm. "Can you help him stay here, Will? He only wants to tend bar and live a quiet life."

"If he comes back, he's welcome here. I'm not the law, Polly, and we're in a troubled time. It might be that nobody even asks him what happened. If the law asks and he tells the truth, I'll do what I can to help him."

"Me, too," said Reed. "That's if he ever comes back."

Polly looked at them.

"Is that stray bitch hound and her three pups still in the stockroom?" Polly asked.

"They are," said Summers. "Is that his

hound?"

"No," said Polly. "She's just some stray who showed up and needed a place to stay. Mortimer took her in, bless his heart. He does that sort of thing, always has. If he left her and those pups here, he's coming back. You can count on it."

"If you see him before we do," Summers said, "tell him to get his bark off. We're not his enemies."

"If I see him first, I will tell him," said Silk Polly. "Now that I know the hound and her pups are here, I'll cook up some pork cracklings for them."

They turned to the front door as it squeaked open enough for Johnny Two to stick his head inside.

"We've got another white flag tied to a rifle barrel coming in, Will."

"I'm coming, Johnny," said Summers. He turned to Reed and said, "Keep these prisoners quiet for now."

"Don't worry," said Reed. He raised his voice for the benefit of the handcuffed prisoners. "I'll see to it these three keep *their mouths shut.*"

From the corral rail, all three battered, hungover gunmen stared at Reed. Lee Ozine, taking issue, half stood from his wooden chair.

"According to the new constitution," he said, "I have a God-given right to say any damn thing I want to say, as loud as I want to say it!"

"Being familiar with our new constitution as I can see you are," said Reed, "if you'll go on to the next page you'll see where it says if you don't keep your mouth shut, I have a right to crack your big head with a rifle butt." He stepped toward Ozine, who sank down into his chair and fell silent. The other two fell silent as well. Reed motioned Summers toward the street. "Go on," he said. "I'll watch through a crack."

"I'll go with you, Will," Johnny Two said, already carrying a rifle.

"All right, Johnny," said Summers, walking toward the door. "Keep to the side. When I need you, you'll know it."

"Are we going to give them the first move?" Johnny Two Red Wolves asked.

"No," said Summers, "not if we see it coming."

CHAPTER 9

The three riders put their horses forward at a walk along the empty street. Will Summers and Johnny Two stood ten feet apart. Each held a rifle firmly in hand, ready to fire. Each wore a big Colt in a slim jim holster. And each remembered how little a white cloth tied to a rifle barrel meant the last time one came to town. From a crack in the livery barn door, Yancy Reed watched. From windows and doorways along the street, the few remaining townspeople watched. At the far end of the street, a wagon left town carrying household goods, a family cow in tow.

"*Hola*, Will Summers!" The middle of the three riders called out. Forty feet away, they brought their horses to an easy halt. One of them led a saddled horse, ready to ride.

"*Hola*, to you, Axel Coyle," Summers called out in reply. He motioned toward the rider on Coyle's left. "Ask your man to

134

lower the white flag, or else get shed of it altogether," he said. "We just had a bad time with one that looked similar."

Axel Coyle lowered his hand at his side. The man with the white flag lowered his rifle.

"None of *my* riders, I hope," Axel said.

"As a matter of fact, it was," said Summers. "But no harm done, except for the noise. They came thinking they would get Dolan and ride out."

"Well," said Axel, with an icy little smile, "I'm relieved nobody was injured."

"Fella named Lee Ozine took a bullet in the shoulder," said Summers. "The other two only got themselves butt smacked."

"Ouch!" Axel winced. "I'd as soon take a bullet wound as I would a bad head thumping, any day."

"I wouldn't want either one, Axel," Summers said, cutting out the small talk. "What brings you here?"

"I come here to get Dolan, just like you knew I was going to," he said. "Are you going to give him up?"

"I have no hold on him," said Summers. "He's a prisoner of Judge Parker's deputies. One of them, anyway. Deputy Claude Parks," he added. "Deputy Edmond Hughes is dead. Your men killed him."

135

"Good," said Axel. "I mean 'good' that Ed Hughes is dead," he added. "I would have given anything to see it. But it wasn't my men that killed him." One of his riders leaned over to him and whispered something. Axel looked back up and said, "I mean, it wasn't my men or *me* who killed him. We were nowhere around." He waved his rifle and flag of truce back and forth, one time, slowly. "Don't forget I'm here under a white flag."

"Red Zorn killed Hughes," said Summers. "Then Zorn was killed straightaway, during the storm that blew through here."

"Who killed Red?" Axel asked sharply.

Summers stared at him for a second and said, "I don't remember. Why? Was he one of your gunmen?"

"No," Axel said firmly. "I told you, we're all clean as a whistle."

"Then I expect it doesn't matter, does it?" said Summers. A tense moment passed. Johnny Two stood firmly in place, his rifle ready to come up firing.

Axel looked ready to turn his rifle from a sign of peace to a carrier of destruction.

"Listen to me, Axel Coyle," said Summers, seeing the peace start to slip away, "it's important you know where I stand before we start splattering each other on

136

the street."

"Oh?" Axel kept his rifle ready, his finger on the trigger, the hammer cocked.

"I'm not a lawman here," said Summers. "My partner, Johnny Two Red Wolves, and I run the public livery and do some horse trading. The judge's deputies came here with Dolan under arrest. They needed the doctor, and they needed fresh horses. The town of Eagles accommodated them."

"So, you're telling me you have no *legal* hold on my brother, Dolan?" Axel asked.

"None whatsoever," said Summers. "And, as far as I know, Deputy Parks has left town."

Axel chuffed and shook his head.

"I always figured ol' Claude Parks has rabbit blood in him. He won't slow down until he reaches Fort Smith." He looked back at Summers. "But why are you telling me all this?" he said. "Is Dolan eating too much? You can't afford him?"

"I wish that was it, Axel," Summers said.

"I'll settle for it," said Axel. "I'm taking my brother and cutting out of here." He raised his free hand and waved it overhead. Riders appeared in a long, jagged line spread out, surrounding the town. Dust stirred at their horses' hooves.

Axel laughed.

"Looks like I caught you off guard," he said. He leaned forward in his saddle and said, "Tell the truth, Will Summers, are your boots still dry?"

Summers only gave the riders a passing glance.

"We're good, Axel," he said. Johnny hadn't so much as cut a glance toward the many riders surrounding the town.

"All right, take me to my brother," said Axel. "You can see I brought him a horse. I wasn't leaving without him."

"I'm glad it worked out for you," said Summers.

"You damn well bet you are, Will Summers," Axel said boldly. "I've got near forty men riding with me. Tell me now, how many guns have you got hiding around here, pointed straight at us?"

"I can't say, Axel," said Summers. "I didn't count."

"Hear that, men?" Axel said to the two men with him. "I told you this is a smart sumbitch we're dealing with in Eagles." He gestured at Summers and said, "No offense."

"None taken," Summers replied, and guided Axel and the two other riders toward the jail. He wondered how Axel would react seeing his brother, Dolan, lying in bed with

138

his head sewed up and bandaged, wearing no more expression than that of a corpse.

When Axel and his two men swung down from their horses at the hitch, Johnny Two slipped in and stood in front of the door to the jail, his rifle still ready. Axel had handed his rifle to one of his men, who wrapped the white flag around the barrel.

"What this?" Axel asked Summers while staring hard at Johnny Two. "Does your partner think I won't kill him where he stands if he doesn't get the hell out of my way?"

"There's something I have to tell you before we go in, Axel," Summers said. "Your brother was wounded during the same rifle fire that killed Deputy Hughes."

"Huh-uh, Summers," said Axel. "If Dolan took a bullet I'll let him tell me about it while we're on the trail! Not you and this Indian *segundo* of yours." He started to take a step toward Johnny Two. "Get the hell out of my way!" he said with his finger on his rifle's trigger.

Johnny Two Red Wolves didn't budge an inch for him.

"Your brother can't tell you, Axel!" said Summers. "Dolan had over an inch of steel removed from inside his head. He can't talk, he can't hear, I don't think he can even think!"

"What the hell are you saying?" said Axel.

"You heard what I'm saying," said Summers. "Dolan don't know who he is, or where he is."

"But he's *alive*?" Axel said.

"If you want to call it living!" said Summers. "Doctor says he's alive. But he looks as dead as any dead man I've ever seen. He just doesn't have any paperwork to prove it."

"You're lying, Summers!" Axel raged.

"I wish I was lying," said Summers. "But I'm not —"

"Who shot him, damn you to hell?" said Axel.

"I don't know," Summers said, "and I mean that. There were riflemen out there firing on this town like crazy. You said they weren't your men. All right, I won't say otherwise. But a bullet came in from somewhere, bounced off the cell bars and nailed him."

"My brother? Shot by a damned ricochet?! What the hell are the odds of that happening?"

"I don't know," said Summers. "I'm going to show you if you're settled enough to see it."

140

"Settled enough to see it?" said Axel. "What the hell kind of thing is that to say?"

Summers motioned Johnny Two Red Wolves to get out of the way.

"Come on," he said to Axel Coyle. "I'll show you what we think happened to your brother."

"Who's *we*?" said Axel. He'd taken a step toward the door, but hesitated and stopped.

"*We* is Dr. Adams and me," said Summers. "I watched him take the piece of steel out of Dolan's head half as long as a framing nail. I have no reason to lie about it. Neither does he." He swung the door open and nodded Axel inside.

"There's something about walking into a jail that makes me edgy as hell," Axel said. He looked around suspiciously. "I feel like a lock is going to click shut behind me."

"I know how that feels," Summers said. "But nothing's going to happen to you here. Leastwise not from me or Johnny Two," said Summers. "Come on in. See your brother."

"What the hell is this — ?" Axel Coyle whispered almost to himself. He'd stepped over to the open cell door and saw the blanket covering Dolan from his feet to his neck, and the bloodstained bandage covering his brother's forehead just above his eyes.

"Dolan!" Axel said. "Can you hear me?" Dolan's eyes, which were half-closed, stared blankly. "Tell me you can hear me!" Axel demanded. "Say something! Bat your eyes!" He started to grab his brother by his shoulder and shake him.

"No, no!" said Dr. Adams. Having heard Axel's raised voice, he'd hurried in from another room. "Don't touch him, young man!" he said firmly.

"He's my brother!" Axel shouted. His hand clasped the butt of the big Colt holstered on his hip. "I'll touch him if I damn well please!"

"In that case, you go right ahead," said the doctor. "I'll get a ruler and measure him for a pinewood overcoat." He stared hard at Axel Coyle. Axel's hand slid off his gun butt.

"You have no right talking to me that way!" said Axel.

"When it comes to your brother's life, I've every right in the world to talk to you how I choose," said Adams. "I didn't save his life for you or anybody else to come in here and kill him."

Axel started to take a step toward the doctor. The doctor stood firm. Summers stepped in between the two.

"Listen to him, Axel," said Summers. "Men like you and I put Dolan here, with this fighting and killing. It's time a man like Dr. Adams steps in and *saves* a life, if he can."

Axel settled, a little, but he looked at his brother and shook his head.

"He looks dead to me, Summers," he said. "And somebody is going to pay."

"Then you best get your riflemen rounded up," the doctor put in. "It was one of their bullets that got him. Or, get the person who built this wall of bars. It was a piece of this steel that flew off and buried itself in Dolan's skull."

"I don't believe you, sawbones!" said Axel.

"I don't give a damn," said the doctor. "If you don't believe that, you won't believe this, either." He looked at Summers and Axel in turn and said, "Only minutes before you came in here, Dolan's head was facing the other direction. And before I came in the room I thought I had heard him mutter the name *Sylvia.*"

"You mean he moved his head?" Summers said, amazed.

"He did indeed." Adams turned to Axel, who looked similarly stunned, as if Dolan's voice had come from the isle of the dead. "Who is Sylvia?" he asked.

"She's a woman my brother had plans to marry," said Axel. "Some drunken sumbitch shot and killed her."

"Well, of course," said the doctor, with a sour note of skepticism. "I would not have assumed that she died of natural causes."

"The hell does that mean?" said Axel.

"Never mind," said Adams.

"Let it go, Axel," Summers interjected. "The main thing is Dolan came around enough to speak and move his head. I never thought that would happen. Dolan can live through this! Right, Doctor?"

"I'm more optimistic than before," the doctor said.

"You better hope to hell he does," said Axel, back to threatening. "If not, it'll mean you were lying!"

"Okay, outlaw, tell me this," said Dr. Adams. "How many people knew the name *Sylvia*?"

Axel fell dead silent.

"That's what I thought," the doctor said. He stifled a yawn. "Gentlemen, I'm going to get something to eat. Axel, can you sit here with Dolan until I return? Make note of anything he might do or say."

"I sure will," said Axel. "And I've got men with me who'll help."

"Good," said Adams. "I might be moving him to my house today. I'm expecting to have some room there after another patient or two have left." He didn't want to mention that there were four patients, all of them wounded posse men.

Claude Parks felt a lot better just knowing he was getting out of Eagles. He and his four wounded posse had slipped four horses out of the livery barn just in time, right before Will Summers and Johnny Two Red Wolves met with Axel Coyle and two of his men in the street out front of the barn. Tom Barton, one of the four posse men, had crawled under a washout space in the rear wall. He'd managed to drag out three good saddles and bridles before Parks spotted the rest of Axel's riders starting to circle the little town.

"You'll just have to ride bareback for now, Tom," he said as the five reined up over a mile out of town and looked back through their roiling cloud of trail dust. "If she keeps fighting you, slap the hell out of her with the ragged end of the rope, why don't you."

"I'll make do," Barton replied, atop a headstrong mare that kept jerking sideways on the hackamore Barton had fashioned from a length of rope. "I don't slap a horse in the face with a rope."

"By God, I do," Parks snapped back, not liking the tone of Barton's voice.

145

"That's you, Parks," said Barton. "I thought we were talking about me. Any *fool* knows better than to whip a horse's face. That's how you blind one, with an eye infection if nothing else."

Parks gritted his teeth, knowing his posse man had just called him a fool in front of the other three. Having seen how quick Tom Barton could cross-draw his big Remington, bad shoulder or no, he decided to let it pass. Under Barton's shirt, a large blood-stained bandage covered his left shoulder. Barton patted a hand on the cream-colored mare's neck, calming her.

"Easy, lady," he whispered to her. "Nobody's going to hit you with a rope. To hell with him, you and I have got to get along." He rubbed her neck. She settled more.

"If you're going to scout for us, get on out there. We can't wait around for you. You'll have to keep up with what's going on," Parks said, trying to claim the last word on the matter. But even that didn't work for him.

"Keep *up*?" A wounded posse man named Harper Dowd gave a chuckle. "Hell, Tom here can ride circles around anybody I know, bareback or saddled. He can *by God* drop over a horse's side and fire a pistol under its belly while it's running —"

"You talk too much, Dowd," Barton cut in. He touched his knees to the mare's sides as he let off of the hackamore. "Come on, lady, show them where you live."

Parks and the others watched the cream-colored mare streak away like a bolt of lightning. Tom Barton, riding bareback, leaned forward, loose and easy, the mare's white mane whipping around his face.

"All right," said Parks, "he's a hell of a rider. I give him that. But we'll see what he does when the Coyles are dogging him."

"Tom Barton has already taken a bullet for this posse," said Harper Dowd. "He don't have to prove a damn thing to me."

"Me, neither," said an older gunman named Neil Tooney. "If we'd had a few more like him we wouldn't be down to four wounded men and one deputy, sneaking out of town like whipped dogs."

"Keep running your mouth, Tooney!" Parks barked. "You'll never ride with another posse out of Judge Parker's court." He turned his horse and stormed away.

"*Ha,* that sure breaks my heart all to hell," Neil Tooney said quietly to Dowd, sitting on the horse next to him.

"We'll be lucky, *damned* lucky, if he don't get us all killed before we get out of here," said Dowd, nudging his horse forward. "If I find myself a flat, straight trail, I'll be gone outta here like last night's whiskey."

"All right, pard. That'll be me spitting and cussing right there beside you," said Neil Tooney.

"I've never been so glad to be leaving a place in my life," said a fourth posse man named Al Slater.

"Watch what you say, Al," said Dowd. "We ain't left here yet. Don't jinx it for us."

"Ha!" said Slater. "The jinx was us ever coming here in the first place."

CHAPTER 10

With the telegraph line between Eagles and
Brayton Siding repaired, Summers had immediately asked Leonard Spires to send an
inquiry to be forwarded on to Fort Smith,
Arkansas, in care of the district court, office
of records. When he saw Spires walking
across the wide street toward the jail, a sheet
of telegraph paper in his hand, he stood up
and walked out to meet him. Some of the
Coyle riders had made themselves at home
in the Eagles Saloon. Summers was good
with that, so long as they started no trouble.

"What have you got for me, Leonard?" he
asked the ancient telegraph clerk as they
met in the middle of the street.

"All right," said Spires, clearing his throat,
"here it goes, short and sweet."

Instead of handing Summers the telegram,
or even reading it to him, Leonard recited
the letter's contents.

"Reply to Will Summers. Deputy Claude

Parks is not, nor has he been for the past six months, an employee of the court." He paused and added, "Ain't that a big solid boot in the rectum?"

"Are you joking?" Summers asked.

Spires squinted at him. "You know me, Will, I'm a rolling barrel of laughs. Always joking."

"Sorry, Spires, I meant nothing by it."

Leonard grinned. "I know you didn't. And I'm not worried about you, either," he said. "I know you'll handle all these far-handed jackasses in proper order, when the time is right."

"I appreciate your vote of confidence, Leonard," Summers replied. "But I have to warn you, things might get worse around here before they get better."

"Better or worse," Spires said, "when you get as old as I am, it's hard to tell which is which. If I can help any, let me know. If not, I'll stay out of your way. Oh, I ought to tell you, when a man is appointed deputy, every court, town sheriff, army post and whatnot is informed right away. That might be helpful to you."

"Obliged," Summers said. "Yes, that might be helpful." He sighed. "*Whew!* How did Claude Parks get to be in charge of a posse hunting Dolan Coyle and his gang?"

150

"Beats the living hell out of me," said the old man. "I expect in Fort Smith everybody knew Parks was a posse leader for so many years, they never wondered when he come asking them to ride with him, they just mounted and rode. Do you think?"

"I reckon so," said Summers. "I should have checked it all out first."

"Check how?" said Spires. "Our lines were down. We were under armed attack. Both deputies had badges, big hats and whatnot. What else would we think? What else would you have done, turn away wounded men? Refused them horses? Not let Doc Adams treat them?"

"You're right," said Summers. "I acted the only way a reasonable man could. I trusted the law." He took the telegram from Spires and shoved it inside his shirt. "I better hang on to this."

"Good idea."

"Now I've got to straighten out the mess."

"Uh-oh! Look what's going on there," said Spires. He pointed toward the Eagles Saloon, where three men were stepping down from their saddles and hitching their horses to a post along the boardwalk, the hitch rail being packed full with sweaty, dusty horses.

But the newcomers weren't the object of the old telegraph clerk's attention. He was

151

looking at four men carrying an upright piano toward the saloon from a closed-down theater across the street.

"If it'll keep them from shooting each other," Summers said, "let them go. As soon as I can, I'll get Axel to gather them all up and get them out of here."

"Good luck," said Spires, and turned to walk back toward his office.

As Spires left, Summers noticed the three men who had just ridden in had not proceeded into the busy saloon. Instead, they'd split up and spread out into a wide half circle out front, where they stood watching the comings and goings through the flapping of the saloon's batwing doors.

He'd wondered when the bounty vultures would start showing up. He didn't like the idea of acting as lookout for a gang of outlaws like the Coyles, but for the sake of the town and its people, what was he supposed to do? *We can't stand by and watch the town get shot up.*

Bide your time, he told himself. *This will pass.*

He walked toward one of the men, who was now standing across the street from the saloon. The man stood comfortably leaning against an overhang support. He straightened quickly as soon as Summers got within fifty feet of him.

"That's close enough, mister," the man said, his thumb pulling back a leather safety loop from around the hammer of his holstered Smith & Wesson revolver.

Summers stopped in his tracks and loosely held his hands chest high in a show of peace.

"No trouble, mister," said Summers. "I'm only here to ask what brings you to Eagles."

"Are you the sheriff, mister?" asked the man, his hand near the big pistol.

"No," said Summers, "I'm just a businessman here. We've had some trouble. I'm here to make sure we don't have any more —"

"Walk on and mind your business, *businessman,*" the man replied. "Your main *business* right now is to stay the hell out of mine."

As the man spoke, he stepped off the boardwalk. Will Summers recognized the look on his face. A fight was coming — *in about half a minute,* if he didn't miss his guess. He braced himself, his boots spread shoulder-width apart. But before another word could be spoken, a rifle shot resounded from the roof of the saloon behind him.

The man's hat spun from his head in a red mist and he fell limply to the ground. The other two men came running in a low crouch, their guns up, scanning the roof-line. Gray smoke curled above the saloon's short clapboard facade. Summers had no choice but to back away himself or get shot down, either by this man's fellow gunmen or by whoever had put a bullet in his head.

Gunshots exploded from the saloon doors, from the roof above, and from along the boardwalk where gunmen appeared now, as if by magic. A little girl, no more than a toddler, had just walked out of the general store, laughing. Now she stood frozen, screaming in fear. Summers ran from the cover of a huge barrel, snatched the child up and kept running, his hat flying from his head. Bullets zipped around them until he dived behind a stack of shipping crates, the child still in his arms.

She let go a razor-sharp scream right into Summers' ear. He managed to hang on to her, even as he peeped around the shipping crates and saw that the two other gunmen were now lying in the street, one dead, one dying. The one still alive tried to push himself up but he couldn't do it. He dropped back down on his face. Coyle gunmen from the Eagles Saloon had started creeping cautiously around the bodies in the street.

Yancy Reed came running from the direction of the livery barn, Johnny Two from the jail. Silk Polly looked on from the barn door, the shotgun in her hands.

Summers rocked the toddler easily in his arms and tried calming her down. He soon noticed there were few familiar faces left in Eagles. The local residents had left town a few at a time. Those who were still here kept inside, out of sight — *out of range,* he thought.

This wouldn't do, he told himself, as the gunmen, saloon girls and brothel women from Brayton Siding gathered around, looking at the three men sprawled in the street, two dead and one still alive.

From the doors of the mercantile store, a woman came running, looking around wildly.

"Greta!" she shouted. *"Baby Greta!* Where are you?"

"Here she is," one of the women from Brayton Siding called out to her. "The sheriff has her! She's all right!"

"Oh my God, there you are," the woman said to the child in Summers' arms. "Oh, Sheriff, God bless you, thank you!" the woman cried. Taking Baby Greta to her bosom, she said tearfully, "I just looked away for a second, an' she was out an' gone. I always bring my older daughter to watch her, but not this time! This is all my fault! I'm Zetra Wilson. We live out that way." She pointed northwest of town.

One of the saloon women called out, "I saw the whole thing. This baby would have been killed had the sheriff not run out and grabbed her —"

"Let's hear it for the sheriff!" a drunken man called out before the woman even finished Summers' praises.

Summers waved a hand and called out loudly above the crowd, "I'm not the sheriff, folks, I just live here!" He looked at a young boy and said, "Will you run and get the doctor? He's at the jail. Tell him we've got a wounded man here." As the boy ran toward the jail, Summers looked around for Reed and Johnny Two, who were standing side by side waiting to hear from him.

"I've seen this kind of thing before," Reed said quietly. "It's the oldest outlaw game in the book." He handed Summers his hat. Summers slapped the dusty hat against his leg and motioned Reed and Johnny Two toward the jail with him.

"You've seen what before, Yancy?" Summers asked as the three walked abreast in the street.

"The way the Coyle brothers and their gunmen are taking this town over," Reed

156

said. The two gave him a look. "Oh, I don't mean taking it by open force. I don't even know if they're doing it intentionally. But a little at a time, they're pushing their way in. I hope I'm not offending you, saying it, Will. But that's what's happening."

"I see it, too, Will," said Johnny. "No offense. They started out laying out in the flats shooting at us. Now, here they are. They've moved into Eagles like they've been here all their lives."

"No offense taken," Summers said to both of them. "The fact is, I've seen it myself. We took in a wounded prisoner until we could either treat him or bury him. Now it turns out that Parks wasn't even a deputy! His posse wasn't even legal." They looked at him, dumbfounded.

"That's right," Summers said. "Our lines are back up to Brayton. I found out this morning. Parks hasn't been a deputy for the past six months. This has all been him not wanting to give up his badge."

"Damn it!" said Reed. "Parks dropped this mess on us and left!"

"That's the whole of it," said Summers. "Now get this. Parks and his four wounded posse men stole four livery horses and left town on them. We've got more reason to hunt them down and hang them as horse thieves than we do to hold a prisoner of the federal district court who we have no charges on whatsoever."

Before they had time to ponder what he had said, they saw the doctor and the boy running toward them. Dr. Adams was carrying a medical bag and rolling down his shirtsleeve with his free hand.

"Go to the jail until I get back," the doctor called out, running past them. "Our *wounded man* is coming around! He recognized his brother this morning!"

"All right, let's go," said Summers. The three ran the last twenty yards to the jail and burst inside as Axel Coyle opened the door for them.

Inside the jail, Axel Coyle, Summers, Reed and Johnny Two Red Wolves assembled at the foot of Dolan Coyle's bunk in the small jail cell. After a moment, a slight blink from Dolan brought Axel forward. "See," said Axel, "he's coming around, just like I said!"

He filled a glass with tepid water from a pitcher and held it steady while his brother took a sip. Summers shook his head slowly. Beside him Johnny Two and Reed stared, speechless. From the bunk, Dolan's eyes, still open only a slit, flitted across their faces, then looked up toward the ceiling.

"I would never have believed it," Summers

murmured. "He's looking around, he drank water . . ."

"It's a miracle," said Axel. "I ain't what you call a religious man, the kind of person who believes in this sort of thing." He gestured at his brother, who lay breathing shallowly and moving his head a little now and then. "But here he is. What they call *proof in point.* My brother, Dolan, beat death all to hell and threw it out the door on its ass!" He teared up a little. Dolan raised a weak hand an inch and beckoned Axel closer.

"What is it, brother Dolan?" Axel said, bending down as tears of joy streamed down his face. "Anything you want, you've got it!"

With Axel's ear close to his lips, Dolan whispered in a low rasping voice, "Shut . . . *the hell . . .* up."

CHAPTER 11

Will Summers, Johnny Two Red Wolves and
Yancy Reed stood in the middle of the street
a few yards from the jail. They watched with
interest as several of Coyle's gunmen carried a large wooden chair, its frame tilted
back, and Dolan Coyle seated with his
hands on the wide wooden arms.

As the gunmen carried him, chair and all
shoulder high, a guitar player appeared as if
out of nowhere, followed by a naked dancer
from Brayton Siding, twirling slowly to the
soft dreamy Mexican music and kicking her
legs straight up, first one, then the other.

Summers looked around toward the saloon, then back at Dolan's unusual entou-
rage crossing the street.

Laughter and music spilled loudly from
the Eagles Saloon, with an occasional
friendly gunshot.

Later that same day, out front of the
Eagles Saloon, four new faces, dusty and

sweat-streaked from the trail, rode in and contemplated the crowded hitch rail for a minute.

"Chauncy," said the leader, a tall man wearing a faded black suit under a riding duster, "turn four horses loose. We need some room."

"Yes, sir, Mr. Ekland," said Chauncy Wade, a man who had recently served three years of a life sentence for murder in Arkansas. He appeared to snap to attention in his saddle. He reined his horse around on the narrow side of the hitch rail, rode along and cut the reins of the first four horses, then shooed them away. The horses jumped back, ran to the middle of the street.

"Hey, that's my horse!" a young trail hand said, stepping out of the saloon.

"Then you better get him out of the street before he gets somebody hurt!" shouted one of the four now reining their horses to the hitch rail.

The young man looked straight at Ekland.

"Who the hell do you men think you are?" he shouted.

"That's not the question, laddie," said Dallas Ekland. "The question is, Do you want to die today?"

Die today?

The young man looked again, this time

161

more closely, at the four men. They sat staring at him, all dressed in dark, dusty, ragged range clothes, armed to the teeth. Shotguns hung under their arms, partially hidden by their trail dusters.

"No, sir," said the young range hand, "I don't reckon I came here wanting to die."

"A wise lad," said Ekland, with no expression on his hard pockmarked face. He and his men each wore a big revolver holstered on their right hip, another in a forward angled holster on their left side, a bandolier of ammunition draped around their shoulder. A rifle butt stuck up from each saddle boot. "Now move that poor animal out of the way," Ekland said, his eyes as blank and dead as a rock lizard's.

One of Coyle's gang, Arvin Yates, who had stepped out of the saloon a moment after the range hand, stayed just long enough to see what was going on. One of the four men looked hard at him as he took note of all their shooting gear and then stepped backward into the saloon.

"More damned bounty hunters are here!" he said in a low tone to two of the Coyle gunmen drinking at the bar. They turned and watched him as he hurried toward the back corner of the saloon, where a large table topped in green felt had been set aside for the Coyle Gang.

When Prince Drako saw Yates coming, he stepped back from a conversation about robbing the town bank and grabbed Yates by the shoulder before he could get past him and head for the back door.

"What are you running from, Arvin?" Drako asked. Yates reached for the mug of beer in Drako's hand. Drako gave it to him and watched him drain the mug in one long gulp. When Yates handed it back, Drako held the mug upside down as if making sure it was really empty.

"All right!" said Yates, catching his breath. "Four more bounty hunters just rode in! I saw them bad-mouthing a drover about his horse being in the street." With frightened eyes, he added, "It's getting awful bad here, Prince. *Awful bad!*"

Drako, a little drunk, patted Arvin Yates on his shoulder. "Well, hell, Arvin," he said. "I hear it's getting bad everywhere. I mean, places where it's never been bad before!"

"I don't know about all that," said Yates. "I just know that I want to warn Axel and Dolan, then I want to get out of here before it's too late!"

Outlaws who had heard some of their words gathered in closer to hear more.

"Relax," said Drako. "If they are stupid

enough to come in here, we'll shoot them, then we'll all have a beer."

"Get the hell out of the way, Drako!" a gunman named Jim Peck shouted. "You're talking out of your mind!" He turned and said to the other men, "All of you clear leather and be ready!"

Guns came up out of holsters, cocked and ready. Gunmen stepped over to look out the window, the front door.

"Yeah, Peck?" said Prince Drako. "If they're coming here, where are they?" He gave a dark chuckle.

A gunman at the window called out, "They're walking up the street to the jail!"

"That's where Dolan is!" shouted Jim Peck. "Let's go!"

The men started toward the doors.

"Everybody, hold your whistle," said Drako. "We moved Dolan first thing this morning." He laughed and said, "You should have seen yourself, Peck, you looked like —"

"Never mind what I looked like, you cackling sumbitch," said Peck, cutting Drako's drunken humor short. "I'll turn your head into a fruit basket!"

Prince Drako's laugh faded. His expression turned serious. Jim Peck stood firm. Before either man could make a move, Eddie Moon came inside from the rear door. "Everybody, rein down in here!" he said, mostly to Jim Peck. "I can hear you crazy bastards all the way outside."

"So what?" said Drako. "Are you afraid we'll scare the bounty hunters away?"

Jim Peck continued standing ready for a fight, until Will Summers and Yancy Reed walked in through the batwing doors, followed by the four men who had ridden in and taken over space at the hitch rail. Reed moved to the side and stood watching the bar, a shotgun under his arm. Summers raised a hand and tried to settle everybody before they started going for their guns.

"Everybody, listen up," he said. "These men work for Southwestern Railways."

"He's lying, they're bounty hunters!" said Eddie Moon, easing back over to the bar, where he'd stood earlier. His hand rested on his holstered Colt.

"Watch your mouth, Moon. I don't *lie*," said Summers. "If they were bounty hunters, I would say so."

Moon fell silent under Summers' gaze.

"And so would we," said Dallas Ekland. He pushed his hat up an inch to better show his face. "Some of you might already know me, I'm Dallas Ekland, security chief. These men are Chauncy Wade, Carlos Sanget, and

165

Beck Tanner. I won't deny that we're lawmen because we are. But if you're not wanted by Southwestern Railways, you've got no problem with us. We work strictly for them. We are not bounty hunters." He looked along the crowded bar, letting everybody take it in. "We like to be thought of as everybody's friend." He offered a wide smile.

"Does that mean you're buying us all a round, Ekland?" Eddie Moon asked. "If you are, don't be bashful, just say so."

"So, what about it, Ekland?" Prince Drako put in. "We're a friendly bunch."

"Yeah," others added. "Show us some good faith. I've never robbed a Southwestern train in my life."

"Nor have I," another shouted.

"All right, bartender," said Ekland to Arnold Mason. "Fix us all up here! Beer all around."

"How about some Tennessee mountain brew?" said the bartender. "Just came in last night. These drinkers all love it. Been drinking it all day." He poured a shot and stood it in front of Ekland. "Take a taste?"

"Of course I will," said Ekland, raising the shot glass and tasting the strong smooth brew. When he set the empty glass down, he smiled and let out a breath. "I should've

166

known, I love anything brewed in Tennessee! Sure, set us all up with a shot. Leave a couple of bottles!"

Uh-oh! Bad move, Summers thought. He watched Ekland take off his faded black coat and lay it over the bar. Saw him start rolling up his shirtsleeves. He picked up the small shot glass the bartender stood in front of him.

"Damn it," Ekland said. He held the shot glass up to his eye. "I always have a hell of a time hitting my mouth with these little fellas. Can I get a water glass?"

Summers walked over to Reed, who said, "Is this man serious? He wants to drink Tennessee whiskey from a *water glass*?"

"He sounds serious to me," Summers said. "Try to keep an eye on him. I heard he came here buffaloing a drover at the hitch rail. He's calmed down, but I'm going to the telegraph office, see about a reply I asked for from Southwestern Railways."

"You already sent them a wire?" Reed said.

"I did," said Summers. "We're not getting stuck again like we did with Parks."

At the bar, Ekland let out a yell and drank down what looked to be three doubles from the tall water glass. The crowd whistled and cheered.

Summers gave Reed a dubious look. "I

167

could be an hour or longer, dealing with Brayton Siding."

"Go ahead, Will," said Reed. "If he gets too frisky, I'll take him down a notch."

Half an hour later, Zetra Wilson walked in through the side door with Baby Greta in her left arm, and a large canvas bag with handles in her right hand. Seeing her come in, Moon hurried her right back out the door and pulled her to the side. He glanced back to see if Ekland was watching, but Ekland was looking at four empty water glasses in front of him, and four empty beer mugs, one lying on its side.

"Zetra! You can't let people see you coming in with a load of whiskey! The hell is wrong with you?" said Eddie Moon.

"Not a damn thing, Moon!" Zetra said. "Manhandle me again, see if I don't bust a jug over your face!"

"*Whoa,* easy, darling!" said Moon, changing his attitude quick. "We just don't want too many people seeing we're selling the Eagles Saloon the same whiskey at a better price."

"See?" said Zetra. "That's how you could've said it to start with. Don't be a straight-up jackass. I'll pack my whiskey up and take it home! I ain't forgot how you tried to cheat me, last time."

168

"Zetra, you are right," said Moon. "I lost my head, and I have apologized. I have just missed you so much, I've been rooster-eyed crazy!"

"That's better," said Zetra. "How is my Tennessee mountain whiskey selling?" She leaned over and peeped inside the crowded saloon.

"You mean *our* Tennessee mountain whiskey?" said Moon. He grinned. "How's it doing? Look at them, darling, they're sucking it down like peppered honey! How many more did you bring us to sell?"

"Here's four jugs," said Zetra, nodding at the canvas bag. "I've got four more in my wagon behind the livery barn. I'll go fetch them once I've been paid for these others."

"*Aw, Zetra*, honey," said Moon, "don't be that way."

"Go to hell, Moon," she said. "Give me my money!" She rubbed her thumb and fingertips together.

Moon sighed. He pulled a folded wad of bills from inside his shirt and counted out the money for four kegs of whiskey.

"I feel like I'm being taken advantage of, paying for these jugs as soon as I buy them."

"And I *know* I'll be taken advantage of any other way," said Zetra, rubbing her fingertips together again, up close to his

169

face. As they stood bickering, a guitar player, an accordion player, and a man carrying a handful of spoons of various sizes walked around them and into the saloon. The man with the spoons wore the dark eyeglasses of the blind, but someone — an unruly child, perhaps — had painted them with large red pinwheel eyes. The exaggerated eyes stared aimlessly at the noisy crowd in the saloon.

"Uh-oh! Looks like music coming," said Moon. "I best get these big boys inside." He picked up the bag of whiskey jugs, but hesitated for just a moment, until Zetra motioned him inside. With Baby Greta hiked up on her hip, Zetra folded the money she'd just counted, pulled back her long trail coat and shoved the money down between her ample breasts. Baby Greta leaned in toward the large breasts, her source of sustenance. "No no, baby," said Zetra smiling, "not now." With one fingertip she gently shoved the child's head back and pulled her coat shut. "Baby Greta want to hear some *music*?" she asked in a squeaky baby voice to which no known species might ever claim kinship.

"Musica!" said the child, approvingly, laying small wet fingers on her mother's cheek.

■ ■ ■ ■

In a corner of the saloon, where the piano from the abandoned theater across the street had been set up, the musicians gathered and sang. They thrust mugs of beer over their heads and waved them back and forth, drawing the interest of the drinkers.

After it was clear they would not be met with gunshots, the musicians uncovered their instruments and the piano player, a woman as thin as a whip handle, with short-bobbed hair, patiently plunked the same ivory key over and over while the others turned their ear and interest in the same direction. The red-eyed blind man stood ready to play, pairs of spoons in various pockets, assembled for a quick change.

Standing against the front wall, Yancy Reed felt great relief as the music got under way. To blend in with the crowd, even though he was the one carrying a shotgun, he held half a mug of beer he'd sipped on for the past couple of hours. He felt relieved when Summers walked in. An Irish reel rolled in the smoke-cloudy ceiling rafters, joined with a Mexican accordion and the jangle of kitchen spoons.

Reed leaned close to Summers, yet still

had to shout in his ear.

"I was starting to think you walked to Brayton to pick up the reply!" Reed said.

"The line being cut for two days has Spires covered up," Summers shouted back. Reed said something in response, but Summers understood not a word of it. He saw only his lips move behind the hard rattle of the blind man's spoons. He shook his head and motioned Reed to the side door.

Through the crowd Summers and Reed navigated, two small vessels pushing for port ahead of a storm. When they stepped out the door and felt fresh air seep into their lungs, they saw Zetra Wilson with Baby Greta in her arms. She stepped back from the open doorway where she had been watching the festivities and listening to the music.

"Mrs. Wilson?" Summers said, taking note of the toddler he had pulled out of the gunfire earlier. At the sight of Summers, the toddler bucked up and down in her mother's arm with a wide toothless grin.

"Yes, Sheriff," said Zetra, "it's me, Zetra Wilson. I beg your pardon, standing in you two gentlemen's way there like we were." She juggled the toddler on her hip.

"No, ma'am, not at all," said Summers, hearing Reed stifle a laugh at her calling him Sheriff.

"Baby Greta has been so cross and nervous after what happened, I thought some music might soothe her."

Soothe her? Summers glanced over his shoulder at the loud wild music, then looked at Reed, then back at the woman.

"Mus-i-ca," the toddler chirped.

"Yes, Little Greta," said Summers, "it's *musica.*"

"Her name is *Baby* Greta, not *Little* Greta," Zetra Wilson said pleasantly but making her point.

"Oh, sorry," said Summers, yet not seeing what possible difference it could make.

"My husband, Reuben Stallard Wilson, speaks Mexican a lot, from work and such. She must have heard *musica* from him."

"I understand," said Summers. He smiled. "Music or *musica,* either one suits me."

Her expression turned brooding, cautious. "Okay then. We'll leave, let you and your deputy go about law business."

"I'm not a sheriff, ma'am," said Summers.

"Oh, I know," said Zetra, yet Summers could see she wasn't grasping it. "Good day now, Sheriff," she said to Summers. "You, too, Deputy," she said to Reed.

"Ma'am," the two said as one, touching their hat brims.

173

"There is a peculiar case," Reed said as the woman walked away a few steps and stopped and stood listening to the music.

"Why do you say that?" Summers asked.

"She says her husband will beat her if he catches her doing something she shouldn't do, that he's a religious zealot. One of them *I'm always right, you never are* kind."

"Oh?" said Summers. "A man bent on proving himself worthy to some higher power?"

"Yeah," said Reed, "you know the type."

"Yep, I'm afraid I do," said Summers. "Where is her husband?"

"That's just it. Nobody seems to know, Will," said Reed. "She's been around here for a few years now, but I've never laid eyes on a husband. Which tells me something's wrong."

"Why?" said Summers.

"Why?" said Reed. "Are you joking? Look at her, Will. She is a knock-down *beauty,* in anybody's eyes! Men kill for a woman who looks as good as she does. Don't you agree?"

"I can't deny Zetra Wilson is a fine-looking woman," said Summers. He paused, then added, "But she has young ones, and a husband, so I don't let myself —"

"Wait a minute, Will," said Reed. "Yes, she has young ones, but how she managed to get them, I don't know. She always says her husband is off somewhere on business. But even if he is, he'd have to be home *sometimes*!" After a pause he went on, "She's gone into making whiskey and selling it around with that barnyard dung weasel, Eddie Moon. And word I get is that he's steadily bumping her night and day, what time they're not brewing whiskey together."

"That's none of my business," said Summers, "and making whiskey ain't illegal, so whatever they're doing —"

"Hold it," said Reed, under a string of shouts and threats spilling out the open door. "Sounds like a fight in there!" They ran in through the side entrance and stopped cold as a tense silence closed in around them.

The crowd had drawn into a half circle on the floor. Some at the back were climbing out windows, hiding in the space under the stairwells, crowding into the stockroom. On the cleared part of the floor, the she-hound stood with one of her pups hanging from her mouth. The pup squirmed, its eyes newly opened, but its mother held on.

Dallas Ekland stood boiling drunk, a pistol half-raised, its barrel pointed in the hound's direction. On the floor at his feet lay Chauncy Wade, a long bloody welt down his right jawline. Carlos Sanget and Beck Tanner stood two feet out from the bar, both with their hands poised at their pistol butts, but neither looking like their hearts were in it.

"Who's going to die first?" said Mortimer Javins, his big Colt lying on the bar top. He had come in quietly some time earlier and stood at the end of the bar, unnoticed, sipping a beer, until trouble occurred over the hound and her pup. Now Chauncy Wade lay groaning on the floor. The crowd watched, frozen with fear and excitement. To break the tension, an old man started moving his feet in a shuffling little dance step. A woman grabbed him and shook him, stopping him.

"What about you, Ekland, you tub of green cow dump?" said Javins. "You made a threat to shoot my hound and her pup. What did you say? *Kill the both of them with one bullet?*"

Ekland's face was running wet with sweat, which dripped from his heavy eyebrows.

"I never knew she was your dog, Mortimer," he said, knowing Javins' reputation from a string of towns across the Southwest frontier. Ekland's big booming voice had dropped, and was starting to quiver.

"You know it now," said Javins. "Get moving on it, so we can send you home in a pine overcoat." As he spoke, he took a wrinkled smoke from his shirt pocket, firmed it up and lit it. He noted a look in Beck Tanner's eyes. He knew Tanner, had seen him build his *own* hot reputation with a gun, in some hard places.

Ekland said, "Mortimer Javins, I'm not drawing on you." He looked all around. "Everybody here, *listen* to me. I'm not drawing on this man today. I'm not drawing on anybody. I got a little drunk. But I'm getting sobered up now!"

Javins drew on his smoke and let it out. His eyes went from Ekland to Carlos Sanget to Beck Tanner, not bothering with Chauncy Wade lying barely conscious on the plank floor. He kept Tanner foremost in his mind as he picked up his Colt from the bar and slipped it easily into its holster, like putting some mindless deadly thing into its cage.

The crowd breathed in relief.

Summers took a step closer to Javins, seeing that something was still afoot between him and Tanner. He gave Carlos Sanget a look that told him Javins would not be alone. Sanget took a step back and placed both hands on the bar top away from his gun. Tanner saw it, too, but it didn't change a thing.

"I want to talk to you, Javins," Summers said quietly, knowing that nothing he said to Javins now would distract him. Javins had this all laid out in his mind. If he didn't, he shouldn't even carry a gun. But Tanner took Summers' words to be all he needed to make his move on Javins.

Rebel Kid my ass, Tanner said to himself. Jumped a step from the bar to the open floor, his hand wrapping around his big Colt to swing it up. Yet Mortimer Javins, *the Rebel Kid,* drew so fast, and fanned two shots so fast that Tanner's boots had not touched the floor before he fell backward, dead, a pool of blood puddling under him. Summers stood watching Dallas Ekland and Carlos Sanget for any further gunplay.

Out of the corner of Summers' eye he saw the hound hurrying through the crowd toward the stockroom, people stepping back to give her room, her pup swinging back and forth in her mouth, its beady eyes open, peering through a veil at its brand-new world.

178

PART 3

PART 3

CHAPTER 12

When the hound and her pup were back in their bedding with the litter mates, the crowd settled down and the band started playing again, led by zippy accordion music. The spoons rattled like playful snakes on the blind man's leg. The new bartender, Arnold Mason, set a fresh mug of beer up for everyone, including Summers and Yancy Reed.

At the bar, Summers said, "Javins, it would be better if we take these mugs out back and talk. The music in here is pretty loud."

"Whatever suits you, Summers. I think the hound will be okay now, for a while anyway."

"You think Dallas Ekland really would have shot her?" Summers asked, just wanting a closer look at how Javins viewed such things.

Javins took his time. He sipped his frothy

beer and blotted his lips on the cuff of his shirtsleeve.

"When a man has a gun cocked and is looking down the sights at his target, there ain't no wait and see. It's time to drop him and send for a shovel." He gazed steadily at Summers. "If I was wrong, you tell me what I should have done."

Summers thought about it. He saw Ekland and Sanget holding Chauncy Wade up between them at the far end of the bar. A string of bloody spittle hung from Chauncy's lower lip. He appeared to be babbling.

"You did the best thing you could do," he said. "Let's go outside and talk."

On their way out, Reed dropped back a step to keep an eye on the three railroad men. Coming in the side door, Johnny Two fell in with Reed. He took in the blood puddled on the floor and said, "You have some trouble in here?" He sniffed the air and caught the lingering smell of burnt gunpowder.

"Not us," Reed said. He motioned Johnny Two on out behind Summers and Javins. "Mortimer Javins had some railroad trouble, but he settled it mighty fast."

"Did he draw that big Colt?" asked Johnny Two Red Wolves.

"Oh, he drew it," said Reed.

"How?"

"How? Fast, that's how. Too fast to even see it happen."

"I meant did he just draw it and shoot it, or did he fan it real quick-like?" Johnny clarified.

"He fanned it," said Reed, the two of them walking on out the door. "*Real* quick-like, all right. I saw him draw and heard him fan two shots into the man's chest. But I can't say I saw much or heard much of anything. Just one fast blur and it was all over!"

"Dang," said Johnny Two. "I wish I'd seen it."

"I wish you had, too," said Reed. "So I wouldn't have to keep telling you about it the next month." They stopped at the corner of the saloon building and saw Summers and Javins talking a few yards away.

"Think we ought to hang back, let them get their talking done?" Johnny Two asked.

"Yeah, let's do that," said Reed. Looking to the right at the far end of the building, he saw Zetra Wilson with Baby Greta on her hip, counting money. From the rear door he saw Dallas Ekland and Carlos Sanget carrying Beck Tanner's body out of the saloon. Young Chauncy Wade staggered along behind them with a wet bar towel pressed against his jawline. At the hitch rail,

183

the two rolled Tanner's body up over the saddle. Chauncy stood to the side with his head bowed.

When Reed saw Sanget pull his rifle from its saddle boot and follow Ekland around the rear corner of the saloon building, he said, "Johnny, I'll be back in just a minute. Keep an eye on Summers and Javins in case they need help. These railroad birds are up to something. I want to find out what it is."

Johnny Two looked over at where Carlos Sanget and Dallas Ekland had disappeared, Sanget with the rifle over his arm.

"Go on, Yancy, I'll stick right here," he said.

Yancy Reed quietly circled the saloon building in the opposite direction of Ekland and Sanget. Although he wasn't sure that being quiet mattered with all the music, foot stomping and howling going on inside. As he peeked around the back corner, he saw a homemade ladder leaning up against the building and caught a glimpse of boots going up out of sight over the top edge.

He thought about Summers and Javins back there talking — *easy targets for a rifleman on the roof,* he thought, stepping onto the ladder.

At the top, he looked out and saw Ekland

and Sanget huddled down against the low front facade, gazing down on Summers and Javins. Under Reed's hand the roof thumped and vibrated with the noise from the crowd, the music and laughter beneath it.

Reed saw the two men talking, yet couldn't hear a word they said. Okay, he decided, if he couldn't hear them, he was sure they couldn't hear him. He hoped so, anyway, as he drew his Colt and crawled up onto the flat roof to inch toward the two from behind.

A full five minutes passed as Reed crept over the hot roof, rising from all fours to walk in a crouch, his Colt out, ready. But seeing how intently the two were staring at the ground far below, leaning out over the facade, he slipped his Colt back into its holster and continued forward.

"What the hell are you waiting for, Carlos?" Ekland whispered. Standing between them unseen, Reed bent into an even lower crouch.

"I'm not waiting for nothing," Sanget whispered back. "I just want to make sure I —"

He didn't finish his words.

Reed grabbed each man by the back of their belts and sprang straight up, leaned forward, and let their weight take them both over the edge of the roof to the ground below.

The loud double *thump* in the dirt caused Summers and Javins to turn to the sound, their hands going to the butt of their side-arms.

"The hell is this?" said Javins, his left hand ready to start fanning the Colt. The two stared at Ekland and Sanget, both of them clawing and pushing and trying to get a hold on the dusty ground beneath them. Looking up, Summers and Javins saw Reed standing on the roof looking down at them.

"Good thing he was up there," Summers said, toeing the rifle that lay in the dirt near Ekland's feet. He waved Reed down from the roof. Johnny Two saw the men fall, heard the *thump* and hurried over, almost in a trot. Chauncy Wade stood back and watched, the bar towel still against his jaw.

Ekland rolled onto his back, trying hard to breathe, his large belly having taken the brunt of the fall. He forced himself up to a sit, but words were still beyond him. He fell over onto Sanget, who was having no easy time of it himself.

Javins watched Johnny Two steady both men into sitting positions long enough for them to get some deep breaths and recover from their fall.

"You said you need men, Summers," said Javins. "Looks to me like these are some pretty good men you've got here already."

"They *are* good men, Mort," said Summers. "We're not outgunned, just *outnumbered.* One thing I never want to do is get good men killed." He sighed. "This whole thing ended up in Eagles because a U.S. deputy wouldn't turn loose of his badge. Even so it would have ended when he left, except we've got an outlaw here who took a head wound from a ricochet. Before he's out of here, if he *lives,* that is, I'm expecting every bounty man and rival gang in the territory to come for him."

"How much is the bounty?" Javins asked.

"Ten thousand dollars," said Summers, realizing that much money could turn a man like Javins either way.

Javins gave a slight whistle under his breath. "That's Judge Parker for you," he said. "He puts the bounty out there, especially for jailbreakers."

"It is a lot," said Summers. "Enough to get a man his own little spread somewhere and live easy." He gave Javins a look.

Javins smiled.

"Don't worry," he said. "I've never collected bounty, and never will."

"I've heard that about you. Didn't know if

you've changed any," Summers said.

"Not a lick," said Javins. "Whatever I started out with inside, I've still got inside." He batted his fist firmly on his chest. "The Rebel Kid, remember?"

"The Rebel Kid." Summers nodded. "What brought you back here today? Nobody knew you were back until you were ready to shoot Ekland."

"I only rode in to check on the hound and her pups," said Javins. "I thought I could slip in and out with no one any the wiser. I would have done it if Ekland hadn't decided to shoot a helpless animal." He looked over to where Zetra Wilson stood with Baby Greta on her hip. "You and this town have always treated me well. As long as I'm here, I'm on your side."

With nothing more to say on the matter, he walked away toward Zetra Wilson, who stood with a canvas bag on the ground at her feet. Summers saw him tip his hat to Zetra, pick up the bag by its handles and walk away with her.

Yancy Reed came around from the back of the building and looked at the two men seated in the dirt. Then with a smirk he turned to Summers. "How did it go with him?" He tilted his head toward Mortimer Javins as he walked out of sight.

"He's with us," said Summers.

"Good," said Reed, "I feel better knowing it. I think there's tension growing among the Coyle gunmen. They've been too good for too long. I look for them to blow up like a powder keg any minute."

"I don't know why," said Summers, "but I get that same feeling."

"Like there's something in their nature they can't even help?" said Reed.

"Maybe," Summers replied.

Reed spit and nodded.

"Yeah," he said. "I'll go with that, unless something convinces me otherwise."

Dr. Otto Adams walked through the side foyer of his house, his black medical bag in his hand, to where Axel Coyle sat twirling his pistol on a short sofa, one of his dusty boots propped up on a small ottoman. He grinned, lowered his boot and stared up at the doctor. His Colt stopped twirling suddenly and pointed in the doctor's direction. His grin vanished.

"How's my brother?" he asked flatly. Out front, Prince Drako set his horse at a hitch rail, holding the reins to Axel's horse beside him.

"Much better than I ever expected," said the doctor. "Your brother is a very fortunate man." He looked at the pistol in Axel's hand and added, "Please point that weapon in another direction."

"Sure." Axel lowered the gun — not much, a couple of inches.

"He's awake," said the doctor. "He remembers events leading up to the incident. He's aware of what's going on around him."

"All good news, eh?" said Axel.

"Yes, all good," said the doctor. "I have to call on a patient, and I'll be back afterward, no more than a couple of hours." He gestured toward the hallway behind them. "Feel free to visit your brother while I'm away. He can have water, nothing more for now. Silk Polly will be here shortly. She's helping out, as you know. While you're here, I must ask that you do nothing that might upset or confuse him. For God's sake don't let him do anything that will get his head wound bleeding. It could kill him!"

"I wouldn't dream of it, Doctor," said Axel. He stood waiting until the doctor left, then walked to the only room in the hallway with its door closed. Opening the big oaken door slowly, he stepped inside. Seeing his brother pointing a hideaway gun in his face, he ducked away.

"Damn it, Dolan, it's *me,* your brother, coming to look in on you! Put that blasted little popgun away!"

"I know it's you *now,*" said Dolan. "I didn't know it when you came sneaking down the hall." He lowered the little gun and put it away inside a long nightshirt. "I figured you might be one of Judge Parker's vultures come to hang me on the spot!" His voice sounded strange, weak.

"Are you all right, Dolan?" he asked.

"Am I *all right*?" barked Dolan. "Well, let's see. I've been shot in the *head.* Had a piece of iron dug out of my *brain*!I've got a crazy old Civil War nurse, carrying a *razor,* comes in every day wanting to shave me and tries to show me her furry part! I've been cooped up in here for seems like six months! But yeah! *I'm great!* Where's my damned horse?"

Civil War nurse? Axel thought about it.

"Are you talking about Silk Polly?" he asked, holding back a little laugh.

"No, damn it," said Dolan. "I'm talking about a damned horse. So's we can get the living, breathing, blue bloody hell *out of here*!"

"Take it easy, Dolan!" said Axel. "I'll get you a horse, soon as you need one."

"I need one right now!" said Dolan. "I've never needed one worse! There's a district court wanting to drag me back to Fort Smith and stretch my neck! While you're at it, reach under the bed and grab my gun belt. Hand it to me. I'm liable to shoot a finger off with this little doodad."

"Okay, okay! I wanted to hear from the doctor first, but if you say you're fit to ride, I'll get you a horse and we'll get you out of here, right now!"

Yet, he hesitated as he tried picturing Silk Polly doing what Dolan said she did. "You mean, you keep seeing an old nurse carrying a razor who comes in here and tries to show you —"

Dolan grabbed the small gun again from inside the nightshirt and cocked it loudly in Axel's face.

"All right, Dolan!" Axel shouted. "Put it down. Drako is waiting out front with his horse and mine. We'll go get you a horse right now!"

"We're going together," Dolan snarled. "You're going to take me to my men."

"You mean *our* men?" said Axel. He reached under the bed, pulled out Dolan's gun belt and handed it to him.

"*My* men, Axel," Dolan said firmly. "Or only one of us will leave here standing up." He drew his big Colt, checked it and holstered it. He hung the gun belt, gun and all, over his shoulder and patted it.

"Yes! Okay, your men," said Axel. "That's

what we'll do. All three of us will go join them! That's even better." He looked nervous and caught off guard. Dolan liked that. The thing about the old barroom dove trying to show him her furry part. *Ha!* He liked that, too. Now that he'd had something stuck in his brain, he could tell people anything. Who would know if it was true or not?

"Are you going to get dressed first? Get your boots on?" Axel asked, looking Dolan up and down.

"Later," Dolan said. "Grab my clothes and boots." He turned on his bare feet and was gone.

Indian Hills, Oklahoma Territory
One day later
Tom Barton stepped down from the cream-colored mare and stood looking out across a stretch of low hills in the direction of the distant gunfire he'd heard since before dawn. There wasn't a doubt in his mind, the gunfire came from a gang of bandidos who had traveled a long way across the border, robbing and killing anyone who got in their path, including Parks' posse men.

He'd acquired four horses the marauders left in their wake. Still had them. He'd fed and watered them and brought them to the camp and shown them to Parks. *Nothing.* Three times he'd warned Deputy Claude Parks that the bandidos were out there. All three times Parks continued to ignore him. So, he had stashed the four horses away from the camp and the men and kept his mouth shut. He looked at the four horses now and shook his head.

Adios, Deputy.

He couldn't care less what happened to Parks, but he felt bad about the posse men. They didn't deserve what was happening to them. Parks did, the others didn't. He rubbed the big mare's nose as he watched the dusty flats.

He could have ridden hard and got there in time to die with the rest of the surviving posse, but it would be for nothing. They had been ill-fated from the start. Still, he felt guilty, not doing something, anything, to help.

Seeing two men stagger into sight from the swirl of harsh sunlight, he swung atop the big mare, still bareback, and rode hard to reach them, the four horses sticking close behind him, no lead rope needed.

The two men, Harper Dowd and Al Slater, worn out and battle-weary, found a surge of energy as soon as they saw Barton and the loose horses running toward them.

As Barton reined the mare down, Dowd fell to the hot sand. Slater pulled at him to get him to stand.

"On your feet, Harper," said Barton. "Pick a horse and get on it."

"And hurry," said Slater. "For all we know they're right behind us! This bunch loves chopping off heads!"

Barton dropped from the mare's back and gave each of them a shove up into a saddle. "There's water in the canteens. Food, we'll have to find some. Anybody else make it?"

"Everybody is dead," said Dowd. "Parks should have listened to you; we all knew it!"

"Too late now," said Barton. "Drink your water, let's get out of here!" He handed each of them the reins to a spare horse. "Hang on to them," he said, "one of them might be supper."

"Where we trying to make it to, Tom?" asked Slater.

"We rode the wastelands and came all the way around these hills," said Barton. "If us and these horses are tough, we'll cut straight up across here and land in Eagles." He touched his heels to his horse and added, "That's if our heads don't end up on a stick."

"Or we don't get et by rattlesnakes and wolves," said Dowd.

"Stay cheerful," said Barton, with a worn-out smile. "They say the Lord loves a cheerful soul."

Chapter 13

The Coyle brothers and Prince Drako had ridden twelve miles out of Eagles, staying on narrow back trails and stretches of rocky ground. They'd slipped unseen into the livery barn and picked up the horse Axel had originally brought for his brother to escape on. Dolan's saddlebags were tied down behind the saddle.

Dolan pretended not to recognize his own saddlebags, yet he pulled out his old pair of British binoculars and draped them around his neck. Then he dropped his gun belt from his shoulder, strapped it around his waist and adjusted it over his nightshirt. He'd checked the big Colt again, out of habit. Still loaded. He closed the cylinder gate and twirled it into his waiting holster. He'd turned and faced Drako, who sat atop his horse, Chico.

"Well, how do I look, *mi amigo*?" he'd asked, spreading his arms a little.

Prince Drako looked a little embarrassed at being asked. He glanced first at Axel, then back at Dolan.

"Well, *uh,* you look, you know. Handsome? I expect, maybe, as some might say, all things considered?" said Drako, awkwardly.

"Handsome?" said Dolan, as if taken aback. "Damn, Prince, I wasn't going so far as to say *handsome."*

Seeing the wild worried expression come across Drako's face, Axel knew it was time to intercede.

"What he's saying is that you look fit and well armed, and ready for anything. You know, like your *old self* again." He looked at Drako. "Right, Prince?"

"Oh yeah, *hell* yeah," said Drako. "Exactly! When I said *handsome,* I meant, you know, in a *rugged, outlaw* sort of way." He looked at Axel for help. But Dolan cut in first.

"Not the kind of man you might try to shoot in the back while he's riding along thinking about the sumbitches he's killed for trying to do the same thing before?"

"Oh no," said Drako, "not that kind of man at all. Nothing like that. I mean . . ." He trailed off, not sure if this was the kind of answer Dolan was looking for. *Hell, he didn't know!*

Dolan had given them both a strange little grin. He'd wiped his fingertip across the tip of his tongue, looked at it and swung up into his saddle.

"Both of you ride up front there, why don't you. I'll ride here and keep watch on our back trail."

Now they were looking out across the low hills and wastelands. The three kept their horses almost abreast, Dolan riding his horse only a step back from theirs.

"Are you doing all right, Dolan, my brother?" Axel asked.

"Couldn't be better," Dolan replied.

"You need to check your head," Axel said, motioning at the dust-streaked bandage circling his head beneath his hat brim.

Dolan reached up and touched the bandage carefully. He looked at his fingertips and saw no blood.

"I'm all right," he said. "I hope you didn't forget that we're headed to see my men," he added unexpectedly.

"I haven't forgot," said Axel. "That's where we're headed. There's just so damn much going on out here, we keep running into every gunman in the territory. I've never seen a place this busy."

Dolan checked to confirm that Drako was in no position to easily get behind him.

"Tell me right now, without lying, *if you can,*" said Dolan, "where are all my men?" He slipped his big Colt from his holster and cocked it.

"Whoa, Dolan!" said Prince Drako. "It's none of my business, but that's awfully cold! You can't kill your own brother!"

"Sure I can!" Dolan said. "Nobody in the Coyle family ever liked him anyway. Our own beloved mother wanted to leave him at a water hole when we came west."

"Look right out there," Axel cut in, wanting badly to change the subject. Ahead of them out on the flatlands floor, they saw a large churning dust cloud, and in front of that came three riders with two spare horses. Axel pointed out toward the brown roiling dust. "That's our men in the rear, chasing what's left of Parks' posse."

Dolan and Drake both looked out with him, Dolan raising the binoculars to his eyes.

"Yeah," Dolan growled. "I recognize one of those posse riding sumbitches. His name is Tom Barton."

"Okay, then." Axel nodded, glad his brother was getting better. "There's a trail out there. You'll see it when this dust clears," he added. "It'll take us to another pissant of a town called Hundly, if we can

200

ever get through this fighting in time."

"In time for what?" Dolan asked. "What's Hundly?"

"Hundly is a rail layoff depot. There's where all the cash goes to pay the troops every month," Axel replied, "but we've got to get it today or forget it for another month. Tomorrow it gets dispersed to several payroll details. Then it's gone."

Dolan was starting to taste the kind of cash that would be waiting in a military payroll town like Hundly.

He patted the binoculars on his chest. "Soon as I can tell that's our men in the dust cloud," he said, "we're riding down and telling them not to shoot. Then we'll ride on out to Hundly."

"Well, hell," said Axel, sarcastically, "why didn't *I* think of that?" He turned serious. "Telling our men not to shoot is one thing, Dolan," he said. "What will stop those three posse men from blowing the hell out of us while our men are *stopped*?"

"I'll stop them, damn their eyes," said Dolan. "Once we get down there, I *will* stop them. You've got my word on it."

Prince Drako and Axel gave each other a dubious look.

"All right," Axel finally said to Dolan. "You're the boss, brother. We'll see if you can do all that without getting us killed."

Three hours later, Tom Barton, Harper Dowd, and Al Slater rested their horses in the sparse shade of a tall rock on one edge of the cutbank arroyo where they lay. The early-afternoon sun burned with no mercy.

"How's it feel?"

Al Slater answered Tom Barton, "It hurts *bad,* awfully bad." He panted between every word.

Barton looked up from Slater's wound.

"We know it does, Al," he said. He had refolded the cloth torn from of an old plaid shirt and placed it back on the wound and buttoned Slater's bib-front shirt over it. "We've got to get you over to that little depot town just over the hills."

"He's talking about Hundly," Dowd put in.

"I know," said Slater. "Has it stopped bleeding on both sides?"

"For now, yes, front and back," said Barton. "Let's hope it stays this way." He looked out over the short cutbank at the dust that followed them. "I don't know why they stopped shooting," he said. "But while they have, we ought to make a run out of here. I'm betting there's a doctor in Hundly."

"Then what are we waiting for?" Slater said. "Pull me up. I can get in a saddle."

"Hold on," said Dowd. "We've got a rider coming — no, two riders," he added quickly.

Tom Barton stood up slowly, rifle ready. He looked, not at the dust behind them, but to where Dowd pointed, out quarterwise to them.

"They're waving a red flag," Dowd said. "Are they surrendering, or wanting to be matadors? I've never seen a red flag mean anything."

Al Slater coughed hard to stifle a painful laugh. Barton gave Dowd a dark stare.

"Sorry, Al," Dowd said quietly.

"*Hola*, posse men!" Axel Coyle called out as the three riders drew closer. "We're here in peace, trying to keep you fellows alive."

"We're already doing that *ourselves*," said Tom Barton. "What else you got?" He levered a round into his rifle chamber, letting the three riders hear it.

Axel gave a laugh.

"That's just like you, Tom Barton. I knew it was you out here all along, being a posse man. I have to say, I thought better of you. A *posse* man? The hell were you thinking?"

"If you come to talk about my shortcomings, take a seat and get comfortable," said Barton. "Being a posse man for Claude

Parks is the worst mistake I ever made, if you want to skip everything else and start there."

"I'm kind of glad to hear you say so," said Axel.

"Oh, why's that?" Barton asked.

"I'm here to deal with you, Barton," Axel said.

"Deal with me?" said Barton. "Deal with me, how?"

"My brother, Dolan, is tired of all the killing. He likes you. He's seen the way you fight. He says, give up this posse malarky and you can ride with us. We pay a lot better, eat a lot better . . . well, you know the rest. Everything is better with us. The main thing is, you'll still be alive."

"That is a tempting point," said Barton. "The thing is, these men would have to agree as well. Give us a few minutes to palaver it out?"

Axel chuckled under his breath.

This gutsy sumbitch . . .

"How about fifteen minutes? It's hotter than a bastard out here."

"Make it half an hour," said Barton. He looked at Slater and Dowd. Slater lay in a full sweat. Dowd looked just as bad, except without a bullet wound in his side.

"What do you say?" Barton asked.

204

Dowd and Slater both nodded.

"Half an hour, Axel," Barton said, "either take it or leave it."

Brazen as hell . . .

Axel chuckled again under his breath, and said, "We'll be back in a half hour. Be smart, all three of you." He and Drako turned their horses and rode back, this time into the settling dust, where Jim Peck stood with his rifle down at his side.

"Well, look here," said Axel. "If it ain't Jim Peck. Jim, did you tire of all the easy living there in Eagles?"

"Hell yes," said Peck grimly. "Give me a scalding hot flatlands and a mouthful of dust *any*time."

"Yeah, I bet," said Axel. He gestured toward five ragged, hard-looking men wearing serapes and tall Spanish boots that were worn down at the heels. "Friends of yours?" he asked.

"You mean, amigos," said Peck. "You can see we're all pals, them and me." He swung his rifle around a little, pointing at the five men seated in the dirt, their hands tied behind them.

"How many you reckon are out there?" Axel asked.

"I left school 'cause I hated *counting*," Peck said, his head cocked to the side. "But

205

I'll venture there's enough to run all of us over if they ever band together. They just keep hitting us in small numbers. Hope nobody ever tells them."

Axel looked at the five men, then back to Peck.

"They're going to hear you," he said in a lowered voice.

"Let 'em!" Peck said. "These right here will never tell anybody. I'm fixing to walk them out and kill them." He grinned. "You want to come see it? I'm leaving them lay in the sun so's pals of theirs can get the message, *Us Coyle Gang outlaws are not out here to be fooled with.*"

"I'll pass, Jim," said Axel. "I'm looking for my brother."

"Yep, he's back there," said Peck. "I have to say I'm surprised he's up and around so quick."

"He's a tough man," said Axel. "But hell, you already know all that."

As the two talked, Prince Drako brought Axel's attention to Dolan riding his horse out of the thicker dust at a walk, his bandanna up across his nose.

"Speak of the devil," Axel said as Dolan stopped close and took down his bandanna. Drako drew his horse over to the side, knowing from earlier experience that Dolan didn't want either of them behind him.

"Why am I the devil, Axel?" Dolan asked bluntly. Instead of looking at Axel, he stared at the five bandidos, watching Peck hurry over and start kicking them to their feet.

"It's just an old saying," said Axel. "You know, like Shakespeare, or something. You know, 'Speak of the devil and here he is'? You've heard it."

"I've heard it twice," said Dolan. "Both times right here, just now!"

Axel gave up on making Dolan understand.

"All right, Dolan, it's just something people say. It don't mean rat-scat."

They both stared off at the bandidos, who walked away in a row, fresh dust stirring up around their boots. Drako put his horse beside Axel's. He waved his hat through the dust in front of his face and put it back on.

"Prince Drako," said Dolan, "if I tell you to put a bullet in that last man's ear, will you do it?"

"I damned sure will," Drako said. His hand wrapped around the butt of his Colt. But before he could draw, a blast from Dolan's own big Colt put a bullet through the man's ear.

"Too late, Drako," Dolan said. "It looks like I beat you to the target."

"That you did, Dolan," Drako said, lowering his Colt back into the holster. "You for damn sure did."

The sun continued to boil in the sky and sizzle on the dry scorched earth below. Dolan, Axel, and Prince Drako rode slowly out of a thin wavering black line in the flatlands. As they drew closer to the small arroyo, they became larger, more human-looking. When they stopped fifty feet back, their images stopped wavering. Their outlines became clearer.

"*Hola,* the arroyo," Axel called out. "We're back. What's it going to be? You want to live, or die out here like jackrabbits on a griddle?"

"You win, Axel," Dowd called out. "We'd rather ride for you and your brother than die for Claude Parks and the Hanging Judge. Is that good enough for you?"

Axel looked at Dolan with a thin little grin.

"It's what we asked for. We're good. Now lay your guns in a pile and keep your hands up high, like you're praising heaven. We'll ride in."

After a pause, Dowd called out, "There they are, all our guns, like you asked."

"Good," said Axel. "We're riding in."

Dowd stood beside Al Slater, who had a

hard time raising his left arm.

"Do the best you can, Al," he said. "A man can't help being wounded."

"I reckon," said Slater, with a painful-sounding groan.

The two men listened to the soft clop of three horses' hooves on the hot blanket of sand.

"Slater here is having a hard time," Dowd said. "He's wounded low in the side."

"Lower your arms, both of you," said Axel.

Dolan sat back watching quietly, his big Colt in hand.

"Where's Tom Barton?" he asked. "He's the main one I want riding for us."

"Tom rode away," said Dowd. "Said he was all done outlawing. Hope it won't hurt Slater and me. We still want to ride for you. Tom went his own way. He said we were both welcome to ride with him, but we told him we want to ride for you."

"What did he say?" Dolan asked.

"He said if we stayed here, you might welcome us, or you might just kill us on the spot. I wasn't leaving my pal here, even if you did — kill us, that is. So there." He tilted his chin up and closed his eyes. Beside him, Slater coughed and groaned.

Dolan raised his Colt and shot each man twice in the chest.

As Dolan holstered his Colt and turned his horse away, Axel and Drako rode over beside him.

"What about these guns?" Axel asked.

"Either of you *need* another gun?" he asked.

"No," said Axel.

"Me, neither," said Drako.

"Then leave them," Dolan said.

"What about the horses?" Axel asked.

"Is this your first shooting, brother?" Dolan asked.

Axel didn't reply, and instead turned to Drako. "Cut their saddles and bridles off. Turn them loose. Maybe they can get away from the wolves for a few days."

"Yeah, maybe," said Drako, lifting a big knife from his boot well. "But I doubt it."

They rode away, Dolan trailing a few yards behind, and the freed horses following a few yards farther back.

"Think he has any hard feelings about you planning this Hundly deal without him?" Drako muttered, staring straight ahead.

"I don't know," said Axel. "If he does, he's had ever' chance to say so, but he hasn't, not a word. He couldn't expect us to hunker down and die because he took a ricochet, can he?"

Prince Drako smiled to himself.
"I reckon not," he said.

Prince Drako smiled to himself.
"reckon not," he said.

CHAPTER 14

In the early shadows of night, Tom Barton stepped down from the cream-colored mare at a small water hole he found among the rocks in a stretch of low hills. He'd kept watch on the sky an hour before sunset, noting where birds swooped down and stayed down. Birds never lied about water, or much else. A mile closer, the mare caught the scent of water and headed there without a nudge.

While the mare watered, Tom wiped her sweaty bare back with a wet bandanna, dipped the bandanna in the water and wiped her down again. He hated thinking he had left the two men behind to die, yet a voice inside him demanded he do so. In his defense, he reminded himself he had laid the matter in their hands. But inside him, that didn't let him off the hook.

He had suspicioned early on that he was riding with an illegitimate posse, led by a man with no authority except what he had taken upon himself. And he had allowed himself to be lied to and misled by that man, he admitted.

He drew a deep cleansing breath and let it out. All right. He had thought about it as long as he could afford to. He refused to think about it anymore tonight. He rested a hand on the mare's neck and looked back in the direction from which they had come. He knew from experience that the way men traveled into the dark was usually the way they made their camp for the night. These were seasoned dark-camp outlaws. They were good. They gave him nothing to go on.

Still, if he was bent on revenge, he knew he could slip in tonight, cut the Coyles' throats and be gone before anyone heard a sound. *But this is not for revenge,* he told himself, still thinking about it after telling himself not to. The mare raised her head, water running from her lips.

Will you take me to Eagles? Get me there even if it kills you? he asked without saying a word aloud.

The mare sawed her head and slung out her sweaty mane.

"All right, I hear you, big girl," he said just between the two of them and the shadowy, dark drifting sky. He ran his hand along her back. "Looks like I've got to hold you to it." He swung up onto her broad back and headed her north toward Eagles.

In the last hour before dawn, in the graininess of a silver-streaked cloudy sky, seventeen of the Coyles' gunmen rode their horses in at a walk and formed a silent half circle in the main street of Hundly. The town, once an army encampment with a military supply rail siding, still had watchtowers standing at either end. Each tower housed a Gatling gun, a full crate of ammunition and room for an operator and his loader should trouble fall upon the frontier town.

The gunmen had no fear of the watchtowers. The first ones coming in looked up and saw the dead operators sprawled over their large, powerful Gatling guns. Had the dim light allowed, the gunmen would have seen the soldiers' throats had been cut. Blood ran freely through the planks and splattered in the dirt below. In one tower, a gunman wearing the operator's cap stood beside the gun. He raised the dead operator's hand and waved it slowly at the men riding by below.

"Crazy sumbitch," Arvin Yates commented to Dan Hurley riding alongside him. "This

214

is no time to fool around."

"I agree," said Hurley, seeing things a little differently, having drunk half a canteen full of Tennessee whiskey he'd purchased directly from Eddie Moon before leaving Eagles. "Some fools can't take nothing serious," he'd added, riding on.

After a minute of peeping through the barred windows of the freight depot below, they saw that no one was up and around. Not a lamp was lit. Without a word Axel Coyle and Prince Drako waved a half-dozen riflemen forward from their horses.

Dolan set his horse back in the darker shadows, watching, and at times running his fingertips up behind his head bandage, still seeing no blood. He still wore his long nightshirt, but he had put on his boots. He had ripped each side of the nightshirt to better accommodate sitting in the saddle.

Doing fine, he told himself.

The riflemen waited until a thick wooden door opened.

"Who goes there?" a young trooper asked. Prince Drako cocked his Colt in the soldier's face.

"Open the door or I'll blast your head off!" Drako said.

"Oh no!" The soldier froze, but held himself together enough to open the barred

215

door with a shaky hand. Armed outlaws ran inside. In seconds four men in their long johns had been handcuffed along an iron hitch rail. More outlaws crowded inside, pillaging an unlocked safe that stood against a wall.

"We're in, it's open!" a young gunman named Felix Hildago shouted from the open doorway. He let out a loud wild yell. This being his first job with the Coyles, he wanted them to see his fervor for the work.

Lantern light started swelling in windows along the dark streets. Even though there had not yet been a shot fired, seven mules in a small corral started braying full blast, as if in a contest to see which could bray the loudest.

"Will somebody get them damn-blasted mallet heads to quieten down!" Dolan shouted to the men.

Axel ran out from inside the depot.

"Brother Dolan!" he shouted. "Tell us how to shut down a mule and we'll be right on it!" The corral of mules continued non-stop.

"Shoot the sumbitches!" Dolan shouted. "Shoot them every damn one!"

"I ain't wasting bullets shooting army mules!" shouted Axel in reply.

Felix Hildago, holding his rifle, ran in

beside Axel.

"Want me to go in there and shoot them?" he said, excited at the prospect.

"Well, you don't want to go in there and only wound 'em, they'll tear you apart!"

"I'm not scared," Hildago said.

"I can see you're not," Axel shouted. A man ran past them with a large grain sack hanging over his arm.

"It's more than we thought, Axel!" he shouted.

"Good!" said Axel. He grabbed a few grain sacks and shoved them at Hildago. "Here, Felix! Forget the mules, they're calming down! Go fill these sacks with cash. Can you do that?"

"You're gawl-dang right I can do that!" said Hildago. He turned and ran into the depot. Axel shook his head and stepped over to one of the soldiers cuffed to the hitch rail.

"I'm going to ask you one time. If I find out you lied, I'll kill you. Get it?"

"Yes, sir, got it!" the soldier said.

"How many troopers are here tonight?" Axel asked.

"Just what you see," said the soldier. "No more than a dozen at the most."

"With this much cash?" said Axel skeptically. "Only a dozen men?"

"That's the gospel, sir," the soldier said. "Nobody comes here. Since the Apache have pulled back, nothing goes on here. Payroll comes in, we never know when, stays overnight and leaves. That's it! I swear it is."

"How many other towns get a payroll transfer?" Axel asked.

"I don't know, sir. A few though, now that the rail spur comes out here."

"Where's the next one?" Axel asked.

"I'd say Cissels, thirty miles north of here. Follow the rails," the soldier said.

"Too bad," said Axel. "We're headed south. Maybe we'll go there another time."

The handcuffed soldier nodded. "It's a long ride to Cissels, considering the payroll money might or might not be there. Things are always changing out here."

"I know," said Axel.

"Hey!" yelled Dolan. "Are you two ol' trail pals?"

"We're just talking here!" said Axel.

"You want to talk? Go talk to the men unloading the safe. Tell them to hurry up! See to it they're not sticking money down in their shirts. Thieving sumbitches," he growled under his breath. He reached his fingertips up to his forehead, under the bandage, and rubbed the dry crusty scab covering his wound. When he lowered his

218

hand, even in the thin moonlight he saw blood on his fingertip and under his nail.

He smiled to himself. *There it is . . .*

Riding up beside him, Axel said, "We've got it all, brother." He patted a stuffed grain sack lying on his lap. Another sack stuffed with cash lay tied down behind his saddle.

"You know where I thought about us going next?" he said to Dolan.

"Where?" said Dolan. "Tell me, since you had yourself such a great time making plans while I laid with a spike in my head."

"A spike?" Axel said.

"Never mind," said Dolan. "Where did you think about going next?"

"There's another pissant of a town north of here called Cissels," said Axel. "It'll get you back up to pace if we hit three or four of these military payroll transfer depots while we're at it."

"Anytime you think I'm not *up to pace,* brother Axel, just holler out, guns or knives. Whichever it is, I'm betting my part of the money in those two bags I can —"

"Dolan, what is that on your head?" He looked closer. "Damn, your head's bleeding."

"No, it's not," Dolan said.

"The hell it's not," said Axel. "Run your hand over your forehead and look at it."

219

Dolan ran his hand under the edge of the bandage and looked at it.

"That's nothing," he said. "It's been doing that for a while. It'll stop."

"It'll *stop*?" said Axel. "Are you crazy? You can't let something like this go! It'll kill you! When we get to Cissels, we're going to round up a doctor there and get you looked at. Your doctor in Eagles said don't let this get to bleeding. Said it will kill you."

"Yeah, but my doctor ain't here, so I expect I can do as I damned well please."

"If you want to kill yourself, go on then," said Axel. "I've done my part telling you!"

Prince Drako came running up, a grain sack full of cash over his shoulder. He broke right into the Coyle brothers' heated conversation.

"Take a look at what I found for us in the safe!" he said excitedly. He held a sheet of paper out to Axel, but Dolan reached down and snatched it first.

"Obliged, Prince!" he said with a snap of sarcasm.

Drako saw the anger and disappointment on Axel's face as Dolan looked at one side of the paper in the dark moonlight, cursed, turned it over and looked again.

"Can you believe that?" said Drako.

"*Believe it*, hell, I can't even see it," said

220

Dolan. He dropped the paper down to Axel. "What the hell good is it to learn to read when it's dark half the time?"

Axel looked at the lit-up depot and called out, "Bring us a lamp out here. Hurry it up!"

In seconds a gunman ran out carrying a lamp. He handed it to Axel and ran back inside.

"Whoa!" said Axel, looking at the letter in the circle of lamplight. "This is a list of every siding and depot in the area that gets a payroll drop!" He looked at Drako in disbelief.

"Yes, it is," said Drako.

"Let me see that," said Dolan, up in his saddle. Axel handed him the lamp and the letter.

"Hell's bells," he exclaimed. "It's only good for the first few days of the month, but in that first few days, we'll take every dollar of it!" He looked at the soldiers cuffed to the hitch rail, making sure they weren't listening.

In the lamplight Drako noticed a widening trickle of blood on Dolan's forehead.

"Dolan, your head is bleeding!" he said in alarm.

Without raising his eyes from the letter, Dolan reached up and touched the trickle of blood lightly.

"It's okay," said Dolan. "Must've just started."

Drako and Axel both saw dried blood under Dolan's fingernail and streaked atop his fingertip.

He's picking at a head wound . . . ? Drako thought to himself. He looked at Axel and could tell he was thinking the same thing.

Axel looked Dolan up and down, setting his horse, in a nightshirt.

Son of a bitch is crazy, he decided. He'd seen Dolan do and say some peculiar things the past couple of years. But this head wound *cinched* it for him. Acting like he was hurt worse than he actually *was?* Hunh-uh. Axel took it to mean that his brother had now gone from being a half-crazy long rider to a full-blown ranting idiot. It wouldn't do.

"You want to start now, ride to the next place on the list after Hundly?"

"Yes," said Dolan. He looked at the list again. "That will be Cissels. It's not too far. We leave here, go back to where we cut the lines coming here. We'll cut out a whole twenty-foot stretch of line, so they can't just shinny up and fix it real quick."

"Now you're talking, brother!" said Axel. He and Drako gave each other a look.

222

Oh yeah! Dolan's crazy as a June bug, their eyes said.

"Great idea," Drako said to Dolan. "Want a couple of us to go back right now?"

"No," said Dolan. "One thing at a time. First we take all this money to a stream somewhere. We'll wet it down and squeeze it as flat as we can get it, then hide it all in some rocks."

Axel and Drako turned silent.

"You sure we want to do all that?" Axel finally asked.

"I'm damned sure," said Dolan. "Now let's stop fooling around here and get going! I want to get home, start digging a well." He turned his horse and rode it away at a walk.

"Dig *a well?*" Drako said to Axel. "What the hell was all that?"

"I don't know," said Axel, sounding concerned. "Before he went to Yuma Prison, he lived outdoors with the rest of us."

"Did you even have a well?" asked Drako.

"Hell no!" said Axel. "We lived on Short Creek in the territory. What did we need with a well?"

Drako shut up, seeing that Axel was getting rattled and angry.

"I'll tell you something else, amigo," Axel said under his breath. "We're not soaking

223

the money and flattening it down, either. That's just more of his damned lunatic talk."

"Fact is, I did hear of a gang of bank robbers out of Texas doing it a couple of years back," said Drako.

"Listen to me, Prince," said Axel. "We are going to cut down more telegraph lines before we head to Cissels. We're going to find us a little cave and bury these sacks of money in it. And that's it. If Dolan doesn't like it, too bad. He's crazy, I'm not. Which one are you going to follow?"

PART 4

PART 4

CHAPTER 15

It was early morning, yet four horses already stood at the hitch rail out front of the Eagles Saloon.

Mortimer Javins set the canvas bag holding three big-boy jugs of whiskey on the wooden steps at the side door of the saloon. He took Baby Greta from Zetra and perched her on his left hip.

"I won't be a minute," Zetra said. She picked up the heavy bag and walked inside. Greta thrust out her stubby, wet little fingers and clutched at her mother.

"She'll be right back," said Javins, as if speaking to a grown-up who understood every word he said. He had no experience in baby talk. Not that he didn't like children, he had just never been around any until now, and he wasn't real sure how this had come about.

He'd been talking to the woman, Zetra, friendly-like. The next thing he knew, he was holding the little one, bouncing her on his hip. He took a cool breath and looked around the sunny morning sky. The next thing after that, he was delivering whiskey, that is, holding the baby while Zetra delivered it. He smiled. That was okay. He hadn't felt this good for a long time.

Inside the saloon, he heard Zetra let out a shriek, heard a jug break on the floor. He hurried inside, Baby Greta still on his arm, and stood looking down at the broken jug and the whiskey on the floor. Behind the bar, Arnold Mason held up his hands.

"It was an accident, Mort, that's all," Mason said. "Take the child outside, please!"

"Yeah, *Mort!*" one of the men said in a mocking voice. "It was just an accident. You and your baby skedaddle on out of here."

Zetra looked up at Javins just long enough for him to see the red handprint on her face, then back down at the wet floor. Javins walked her to the side door, handed Greta to her and nudged her down the steps.

"I'm not hurt, Mort," she whispered. "I mean, don't kill him or nothing."

Without answering her, Javins stepped back inside, took a big mop from behind the end of the bar. He walked to the mess on the floor and stood over it.

Chuckling among themselves, one of the three men pushed away from the bar and said, "Watch this." He walked to the mess and stood facing Javins over it.

"Leave it alone, Mort," said Mason. "I'll get it later."

"Yeah, *Mort,*" the same man said in the same mocking tone of voice. "You don't have to clean it up."

"I know," said Javins, "*you* do." He leaned the mop against the bar, closer to the man.

"*I* do?" the man said.

"That's right, you do," said Javins.

The man's sarcasm turned dark.

"Maybe I should take you apart," he said. "Teach you some manners."

"Did you hit that woman?" Javins said.

"Yeah, I might have," the man said. "She spilled all that whiskey. All's I did was tried to feel her teats, you know, friendly-like, for fun —"

"She tried to stop you, and you backhanded her," said Javins.

"Well," the man said. "That sounds about right —"

Javins backhanded him, hard. The man staggered backward two long steps and fell to his knees. He shook his head, steadied himself. Wiped blood from under his nose, looked at it.

229

"Is that how you did it?" Javins asked. "Is that how you hit a woman?"

"Why you —" He drew his gun, fast, but as he drew it, he saw Javins' Colt come up, slick, silent and cocked. The man froze.

"Come on now," said Javins. "Pull that trigger. I'll stick half your teeth out the back of your head."

The man hesitated. That was all it took.

"Well, hombres," said Javins, "it looks like your pal here is nothing but a yellow coward. Are you all the same?"

Outside the saloon, as shots exploded in loud rapid succession, Baby Greta grabbed Zetra around her neck and squeezed hard. Yet, it was only an instinctive reaction. It was over in a second and appeared to be forgotten by the child a minute later.

"There, there, my Baby Greta," Zetra said, hugging the child. "That's only *gunshots*," she cooed in a baby voice. "Only gunshots, yes!"

Walking back up the steps she leaned around the doorframe and peeked into the silent saloon.

"Everything all right in there?" she asked. "Mort? Mason? Anybody?"

"We're all right," Javins called out.

"Can we come in?" said Zetra.

"It's a mess," Javins warned.

"That's okay," said Zetra, already stepping inside. The smell of burnt gunpowder shook her for a moment. She cupped a hand over Greta's face.

"I should have warned you about the smell. It's too strong for her."

"We're not staying," said Zetra. "Just wanted to make sure you're all right."

"I am," said Javins, standing at the bar, reloading six spent shells. Zetra saw smoke curling around the back of his hands and glanced down at the three bodies sprawled brokenly in poses of death.

"Ma'am," said the bartender, setting the empty canvas bag on the bar, "I'm paying you for the jug that broke. It wasn't your fault." He laid cash beside the bag.

"Thank you, Arnold," she said, scooping up the money and shoving it into her clothing.

Johnny Two ran up and came to a halt on the steps outside the open door.

"It's me, Johnny!" he called out. "I'm coming in. Don't shoot."

"Johnny Two, it's Arnold Mason," the idle bartender replied. "Come on in. Everything's all right in here." He looked at Javins and Zetra. "Thanks to Mort Javins, that is," he added.

"Man, oh man!" Johnny whispered, looking around at the dead men, at all the blood slung and splattered everywhere beneath a low drift of smoke.

"Mort couldn't help it, Deputy!" Zetra said. "This was self-defense. I saw the whole thing!"

"I'm not a deputy, ma'am," Johnny said.

"I saw it, too, from right here," Arnold Mason said. Johnny turned to him and Mason went on. "It all happened mighty fast." He pointed at the bodies. "He drew first, or I should say, he *tried to*. None of the three were fast enough to get it done."

As the bartender spoke, Johnny Two started walking from one body to the next. He looked in amazement at the two bullet holes in each man's chest. "I see," he said, as the bartender finished his account. He stood a moment longer, looking all around the place, seeing no new bullet holes anywhere. He didn't know what to say.

He walked to the front, opened the main door and rolled it partly open. A breeze swept in as if it had been waiting its turn. Smoke caught the cross draft and started moving out.

Johnny Two saw Javins loosen his gun belt and stopped him.

"You don't need to do that," he said. "I'm

not arresting you. Like I said, I'm not a deputy anyway. I'm just taking what you've told me here and telling it to Will Summers. If he's got questions, he'll come ask them."

"Obliged," said Javins, refastening his gun belt.

Actually, Johnny did have another question, but he kept his mouth shut, *he who was not a deputy,* asking for Summers, *who was not a sheriff.* He wanted to ask Mortimer Javins: *Mister, how does any human get fast enough on the draw to empty a six-gun into three men who are out to kill him?*

Another time, maybe, he told himself. He touched the brim of his hat toward everyone and left. As he stepped out the side door, he heard Baby Greta say, "Bye-bye."

The three grown-ups chuckled. Then Javins said, "I better go calm the mama hound. She gets upset at gunfire near her pups."

Yancy Reed had ridden out before dawn and gave his horse a good straight run as the sun came up. As he set his horse atop a hill letting her cool off, he spotted a horse and rider streak along the trail below. Their wake of red-brown dust reached back a long way, fading up into the sky.

More saddle trash, he thought. Yet looking

233

closely he saw the rider had no stirrups supporting his feet. He saw the horse wore no bridle, only a rope hackamore. The rider held the hackamore in one hand and held his other hand farther up the big horse's neck, entwined in its thick flaxen mane. Being familiar with the long barren land behind the rider, and considering the dust they'd stirred up, Reed shook his head.

"There's a hard-riding man, Rudy," he said to his horse. *Indian?* he asked himself. *Yep,* he replied, *Cherokee, most likely.* But he saw no long hair, no tribal dress. What he did see, and suddenly recognized, was the cream-colored animal beneath him with the long flaxen mane.

"C'mon, Rudy," Reed said, reining his horse around and putting him down toward the trail. "Let's catch us a runaway posse man."

But the runaway posse man was having none of it. As soon as he realized someone was dogging his trail, he started slowing the big mare down. He took no shots back over his shoulder and did not attempt to dart up into the rough rocky hillside to shake him loose.

All right, posse man, you want to talk, let's talk. Yancy slowed Rudy to the point that the rider had to see he wasn't being aggressively pursued. The more the rider slowed down, the more Yancy slowed down behind him. Finally, the mare stopped. The rider raised his hands loosely.

"I know you," he called out. "You're Yancy Reed, the gambler. One of Will Summers' deputies."

Yancy waited until he got closer and pulled Rudy up almost beside him.

"Take your hands down, posse man," he said, friendly enough, he thought, considering how Parks had lied to everybody and got some men killed. "You're almost right, except I'm no deputy and Summers is no sheriff."

"So, am I right that you're Yancy Reed?"

"Only if I'm right that you're Tom Barton," said Reed.

"We're both right," said Barton. "In my case, it's about time. I've had the Coyle Gang trailing me all night, and yesterday. How many are there in that gang anyway?"

"Too many for me to count," said Yancy. "I doubt if the Coyle brothers even know."

"I hear you," said Barton. "I'm lucky to get away from them." He patted the big mare's damp withers. "I rode this gal hard all night, knowing they'd kill her as well as me if they caught us."

Reed let out a breath.

"I hate to step on your horse story, Barton, but the mare you're riding is stolen."

"Stolen?" Tom Barton looked like he'd been kicked in the chest. "I took her and some other horses out of the public livery corral under order of Deputy Parks. He would have paid for their use as soon as we brought them back."

"*Whoa,* Tom Barton," said Reed. "Run what you just said back and forth in your mind a time or two." He chuckled.

Barton took a breath.

"You're right," Barton said. "Turns out, nothing Parks ever said here was true. He got me to steal those horses, if you look at it a certain way."

"You ever hear the old expression, 'He lies so much he has to put his boots on backward'?" As Reed spoke, he pulled a pint bottle of Tennessee whiskey from inside his trail duster and handed it to Barton.

"I've heard it, but I've never made much sense of it," said Tom Barton.

"Well, I must've said it a thousand times," said Reed, "and neither have I."

Barton took a shot of whiskey and let out a whiskey hiss.

Reed did the same. He corked the bottle and put it back in his duster. "I'm headed back to Eagles," he said.

"I'm headed there, too," said Barton. "I need to get this gal rubbed down, watered and fed." He rubbed the big mare's sweaty withers. "I'll deal with giving her back when the time comes."

"I understand," said Reed. "I know Lowes Bratcher. He never broke either one of these cream-colored mares. Did you break this one, riding bareback, using a hackamore?"

"She didn't need much breaking," said Barton. "She's a big smart gal. I handled her easy-like. We were running this rocky red dirt like we'd done it for years." He paused, then said quietly, "I'm going to miss her."

"Maybe when Lowes Bratcher gets back, you can see what it would take for you to own her."

"Yeah, you think?" said Barton.

"It's worth a try," said Reed. "Where do you live these days?"

"These days? Wherever I can make a camp without getting run off or shot at." Barton gave a slight smile.

"You're a good horseman; you ought to see about taking care of Bratcher's horses," said Reed. "Ride this mare when she's not bred. Keep her in when she's ready to foal."

"Think he might hire me to do that, take care of his horses?"

"If you handle the other mare as well as you've handled this one, you might have a harder time getting him to let you go."

"Hear that, lady?" he said to the big mare. "We could ride these hills flat, you and me."

CHAPTER 16

Will Summers, Johnny Two and Dr. Otto Adams stood in the street out front of the jail as Reed and Tom Barton rode into Eagles. Except for the three in the street and the two riders coming in, the street and the town stood otherwise empty. A thin spotted cat sat in an awkward-looking position, cleaning itself, licking a hind leg it held up above its head.

"Beats anything I've ever seen," the doctor said, shaking his head. "Ten years back, three gunmen come here, said they would tear this town apart. Every man and woman who could hold a gun, held one. They shot the gunmen to pieces. Strung them up on poles before they died and let them hang there. Put up a sign daring anybody to come for them. Said they would get the same thing." The doctor considered and said, "The townsfolk couldn't get out of here quick enough."

"I heard about that time," said Summers. "Maybe it would be that way this time had the Coyles come in making threats. But they didn't. The gunmen kept the fight between the posse and themselves. Their leader needed help, Eagles gave it to him. Now he's gone because you saved his life. If it ends this way, let's count ourselves lucky." He watched Reed and Barton ride closer along the empty street, and added, "But I don't think we're done with the Coyles yet."

Johnny Two stood to the side reading a telegram from Judge Isaac Parker's court in Fort Smith. Carrying the telegram down at his side, he walked over to Summers. Seeing that Johnny Two wanted to talk to Will, the doctor excused himself. "I'll be at my office if you need me."

"Obliged," said Summers. He turned to Johnny Two, who spoke before Summers could get a chance.

"Will, does this mean what I think it means?" He held the telegram chest high.

"If you think it means I'm now a federal deputy of Isaac Parker's court, you're right," he said. "To turn it down I have to reply by telegraph. Otherwise, I have accepted it." He gave a sharp little grin. "A badge is in the mail, unless I say otherwise."

"You mean just like that, you've become a

lawman by way of the *telegram*?" He glanced up at the telegraph lines running out of town as if an explanation lay up there.

"It's this new world we live in, Johnny. We'd just as well get used to it."

"Are you going to take the job, Will, or are you going to turn it down?"

"A few days ago I suppose I would have turned it down," said Summers. "But I have another telegram that came in right before that one. After I read it to you and Reed, you'll both understand why I might take the job." His last few words became quieter as Reed and Barton stopped their horses three feet away from him and Johnny Two.

"I met up with one of Deputy Parks' posse men a few miles out," said Reed.

"Tom Barton," said Summers, recognizing him right away, as well as one of Lowes Bratcher's future brood mares beneath him. "I figured you fellas would be well headed for Fort Smith by now."

"Will Summers," Barton said, touching his hat brim in respect. "Fort Smith never happened," he said. "We run into the Coyles and fought them the whole time. They whipped us bad. As far as I know, I'm the only posse man left. Two of us surrendered, but I reckon they're both dead now." He wasn't going to mention the circumstances unless pressed. "Parks' head went up on a pole."

"Too bad," said Summers. "I see you brought back one of Lowes Bratcher's young mares your posse men must've taken by mistake?"

"I *am* bringing her back," Barton said. He rubbed the mare's withers. "I can't stand to return her, though, she's been such a fine animal."

"I told him, he might talk to Lowes about working for him," said Reed, "tending all his horses and whatnot."

"It's going to be a while before Bratcher gets back. I'm paying a stable boy to feed and water. I might have a little money to pay you for exercising, and riding. Keep the horses from going green." He looked at Barton. "You can live in the bunkhouse there for the time being."

"Much obliged," said Barton.

"Let me ask you something," Summers said. "Are you a posse man for Parker's court, as needed? Not just for Claude Parks hunting the Coyles?"

"That's right," said Barton. "I've been with the court for a long time, as needed. I've got paper to say so."

"Okay," said Summers. "While I've got the three of you here, let me tell you what's gone on with the Coyles." He flipped open the other telegram.

"I'm going to pass this around and have each of you read it for yourself. But here's the gist of it.

"Judge Isaac C. Parker of the U.S. Court for the Western District of Arkansas has appointed me federal deputy by way of telegraph. To refuse it, I need to telegraph back and tell him so. If not, I become a U.S. deputy given the task of bringing in the Coyles and members of their gang for the robbery of the government payroll at Hundly, Oklahoma Territory."

He looked at the three men in turn. "I've decided to take this appointment. And along with the deputy title," he said, holding the telegram up for them to see, "I'm given the authority to hire as many deputies as I need, within reason. If you three will work for me, I'd like to hire you right now, while we're all three here together."

Johnny Two handed Summers back the other telegram and spoke out.

"Are you going to be taking on any more posse men?"

"If it's somebody good, Johnny, yes, we can take on more help."

"Mort Javins, the Rebel Kid," said Johnny Two. "I saw him shoot. He is so fast, and accurate, I've never seen anybody like him."

"The Rebel Kid," said Tom Barton. "I saw him in a gunfight many years ago. I can't think of anybody faster, more deadly than him, with any weapon — six-shooter, rifle or knife. Yeah, I say hire him."

"Okay, Mortimer Javins is in, if he wants in," said Summers. "All of you go get him. Tell him I've got work for him. After killing three of the Coyles' gunmen, he knows more gunmen will be looking for him. Just say we're on his side. He'll figure it out."

"We should have left well enough alone, Axel. This was a hell of a mistake!" Prince Drako shouted as they rode for their lives from six cavalry troops. "Whatever you're thinking about doing to your brother, go ahead 'n' do it, before he gets us killed!" Bullets zipped past them. One man fell dead from his saddle in a red spray of blood.

"Damn this! And damn Dolan!" said Drako. "If you don't kill him, *I will!* That crazy sumbitch!"

"Watch your mouth, Prince!" shouted Axel Coyle. "That crazy sumbitch is my brother! Anybody kills him, it's me!"

Rounding a turn in a hill trail, four of the Coyle gunmen ran out of the rocks and began firing rifles at the cavalrymen. A trooper flew from his saddle. Another's horse tumbled beneath him and spilled forward, sending the hapless man tumbling and bouncing hard over the rocky hillside.

The Coyle riflemen continued firing at the soldiers until the intensity of it forced the remaining troops to turn away and take their horses up into rock for cover. With the riflemen throwing a hard barrage of gunfire and pinning the soldiers down, Axel and Drako took their time. They rode easily up the rugged hill trail. At the top they rode over to Dolan, who was sitting on a rock with his horse's reins in hand, still wearing his long nightshirt.

"I hope you two found a good hiding place to stash the payroll money before we hit Cissels," he said.

"We did," Axel lied. "Just like you told us to."

"Yeah? Where'd you hide it?" Dolan asked. Axel didn't want to prolong this conversation, but he knew if he didn't say something, Dolan would keep at him until he did.

"We picked out a cave and buried it inside," he said, leaning in closer, lowering his voice, lying with every breath.

"Did you wet it down good?" asked Dolan.

"Didn't get a chance," said Axel. "But it'll be safe enough for now."

"It might be quite a while until we get back this way," Dolan said, laughing. "These soldiers out of Hundly act like all the money there is *their* money! Greedy bastards!" He laughed louder.

Drako and Axel both stared at the dried blood on Dolan's forehead.

"Your head's been bleeding again, brother," said Axel.

"I'm all right," said Dolan, dismissing the matter. "When I get back to Eagles, I'll have Dr. Adams fix me up. I'll lay around there a few days, get feeling better."

"You think these soldiers will let you just lay down in Eagles and take it easy?" Axel asked, tiring of his brother's nonsense. "You have a hanging sentence waiting for you in Fort Smith, and now you're robbing army payrolls!"

"Ah yes, that's all true," said Dolan, raising a finger for emphasis, "but none of it is in Eagles, and that's where we're headed as soon as our new wagon shows up. The law can't touch me in Eagles. As long as Will Summers is the sheriff there, we've got it made."

Axel took a couple of steps back and stood beside Prince Drako. He looked grimly at his brother in the long nightshirt, now dusty and soiled from being on the trail, and at the dried blood on his forehead.

"Prince, this is all too crazy to even try to explain," he said out of the corner of his mouth. "I don't even know where to start." The sound of rifle fire between Coyle's gunmen and the U.S. Cavalry resounded on the trail below.

On the empty streets of Eagles, Summers found it ironic that his first act as a deputy U.S. marshal was to make his rounds and see to it that anyone left in the town he was hired to protect got out, as quick as possible, and stayed out — until further notice.

He didn't have to tell the bartender at the Eagles Saloon that trouble was on its way. He knew that Arnold Mason had seen it all building up from the day he'd taken the job; still, Summers would stop by there first. On his way to the saloon, Yancy Reed rode up to him from the livery barn.

"I just spoke to Javins," said Reed. "He's with us."

Summers nodded, feeling relieved. He gave Rudy an easy slap on the rump and watched as horse and rider galloped away for their morning ride.

Summers walked on across the dusty street, into the empty saloon through the batwing doors. He stopped at the freshly wiped bar, smelling hot brewed coffee.

"Morning, *Sheriff,*" Arnold Mason joked. "What can I do for you?" As he spoke, he set a mug of steaming coffee down in front of Summers.

"I want to let you know I've been *promoted,*" said Summers. "I'm now an appointed U.S. deputy of Judge Isaac Parker's court. So, no more sheriff talk, please."

"Well, congratulations, Deputy Summers!" Mason said.

"Obliged."

"I know you're not an early drinker, so I hope this coffee will do."

"*Gracias,* it always does," said Summers. "My first official act is to remind you that the Coyles are likely on their way here. If you plan on leaving, now is a good time to do it."

"I think I'll just stay here if it's all the same to you," said Mason. "Whatever they've been doing out there, I bet they've worked up a powerful thirst. It'll help make up some for the slow business they've caused here."

"I can't tell you what to do," said Summers. "But if I was you, I'd leave."

"No, you wouldn't," said Mason. "You already knew trouble was coming. You could have left before you were made a deputy,

248

but you didn't."

"That's a little different, Mason, but I've got no time to argue right now."

"Good," said Mason. "I don't want to argue, either." He poured himself a short glass of beer from a tap. "I don't blame myself for the trouble drinking causes here." He took a sip and licked a streak of foam from his mustache. "But to be honest I know that most trouble that happens in this town comes from pulling those tap handles or jerking these bottle corks." He gestured around at the mugs and glasses and bottles on the wall.

The two gave a dark little chuckle.

"So, anyway, I'm keeping Eagles Saloon open as long as I can. If trouble forces me out, you'll know when you hear two shotgun rounds go off." He raised his short glass of beer and clicked it against Summers' raised coffee mug.

"Mason," Summers chuckled, "you've only been back tending bar a week. You don't owe this place a thing."

"I know," said Mason. "Don't forget, I worked here years ago. Now that I'm back, I feel like I never left."

They both looked up and saw Mortimer Javins, carrying a ragged quilt over his forearm, enter through the side door.

"Bartender," he called, "I've got to go in your stockroom, get my hound and her pups out of here."

"Sure thing, you go right on ahead," said Mason. "That's a good idea." Summers smiled to himself. It couldn't be helped, he thought. Once people knew Mortimer Javins was the Rebel Kid, their voices just seemed to naturally grow more pleasant toward him, their attitude more affable. Mason saw the slight smile on Summers' face.

"What?" he asked, but he knew what it was. His face reddened a little.

"Nothing," Summers said, looking down at his coffee mug. The steam had dissipated down to a thin curl. He swirled it a little and took a sip.

Zetra Wilson came in next with Baby Greta hiked up on her hip.

"Mort is back in the stockroom, Mrs. Wilson," Mason said.

"I know," said Zetra, stopping just inside the door.

"You and the little one are welcome to come wait inside, ma'am," said the gracious bartender.

"Thanks," Zetra said. "Here he comes."

Javins emerged from the stockroom with the quilt tied over his shoulder, the pups squirming inside. Three feet behind him the she-hound followed the tot-quilt, her nails clacking along on the wooden floor.

"Much obliged," Javins said to Mason. Then he looked at Summers. "Did you talk to Reed?"

"I did," said Summers. "Much obliged for your help."

"He told me you have a place where I can keep these little fellas for now. I'm much obliged to you for that."

"So am I," said Zetra.

It took Summers a second to understand what Javins and Zetra were thanking him for. Then it came to him. He'd told Reed of a place they might run to if things got too hot between them and the Coyles. It was an old cabin hideout Summers owned in the hills east of town. Longtime townsfolk, like Silk Polly and Leonard Spires, knew the place as Gunman's Pass.

"Glad to do it," Summers said.

When Javins and Zetra had gone, Mason gave Summers an inquiring look.

"I keep a place up in the hills," Summers said, inclining his head. "It's a cabin built on the site of an old ruins."

"All right, now it rings a bell," Mason said. "I heard about a big gun battle you had up there with a gang of outlaws. Gunman's Pass, they call it, right?"

"That's right," said Summers. "It's a nice quiet little place. I still go up there some, not as much as I used to."

"Well, now it looks like you've got a litter of hounds boarding with you," said Mason.

"I don't mind," said Summers.

A silent pause set in. After a moment, Mason said, "All right, I'm going to ask you about Gunman's Pass. If I get too personal just tell me to shut up. Fair enough?"

"Fair enough." Summers nodded. He motioned for a shot glass. Mason set one up and stood an open bottle of rye beside it.

"All right," said Mason quietly, "I heard *six* men against just you and your six-shooter. Is that right?"

"Yep," Summers said, and he stopped there. He filled the shot glass and threw back a drink.

"The story I heard was you killed four of them with your Colt. Then you ran out of bullets and hunted down two of them and killed them with your bare hands?"

"A knife," Summers said, solemnly. "I had a knife."

"*My God,* Summers . . ." Mason whispered.

Summers filled the empty shot glass and

tossed back the fiery rye.

"Tell me, Will," said Mason, "does a man ever get over that hard kind of killing?"

Summers remained silent for a moment, the empty glass at his fingertips. Then almost in a whisper, he said, *"Shut up."*

CHAPTER 17

The rifle fire between the outlaws and the cavalry troops had waned along the lower trails. Dolan, Axel, Drako, and many of their men had straggled in and gathered on the hillside. They boiled coffee, ate jerked meat and waited. After another hour, Dolan stood up in his nightshirt and pointed down the steep rocky hillside.

"Men! Here comes our new wagon," he shouted. The men quickly grabbed their horses and headed down the trail to where the wagon had turned and begun rolling slowly uphill, four mules pulling the big wagon over the rock-strewn trail through deep washouts and potholes.

"Stop that wagon, you stupid sumbitches!" Dolan shouted, pulling his gun and pointing it, just shy of firing it. Riders who'd been goading the braying mules stopped and stared up at the big man who appeared to have forgotten to dress himself.

"Hold up right there, damn it!" Dolan bellowed. "We'll come down!"

"Okay, now I understand," said the gunman driving the wagon to one of the horsemen riding near him. "He doesn't want to wear them mules out on these sawtooth hills. Must be saving them for later."

Dolan Coyle rode in hard, his nightshirt flaring out around him. He slid the horse to a halt and jumped down from his saddle and threw open the back canvas of the big wagon.

"Oh my! Oh *my! Oh my!*" Dolan jumped up and down in the dirt, staring wide-eyed at the big brand-new Gatling gun facing him from inside the wagon bed. His shouting was so loud, two of the four wagon mules started braying, stiffening their necks up in the air and kicking at the other two. The heavily loaded wagon rocked back and forth.

"All right, that's enough!" Dolan shouted. He held his hands out as if to calm the excited animals.

"We've got trail dust rising back there," Drako called out to Dolan and the others around the wagon. "Better get them moving!"

"Okay, you heard him," said Dolan. "Keep this wagon down here a few more miles, rest these mallet heads some. There's a trail a few miles ahead where the hills are not as steep. We'll take them up when we get there."

"No matter what kind of a fool he looks and acts like," Axel said under his breath to Drako, "he gets something in his mind, he sticks with it."

"Yeah, I reckon," said Drako. "Any other time I might ask why the hell do we need a Gatlin' gun. Way things are getting to be, I can't help but think we've needed a Gatlin' gun long before now."

"Yeah," said Axel. "I hate to think what we'll be needing later on."

"Everybody, listen to me," Dolan called out. "This Gatling gun cost me more than this wagon and all four mules! As soon as my brother, Axel, brings me my trousers, we're going to take this gun somewhere and see how it works. If any of you have somebody you'd like to see these big bullets cut to pieces, now's the time to let us know!"

Three hands went up among the gathered horsemen.

"Hold it, damn it!" said Dolan. "Fellas, I was only funning with yas! We're not going to shoot anybody tonight. I admit that I, myself, can't wait to see what this big gal can do to a couple hundred pounds of wild meat on the hoof. But not tonight! No violence tonight, men! Tonight, we see how reliable this gal is! After that we can kill any sumbitch who gets in our sights."

"Oh yeah, Prince," Axel said as he reached back and pulled Dolan's trousers out of his saddlebag, "Dolan's mind is gone." He tapped his forehead. "And I ain't blamin' it all on his head wound. First chance we get, you, me and this big gun are out of here."

Drako rose a little in his stirrups and looked all around as if taking a head count.

"How many men did we start out with?" he asked.

"I don't know," said Axel. "Twenty? Twenty-five?" He stood in his stirrups and looked around also.

"How many you see now?" Drako asked.

"A dozen maybe?"

"Maybe," said Drako. "Ol' Dolan has thinned us down a lot."

"All right, you bunch of outlaws," Dolan shouted with a loud laugh. "Let's take this gal out and see what kind of job she can do!"

In the middle of the night, the gunmen and the big mule-driven wagon had traveled through the dark rugged land. Finally, Dolan Coyle looked down from atop a ridge at a narrow wooded valley lit up by lamps and lanterns and bonfires of all sizes.

"Here we are, men," Dolan called out from the saddle. He gestured at the lights and said, "Any of you who don't know, there sits the Little Diamond Brothel." The men drew their horses closer around the big wagon and gazed down as if in awe.

"I've heard tell of it, but never seen it," one of them said quietly. "It's not on any map I've ever heard of. Leastwise, I've never found it."

"Now you have!" said Dolan. "And some-day you'll be able to tell your grandkids, or cellmates maybe, that you were here the night a Gatling gun chopped the Little Diamond Brothel and Road House to the ground!"

Instead of the cheers Dolan had expected, a seriously dead silence fell over the group. Finally, a hesitant voice said, "Dolan, you don't aim for us to shoot the place into the ground, do you?"

"What did I say, huh?" Dolan replied. "Hell yes! Turn it into sawdust and sweep it across Kansas!"

"Holy Moses and Joe!" said another man. "Can't we just chop down some trees with it?"

"No! Hell no!" said Dolan. "There's not a

tree in this world that ever cheated me at cards or sold me a bottle of watered-down *laud*. I went years thinking I'd never get revenge, but here I am!"

As Dolan continued to rant, Drako whispered to Axel Coyle, "We rode all this way, robbed a payroll, fought the U.S. by-God Army, and bought a Gatling gun, so's we can destroy this harmless little whorehouse that's never hurt anybody?! Because your shot-in-the-head idiot brother got cheated here one time in a card game?"

"You heard him, Prince," said Axel. "If you need to ride down and make friends with one or two of the ladies before we commence shooting, you best hurry on. Whatever half-ass plans he's got in mind can change quick."

Prince Drako looked down at the ground.

"Had I known we were coming here, I might have rode down and stood tall, so to speak." He let out a sigh. "Not now, though. My heart wouldn't be in it."

"All of you listen up here," Dolan called out. "We need to get this gun in closer and on some solid ground. About sixty to eighty feet away from the place! I'll warn everybody to get out, then we'll let 'er rip." He looked at Axel and Drako and gave a sly wink. "Aside from getting revenge over that crooked card game, I expect this big gun will scare off any soldiers still dogging our trail and send us safely back to Eagles."

"See?" said Axel to Drako. "This slippery bastard always has a reason for doing what he does." If they listened close they could hear the slightest sound of renewed rifle fire in the distance.

When the Gatling gun had been safely and quietly moved to within a hundred feet of the Little Diamond Brothel, Dolan issued an order for the patrons to evacuate, with a dark threat of the ugly fate awaiting them should they decide to stay inside.

Women in various stages of undress ran out the front door with dresses and under-garments slung over their arms and shoes clutched in their hands.

"Don't shoot!" they shrieked and shouted, their male customers staggering along behind them, dropped boots littering their wake across the wide yard.

"Don't forget to take your horses," Prince Drako called out, stifling a laugh. "This big gun will turn them into red mush right before your eyes!"

"Fire!" Dolan hollered. He swung an arm as if it were holding a battle sword. Two shots erupted from the big gun, then it stopped. *A jam!* The operator and his ammunition feeder made a quick adjustment and got ready to fire again.

"Fire!" Dolan shouted in the same tone of voice, with the same swing of an arm. *Nothing!* Not a shot. But the gun seemed to have alerted the distant cavalry riflemen. Their firing increased, and this time sounded closer.

"*Uh-oh,* they're back in the game!" Dolan shouted. He ran forward to the big gun, kicked it, cursed it. "Get this rotten sumbitch working! Before they attack and ride us down!"

Seeing the gun operator back in position with his loader beside him, "Fire!" Dolan shouted for the third time. This time the gun let out three quick shots, stopped, then fired repeatedly, the vibration sending the operator's hat down onto the bridge of his nose.

"*Ah!* Shoot 'em, men, shoot 'em!" Dolan bellowed at the gun crew.

At a distance of one hundred feet, the big bullets caused devastating damage to the thick log-and-brick wall of the storied brothel. A piece of brick even flew back and hit one of the men in his chest and left him folded up on the ground, knocked out cold.

"Keep it firing! Keep it firing!" Dolan

shouted, even though the gun crew couldn't hear much of what he was saying. The big gun moved back and forth, knocking out the brothel wall five feet above the ground. Where the wall had already crumbled, it was possible to see the interior of the rooms being chewed to pieces. Broken furniture jumped and moved, dancing to some strange music.

Axel leaned in his saddle and shouted to Prince Drako.

"Let's ride out of this a little!" he called out above the heavy steady blasts of gunfire. "If we're here and it breaks down, he'll call on us to repair it."

"Hell yes, *let's go!*" shouted Drako. He looked all around, then pointed to an old log cabin with its doors swung wide open. Some of the women and their customers had spread blankets on the ground and moved the party outside without slowing down. Clothes lay strewn in the grass and dirt. A man's striped dress shirt, caught on a strong breeze, appeared to be chasing a flimsy blouse across a nearby field.

"I could stay here awhile," Drako said with a grin.

"Lord, yes!" shouted Axel, as two women came walking toward them wearing short summer underwear and carrying a long bottle of whiskey and two glasses.

Four miles behind the big gun wagon and Coyle's gang, the U.S. cavalrymen had heard the firing stop. A forward scout named Owen Dunes rode in on a wounded horse and sought out the leader of the troops, Captain Daniel Turr.

"My goodness, we thought you were dead!" said Captain Turr as the exhausted scout lowered a canteen from his lips and wiped his mouth. Dunes started to offer a salute but the captain waved it away.

"This is not the time to stand on formality, Dunes," said the captain. "What is going on up there? Are they fighting toward us or away from us?" He glanced around at his mounted staff, who, seeing the scout had returned, had sidled up near him.

Dunes looked up at the captain and said, "Begging your pardon, sir, may I first get help for this animal? I fear he's dying, sir!" He motioned to the blood running down the horse's leg from a gaping bullet hole.

"Of course, Dunes," said the captain. He turned to his left. "Take the scout's horse back to our horse attendants, Sergeant. See to it the animal gets the best of care."

"Yes, sir," said the sergeant. He took the horse's reins from the scout's hand and rode away with the limping animal.

The captain looked down at Dunes expectantly.

"And now, scout?" he said coolly.

"Captain," said Dunes, "they've taken a hard beating. When I started riding back less than an hour ago, they had started breaking up, losing positions they'd held firmly to start with."

The captain offered a satisfied smile and looked around to make sure his staff officers had heard it, too.

"From that time to this, sir, I've heard the firing fall off even more. Sir, if you will permit me to say . . ." He trailed off, waiting for the captain's permission.

"Yes, please. What is your personal assessment, scout?"

The scout offered a slight smile.

"Sir. They sound to me like all they want to do now is go straight home."

The men gave a grateful sigh. "Thank God," said a young lieutenant. "The less 'letters home' I have to write, the easier my job."

The scout gave him a hard look.

"Anything further to report, Mr. Dunes?"

The scout reflected that it was always a good sign when the captain went from calling him *scout* to calling him *Mr. Dunes.*

"No, sir," said Dunes. "I should mention that a large freight managed to get to them somewhere along the trail. It looked pretty heavy. Had four mules pulling it."

"Probably food supplies," the captain said. He smiled again. "I say, *good for them.* By now they have had time to enjoy their last meal before we fall upon them and beat the living hell out of them!"

The captain's staff cheered, clapped and hurrahed as he waved his hat above his head.

"Rally the men on me!" he shouted to his officers, who each sat mounted in front of a column of riders. At the sound of the captain's voice, they relayed the order and rode their horses forward at a steady formal gait.

"Now then, Mr. Dunes," Captain Turr said, as the scout mounted a fresh horse beside him. "Show us to the heart of the battle."

"Yes, sir," said Dunes, gigging his new horse forward. Armed, formed and ready, they rode on.

CHAPTER 18

Under a half-moon, the long column of cavalry pressed up along the hill trail. They moved quietly, their yellow-gold bandannas removed from around their necks and shoved down out of sight inside their tunics. Officers who ordinarily wore gray Stetsons replaced them with their dark blue garrison caps. Instead of hanging their rifles from saddle rings, they carried them across their laps to muffle any noise.

When three rifle shots resounded from alongside the trail behind, Captain Turr said to the young lieutenant riding beside him, "What the devil was *that*?"

"Rifle fire, sir!" the lieutenant replied. "Much farther back behind us! Nothing close, I'm certain!"

"Damn it, man!" said the captain, still trying to keep his voice lowered. "I know it's rifle fire! What the hell is it doing behind us? Are they running away so slow we've passed them?"

"Sir, I —"

"There it is again. That's a heavy volley!" the captain said. Before the words had even left his mouth, more rifle shots blinked along both sides of their back trail like angry fireflies. Now, across the trail from the column, gunshots blinked everywhere on the hillside.

A horse fell, whinnying in pain. The rider scooted away on his hands and knees, crying, "My horse!" Two troopers jumped down from their saddles and dragged him off the trail into a drainage ditch.

"It's an *ambush*!" the captain said, still keeping his voice down.

"Men!" shouted the young lieutenant before the captain could say anything more. "Take cover off the trail! Get your horse down! Get into the ditch! Hurry, men! Fire at will!"

"Yes, men!" the captain echoed the younger officer. "Fire at will! Get your horses down!"

"Is this where our good captain gets us all killed, Williams?" one man asked another darkly, as they pulled their horses into the safety of the ditch.

"I hope not, Benham!" Williams replied amid relentless gunfire. "I figure when the firing slows, we'll charge toward the hilltop, take the higher ground."

"Lucky us," said Benham. He'd laid his horse down on its side and stood above it, his left foot near the flattened stirrup, firing out at the gun positions on the hillside.

"If Turr doesn't get us out of here when these outlaws stop to reload, I'm headed down this hillside on my own. Are you with me?"

"Hell no!" said Benham. "If this lower side of the hill was safe, outlaws would be on it, shooting at us!"

"Suit yourself," said Williams. "I'm going."

"You'll be a deserter!" said Benham.

"I'll be alive!" said Williams.

"Not if you get *caught*!" said Benham. "They'll hang you out here on the nearest tree."

"Yeah, well, I'm going, you just watch," said Williams.

Farther along the ditch, Captain Turr and his lieutenant, Charles Goss, huddled over the high ditch bank.

"We must immediately take the top of this hill, Lieutenant," Turr said as the heavy rifle fire slowed. "Divide our command into three fighting units. We are the head unit. Have the other two units remain here and provide cover while we get up close to the top. Then we will cover the next unit as it advances, and so —"

He stopped short as the first two shots from the Gatling gun roared on the hillside above them.

"What was that?" barked Turr.

"Sir, I have to say, it sounded like a Gatling gun to me. A jammed Gatling gun, I might add."

"Lieutenant, you heard my plan, three units, one covering the other, pushing up the hill?" said the captain.

"A Roman three-tentacle phalanx," said Goss. "Yes, sir. We studied the various phalanx formations at West Point."

Captain Turr stared at him for a moment, then shook his head as if to clear it.

"Yes," he said, "yes, as you say, a Roman phalanx. Very similar." He coughed and cleared his throat. "I don't need to elaborate on it, then?"

"No, sir," said Lieutenant Goss. "Rest assured I know the staging of the formation."

The Gatling gun belched out three more shots, then stopped again.

"My goodness, man!" said Captain Turr. "That is a Gatling gun! No mistake about it!"

Almost before he'd finished his words, the

269

big gun fell into relentless rapid fire, as if it would chop down the entire hillside before them.

Amid the deafening gunfire, the captain, his lieutenant, and all of the dismounted men stuck close to the side of the ditch, even though they judged the big gun to be a few miles away, and getting no closer.

"Lieutenant Goss!" shouted the captain. "Cancel my order to attack."

"Sir, you've given no order to attack yet," Goss shouted back above the sound of the big gun.

"Even better!" said Captain Turr. "Here's my new order. Everyone lie low here until I say otherwise!" He paused and scratched his goatee. Then he added, "That includes us, Lieutenant! We must keep our heads. The men are counting on us. Besides, I have to say, I've never seen one of these big monsters that can fire long without jamming, overheating, or breaking down. We must bide our time here. This *will* pass!"

Four of Coyle's newer gunmen rode into Eagles at daylight. They came into town through a back trail and set their horses near the livery corral, then gazed back in the direction of the trail that had brought them from the Little Diamond Brothel.

"I can't believe what we did to that poor little brothel," said one, a former California bank robber and paid killer named Bobby Hood. "I never even had time to make any friends there."

"Neither did I," said Fred Byers. "All my life I looked for the place and never found it. When I do find it, all I get to do is watch it get shot to the ground. Hell, am I supposed to call that a *good time*?" He spit and wiped his parched lips. "Wasn't I supposed to get something out of that? I didn't get a chance to spend any of the money I made robbing that army payroll."

"That is a damn shame," said a Kansas gunman named Ike Reno.

Byers shrugged.

"I learned it's not a good idea to try cheating Dolan Coyle," he said. "Especially if there's a Gatling gun sitting nearby."

They stifled their laughter.

"Did you see how crazy Dolan looked, firing back and forth into that wall until it fell?"

"I saw it!" said Lon Riggs. "That was one of the craziest things I ever seen anywhere."

The four stopped laughing when Yancy Reed and Johnny Two walked up to them from the livery barn, each with a double-barreled shotgun in the crook of their arm.

"Uh-oh," Bobby Hood murmured. "What have we got here?"

"Hombres," said Reed, sociably enough, yet without touching his hat brim. He and Johnny Two stopped ten feet back. Behind them the upper loft doors of the big barn were standing wide open, for no visible reason. The four gunmen took notice just as it was intended for them to do.

"Hombres," Bobby Hood acknowledged. Neither he nor the others offered any further reply.

At the corner of the alley next to the Eagles Saloon, Tom Barton stepped into sight, his hands holding a rifle at the ready.

At the same time, Mortimer Javins emerged from the front door of the saloon and stood on the boardwalk. He looked unimposing in a long black duster . . . which he opened slowly to reveal the big Army model Colt on his right hip and a cross holster on the left side of his belly with the butt of a big bone-handled Colt protruding from it. Javins laid his left hand on the belly Colt as if on the unlikely chance he might ever need it.

"Well, now," said Ike Reno, with a dark smile spread beneath a thin mustache, "all of this makes me feel a mite bit unwelcome here."

"If you're through scaring us here," said Lon Riggs, "let me ask you as friendly as I can, Why do all of you have so much bark on at us long riders? We were told we'd be welcome here, that Dolan even has an old friend here running things."

"No," said Reed. "Dolan doesn't have anybody here running things for him. Dolan, he took a ricochet here a few days ago. Our doctor treated him, and now he's all fixed up and gone his way. That's the whole of it."

"Hell's fire, boys," said Bobby Hood. "That sounds like the kind of thing that ought to make people friends for life, not have them walking around with a mad-on like a bunch of stiff-legged dogs."

The gunmen chuckled a little. Even Reed and Johnny Two let go a short laugh.

"It would have been all right," said Reed, "but now the man that handles the law in Eagles has been appointed a U.S. federal deputy by Judge Isaac Parker, and you can see how that changes things."

"Well now," said Bobby Hood, "just where is this *Summers* fella, I believe his name is?"

"Yes," said Reed, "Will Summers is his name."

"And just where is this Will Summers?"

asked Hood. "He's not the bashful type, is he, afraid to show his face? Afraid he might do or say something to cause somebody to grab up a shooting iron and splatter him all over the countryside?"

Instead of chuckling, the gunmen just stared this time. Yancy Reed and Johnny Two saw that the joking had stopped. Now they would see just how serious these four were going to get without the odds stacked in their favor.

Reed raised a hand and Tom Barton and Mortimer Javins took a step forward. The gunmen quickly looked around from their saddles.

"What's this?" said Hood. "You jakes think you're going to slip up around us?"

"We're not slipping up," said Reed, calmly. "I just figured if you're all through smearing your bull-dobble all around, we'll go ahead and empty these shotguns in your bellies, get this meeting over with." He motioned Barton and Javins another step closer. "What do you say, Johnny? Kill them or run them out?" he asked without taking his eyes off Bobby Hood.

Barton and Javins stepped even closer.

"You know my answer," Yancy said, and cocked both big hammers on the shotgun. "I've got two loads of broken roofing nails.

Just say the word."

Riggs, Reno, and Byers tensed, ready to fight. Again Barton and Javins stepped closer, this time quickening their pace.

"*Whoa,* everybody," said Bobby Hood, sweat running down his face. "What the hell is all this? We were all funning back and forth. All of a sudden somebody's wanting to kill somebody! Why? Damned if I know. But Dolan said meet him and the rest of 'em here, not start killing!"

Reed jabbed his thumb west of town.

"You can meet the rest of 'em out there. They made a camp less than a mile out while they waited for Dolan to heal some. You can tell him I said if he's smart, he'll realize why Will Summers is not here to meet him. Now that Summers is a deputy marshal, he'll have to arrest Dolan on the spot. It sounds like he's trying hard *not to.* Can you remember that?"

Bobby Hood said to the others over his shoulder, "Let's get out of here. If Summers is a deputy, and Dolan is wanted by the law, it makes sense they keep a distance between them."

"Now that you're getting the message," said Reed, "get out of here."

As the gunmen headed out of Eagles toward

the camp west of town, Will Summers stood up atop the old Quaker Missionary Church and watched them go. He waved his hat at his four deputies, walked to the back of the roof and climbed down the ladder. The five of them gathered on the street under a canopy in front of the blacksmith's forge and bellows.

"This place looks like a ghost town," Summers said, gazing down the empty main street. "I've never seen the townsfolk so edgy over a gang of outlaws."

"There's just so many of them, Will," said Reed. "I don't think Dolan or Axel, either one, knows how many men they've got riding with them."

"You're right, Yancy," said Summers. "At least they've got less today than they had yesterday. I got a telegram from Brayton Siding. The gang robbed an army payroll and shot it out with a battalion of cavalry troops. Unfortunately they somehow managed to get their hands on a Gatling gun, and now they're headed this way, with the cavalry on their tails."

All his deputies looked worried.

"Will," said Johnny, "if they come here for a fight, we can't stop them. They'll tear this town to the ground."

"That's right," said Summers. "That's

why we're not letting them come here. We're going to lead them all up to Gunman's Pass. Anybody who wants out, get out now. Nobody's going to blame you if you do."

"I'm still in," said Reed.

"Me, too," said Johnny.

"I didn't come *in* looking for an easy way *out*," said Barton. "What about you, *Rebel Kid*?"

"I always figured I'd go down shooting," said Javins. "Nothing suits me better."

CHAPTER 19

Six miles along the trail out of Eagles, eighteen exhausted men rode along in a column of twos, keeping an eye on their back trail. In front and behind, men held hidden firing positions among the rocks and brush.

A few miles away, Bobby Hood, Lon Riggs, Ike Reno, and Fred Byers met the large body of the Coyle Gang on their way back to town. After their spree of robbing, pillaging and shooting down the Little Diamond Brothel and Road House, a half-dozen worn-out outlaws kept their equally worn-out horses closely sidled up around the big gun wagon.

"I'm glad to be getting back to Eagles," said Dolan, who was sitting beside the driver. He grinned. "Back to where it's safe!"

Riding alongside the wagon, Axel said, "I don't know how safe it's going to be now that you've got the whole U.S. Army down our shirts."

"They're *gone*," Dolan chuffed. "They started dropping off of us as soon as they heard our *rat-tat-tat* gun looking for them."

"You beat all, brother," said Axel. "You think we're going to be welcome in Eagles once they hear that the law as well as the army is looking for us?"

"The *law*!" Dolan scoffed. "There's no law in Eagles, just Will Summers telling everybody how he wants things done. He's no more a U.S. deputy than I am a bullfrog! He said as little to those four tramps as he could until he can talk to me in person. Pretty smart of him, I think, don't you?"

"Maybe, but still," said Axel, "the army?"

"Ease up, brother Axel!" said Dolan. "Summers knows as well as I do that the army will get tired of looking for us in the kind of places we know to hide. He knows we'll lay low a few days, then do as we damned well please."

"The four men who rode in here a while ago must've heard something different. They talked like they almost had a fight with his so-called deputies before they left town," Axel said.

Dolan chuckled.

"A *fight*? Hell, those four saddle bums can

pick a fight with a preacher on their way to church."

"I can see there's no use in talking to you, Dolan," said Axel. Seeing that the trickle of blood on Dolan's forehead looked fresh, he added, "How's your head?"

"It's doing real good."

"Why do you keep picking at it, making it keep bleeding?"

"I *don't*!"

"The hell you don't!" said Axel. "I'm not blind! Look at the blood on your finger. Look under your nail!"

"Both of you, take it easy," said Drako. "This kind of arguing never causes anything but trouble! We need to be pulling together!"

"Yeah," said Dolan, "before somebody gets killed."

Hearing a noise inside the closed mercantile, Will Summers took a step back onto the boardwalk, opened the door slowly and slipped inside. Following the sound of whispered voices in the stockroom, he eased his Colt from his holster and stepped in through the open door.

"What are you two doing in here?" he asked, his voice loud enough to startle the two soldiers in ragged, dusty uniforms. They raised their hands, quickly and instinctively, dropping the armloads of clothes to the plank floor.

"Mister, don't shoot!" the taller of the two cried out, spewing crumbs from hardtack that had clearly come from an open tin sitting atop a stack of trousers. "We're just soldiers separated from our unit!"

Summers lowered his Colt a little, but kept it ready. He saw the back door opened a crack. "This door wasn't locked?"

"It was," said the same soldier. "But it only took a little jiggling back and forth. We already wish we hadn't done it!"

"Like he said," the other man put in. "We were in a fracas last night. Lost our horses, our guns, got separated from our company." He spread a hand. "We're in a bad shape here!"

"Stop your lying," said Summers. "You've torn the stripes off your trousers and rolled them up and stuck them in your pockets. Pull them out!"

They both pulled the rolled-up yellow stripes from their pockets and let them unroll down their legs. "There," said the taller one, "you've caught us. Now, we'll likely hang."

"Maybe not," said Summers. "Put on a pair of new trousers and boots. If the army's on their way here, you better hurry. If the outlaws you were fighting are on their way, you better hurry *even more.*"

"You got that right," said the taller man. "I'm Jess Williams. This is Bean Benham. That's our *real* names, too."

"Howdy do," said Benham, his mouth still half-full of hardtack biscuit.

"I'm U.S. Deputy Will Summers," said Summers, trying out his new title.

"U.S. *deputy marshal?*" said Williams. "I'll be damned."

"I just started yesterday," said Summers. "I'm looking for information. The more you can tell me about the outlaws and the army, the more I might be able to help you keep from hanging. What happened out there last night?"

The two got dressed in civilian clothing as they explained.

"We were outnumbered from the start," said Williams. "I've never seen a gang of gunmen as big as this one the Coyles have put together. They go where they want, take what they want. We couldn't stop them! Bean and I couldn't even run away from them! We tried to retreat, but ended up riding off a cliff in the dark!"

"Yeah," said Benham. "Horses and all! We all fell fifteen, twenty feet or more. Lucky it didn't kill them poor cayuses. They came up at a hard run, but they wanted nothing more to do with us after that!"

"We come across Indian Territory last night, on foot, in the pitch dark!" said Williams. "We heard a Gatling firing. That was more than a little unsettling!"

Johnny Two found the rear door of the mercantile store partly open. He eased inside and found Summers and the two deserters talking quietly in the stockroom.

"Will," said Johnny Two, "there's a six-man cavalry detail out front. They want to talk to you." He looked concerned.

"A cavalry detail?" said Summers.

"Yep," said Johnny Two. He looked back and forth at the two soldiers.

"Oh, God *no*!" shouted Benham, on the verge of running out the rear door.

"Don't let them take us, *Marshal Summers*!" said Williams. "*Please!* They will kill us! We know they will!"

"Easy, soldiers, both of you!" said Summers, peeling Williams' hands off his forearm. "We don't know what they want. Stay calm! You're not wearing a uniform. This could be about anything. Hold tight. Let me find out."

Johnny Two stepped in between the soldiers and Will Summers. "I'll keep these two inside until Reed gets here," he said.

"Good," said Summers.

"Wait!" said Benham. "Who is this Reed? Why is he on his way here?"

"Don't worry about it," said Summers. "Calm down!"

He turned and walked out the back door. Before his boots had touched down from the boardwalk, four of the six-man detail were hurrying toward him from the direction of the mercantile's hitch rail.

"Deputy U.S. Marshal Will Summers?" said the young lieutenant at the head of the detail.

"That's me, Lieutenant. How can I help you?"

"First of all," said the young officer, "I understand congratulations are in order?"

"Obliged, Lieutenant . . . ?" he said.

"Lieutenant Brewer. These troopers and I are searching for deserters from last night's skirmish. Our scouts sighted a dozen or more who left under the cover of darkness."

"A dozen *or more*?" said Summers.

"Yes," said Brewer. "We ask that if you see any of them, report them to the nearest federal officer, which in this case is *you*." He smiled and glanced around. "Is everything as it should be here, Marshal Summers?"

"Not to my thinking," said Summers.

"We've had trouble with a big outlaw gang, with bandidos, you name it. That's part of why I'm here. We've a lot going on to keep us busy."

"I can leave a few men here to assist you," the officer said.

"Much obliged, but no thank you, Lieutenant. I have four good deputies," said Summers. "I'm sure we will be all right whatever comes our way."

Summers stood out front of the mercantile watching until the soldiers were out of sight. When he turned to the mercantile, Johnny Two had stepped out and off the boardwalk and stood beside him as Yancy Reed came walking to them from the saloon.

"When I saw the cavalry, and Johnny gave me a wave, I figured I better stick close by and see if you needed me," Reed said to Summers. "What was all that?" He nodded in the direction the soldiers had taken out of Eagles.

"They're searching for deserters," said Summers, "like the two we've got inside."

"Yeah?" said Reed. He chuckled. "First full day on the job, you've already captured two deserters from last night's big battle? Congratulations, Deputy!"

"Obliged," said Summers, in no mood for idle conversation. "Walk them out the back

285

way to the jail, the two of you," said Summers. "Try to go unnoticed if you can."

"Sure thing," said Reed. "The way we'll handle them, nobody will suspect they're prisoners, let alone deserters."

On the way to put the two deserters in the jail for their own safety, Silk Polly strolled out of the Eagles Saloon twirling a parasol above her head in the morning sunlight. "Yoo-hoo," she said, giggling.

"Oh no, look at this," Reed said to Johnny Two beside him. "How are we going to be unnoticed with Polly pointing us out like a circus act?" He looked more closely at Polly and said under his breath, "Is she drunk?"

"I'm never able to tell," Johnny said, seriously. "Don't let her see you watching her though, or she'll get worse."

"Oh no!" said Reed. "She has pinned her skirt up at the waist! She is taking her blouse off!" He turned his head forward and lifted his eyes skyward. "*Please,* can we get this over with?"

"*Amen,*" whispered Johnny Two as Polly danced in the street, twirling her parasol.

"What's going on back there?" asked Williams. The four stepped onto the boardwalk out front of the jail.

"Nothing," Johnny said sharply.

He shoved the door open and guided Reed and the deserters inside. Reed started to close the door, but Polly bounced through like a young rabbit.

"Excue-*ees* me!" she said, melodiously.

"Sure, Polly," said Reed, looking out, back and forth, then closing the door.

Johnny Two went to the cell, lifted a looped length of heavy chain on the door and pulled the door open with it.

"Inside," he said. The men hesitated.

"I'm sure our deputy marshal explained that this is for your own good? Just until all the troops have gone through and headed back to the fort at Brayton?"

"He has," said Williams. "But what about this fella?" He hitched a thumb at the sleeping man curled up like a baby under the bunk on the right, his flop hat pulled down over his eyes.

Johnny moved past the two deserters and walked to the bunk. He stuck his boot toe under the man's hat brim and lifted it.

"It's Eddie Moon," said Reed. "I'd recognize him or his breath anywhere."

Johnny looked at the two deserters.

"Moon is one of the Coyle Gang, but he's not dangerous. He won't crowd either of you."

"Well, should he try," said Williams, grow-

287

ing bold, "he'll find that the U.S. Army turns out some damn fine fighting men."

Johnny Two and Reed stepped out of the cell and closed the big iron door by the loop of chain.

"Oh yeah, we all know that," said Johnny, throwing a look at Reed.

"Should I stay and dance awhile longer?" Silk Polly smiled, twirling her parasol in front of her naked breasts.

The two deserters stood silently watching, stunned, as Polly artfully careened around the small space in front of the cell.

Johnny stepped forward with the small tin of hardtack Reed handed him and stuck it through the bars.

"Here," he said. "Keep eating these until we can bring you something more substantial." He inclined his head toward Polly. "She'll stop before long, if you want to just let her go."

"Obliged, Deputy!" The two soldiers reached into the biscuit tin and ate as Silk Polly wiggled, twisted and twirled.

CHAPTER 20

In the early afternoon, Summers, Johnny Two and Yancy Reed stood out front of the jail and watched seven soldiers arrive in the back of a freight wagon covered with battle scars. Four more arrived on horseback and hitched their horses at the rail alongside the wagon.

Less than an hour earlier, Summers and Reed had watched men from the Coyle Gang ride in from the same direction. But instead of fighting one another, they were all drinking together.

"Think about this," said Yancy Reed, as music blared from the open doors of the Eagles Saloon. "These soldiers and gunmen were out along the trail down at Hundly and the Little Diamond Brothel last night, killing one another. Now you'd swear they're all *kin*."

"Johnny," Summers said, "when you get a chance, how about walking past that freight

289

wagon close enough to see what's inside?"

"You got it, Will," Johnny said, and headed that way. Summers looked up at the sound of the jail door closing and saw Silk Polly slip out onto the boardwalk, the wide-open parasol spread before her.

"Miss Polly," said Summers, "are you all right?"

"All right! *Ha!*" She giggled and twirled her parasol back and forth. "I'm naked as a *baby bird.*" She grinned drunkenly. "Want a little *look-see?*"

"No, I'm good," said Summers, who could see she was scantily dressed, not naked.

"Are you drunk, Polly?" he asked, taking a step toward her in case she needed help.

"I am indeed," Polly said. "I slipped Eddie Moon's bottle of Tennessee whiskey from his hip pocket and sucked it down proper-like!"

"How did Eddie Moon get it?" Summers asked.

"Said he makes whiskey now, and always keeps one with him," Polly replied. "Said he keeps one with him 'cause you never know when you're gonna be arrested!"

"I suppose he's right about that," said Summers. He stepped onto the boardwalk and carefully took Polly's arm and opened the door. "Come with me, Miss Polly."

"Where are we going, Will?" Polly asked.

"Right back inside here. I can't leave you to maybe get run over. There's quite a crowd in town."

"You're always such a gentleman — I could just kiss you!"

"I can't do that, Polly. I'm on duty."

"But you're on duty *every* time I see you."

"And that's the bad part of wearing a badge," said Summers, opening the door. He smiled, almost laughed.

"What's so funny?" Eddie Moon asked from inside the cell.

"Nothing that concerns you, Moon," said Summers. "Since you're here, tell me what you had to do with the payroll robbery in Hundly." While he spoke, he walked Polly into the other cell and eased her back onto the bunk. She was snoring lightly before he'd even covered her with a blanket.

"I didn't have a *damn* thing to do with it," said Moon. "Can't a man come to town without getting accused of something or other?"

"Not in your case," said Summers. "You've been too wrong for too long. You're always guilty of something."

"Not this time," said Moon. "All I'm guilty of is taking up with a low-down Jezebel who deceived me, took all the money I

291

earned selling whiskey for her and dumped me for the new bartender at the Eagles Saloon. He's a lucky man if I don't kill him deader than last winter."

Summers started to tell him that bartender was the Rebel Kid, but decided to keep his mouth shut, for now anyway.

"Is she the wife of Reuben Wilson, lives north of town?" Summers asked.

"She said she is, but I figure they're as married as a rooster and a hen. She lies worse than any woman I ever seen. Said she has five offspring, but she lied. The four oldest belong to her sister up the road. Youngest one might be hers, but mostly she likes keeping it on her hip, says it makes people want to buy more whiskey from her."

"You live an interesting life, Moon," said Summers. "Where are you living after last night's payroll robbery?"

"Whoa, now," said Moon. "I wasn't in on any of that. I don't even like being around them big Gatling guns, the loud sumbitches! Soon as I figured Dolan Coyle was going to rob the army payroll, I cut out. I had a feeling Dolan would get himself a Gatling gun, and if he did, I knew he was going to shoot down the Little Diamond with it." He grinned and tapped his temple. "I've watched the Coyle brothers long enough, I can see what they're fixing to do before they do it. That's how I manage to stay ahead of everything, with my wild bunch of pals."

Noting that Moon had awakened sober enough to carry on a conversation, Summers asked, "If I turn you loose, will you be able to stay out of trouble?"

"Sure enough," said Moon. "But I've got nowhere to go unless I find my horse and ride out west to the Coyle camp."

"The place where they lay shooting at the town during the storm the other night?" said Summers.

"Yep, that's the place," said Moon, "except I was laid up chasing butterflies with Zetra Wilson at the time. So, I did no shooting that night." He added in reflection, "Zetra Wilson, *mm-mm.* I have to say, even though she's the most meanest, lying, *deceitful* woman ever run out of hell, she *does* have her ways. She can be sweeter than a bucket of warm honey —" He stopped abruptly when the door swung open and a young soldier ran in.

"Sheriff! Marshal! *Whatever* you are," the soldier said. "Your deputies sent me! There's about to be a killing at the saloon."

Even as he spoke, gunfire erupted out on the street. Summers gave the sleeping Silk Polly a quick look. Then Moon.

"Don't worry about her," Moon said, watching Summers pull down a shotgun and throw a ten-shot bandolier over his shoulder. "I'll pull the door to if I leave."

"Obliged, Moon," said Summers. He hurried out the front door, the soldier right behind him.

On their way to the saloon, a loud barrage of gunfire erupted inside. Even in the afternoon light a bright glow of burnt gunpowder pulsed with the explosions. An outlaw flew screaming and flailing through the large window, knocking out glass, window frame and all. Three soldiers sprang out through the broken window and fired at the man as he wobbled upright in the street and took off running.

"We ain't hitting *nothing*!" one of the soldiers shouted as they began reloading their pistols in a cloud of gray smoke. Across the street, the fleeing outlaw dived atop his spooked horse amid a row of other spooked horses and batted his spurs to its sides. The horse whinnied loudly and took off . . . but its reins were still wrapped and tied to the iron hitch rail.

Four other wild-eyed horses, all still hitched, bucked and pulled at the iron rail until all were released except the outlaw's

shaken mount. The freed horses ran, terrified, through closed storefronts and the
stage depot.

The outlaw hung on with both hands as
the iron hitch rail flew back and forth at the
end of the long reins. Three times the rail
barely missed the outlaw's head. The fourth
time the rail swung straight up. With
uncalled-for accuracy, it came down like a
battle club with a loud, long metal clang,
then landed in the dirt next to the unhorsed
outlaw. With the weight off his back, the
tired animal stopped rearing and stood
looking down at his erstwhile rider.

"Darndest thing I ever seen in my life," an
old man said. He walked up to the horse,
cut the iron rail free from its reins and carried it back over to its posts. He dropped
the battered rail on the ground and walked
away.

Standing beside Summers in the middle
of the street, the young soldier stood pant-
ing, settling himself.

"I agree with that old man," he said. "That
is the darndest thing I've ever seen in my
life, too."

Summers smiled. "The way things have
been going, Trooper, if you hang around
long enough, this sort of thing starts to look
like an everyday occurrence."

Stepping into the saloon, Summers saw Johnny Two and Yancy Reed at the far end of the bar pointing their shotguns at the gathering of soldiers facing a dozen of Coyle's outlaws. Men on both sides held smoking six-shooters. Arnold Mason stood behind the bar, wiping blood from his hands on a clean bar towel. Instead of getting the two angry drunken groups stirred up again, Summers turned to the bartender.

"What happened here?" he asked.

Both sides grumbled until Summers and his two deputies stared them into silence.

"All right," said Mason. "Here's how it started."

"That's a damned lie!" an outlaw shouted before the bartender said another word.

The place fell silent. Summers stepped over to the man as the crowd parted.

"Another word out of you," Summers said, "and that will be my boot you feel kicking your mouth shut. Do you hear me?"

"Yes, I do," said the red-eyed drunken outlaw. "I spoke a little too soon."

"You did," said Summers. He turned back to the bartender.

"All right," Mason said, pointing from one side to the other. "This one here shot this one over here." Summers looked closely at the two wounded men. One held his bleeding forearm; the other, a trooper, held his bloody leg squeezed tight.

"I'm bleeding here," he said.

"Yes, you are," said Summers. "Can you walk to the doctor's?"

"How would I know?"

"All right, some of you help your fellow trooper to the doctor's, straight down the street, with a sign out front."

"Let's go, Sherwood," said a soldier.

While four soldiers carried the wounded soldier out, Summers looked at the other wounded man, a new outlaw with the Coyle Gang.

"What about you?" Summers asked him.

"What about me, what?" the man asked in a surly tone of voice. Blood dripped from his wrist. Summers gave Yancy Reed a look. Reed stepped over in front of the wounded outlaw.

"How about a taste of this shotgun butt, badman?" he said, the big double-barrel's butt already drawn back for a hard swipe.

"That's no way to treat a wounded man," the outlaw said.

"I don't like wounded men," said Reed. "They get in the way and always leave a mess." He let the man see him standing ready to punch the shotgun in his face.

"All right, I heard what he asked me," the

outlaw said in a more subdued voice. "Can I just get a towel?" He looked at the bartender.

"One towel," said Mason, pitching him the towel he'd wiped his hands on. The outlaw caught it and pressed it to the bullet wound in his forearm.

"Is that all there was to it?" Summers asked everyone listening. "One man pulled a gun and shot the other for no reason? Now, all of you want to go to jail and spend the night instead of being out here drinking your fill, raise your hand."

No hands went up.

"That's what I thought," said Summers.

"Hell, this is all dancing-squirrel crazy," said another one of the newer outlaws. "Fact is, I don't recall who started it, or why. If I can get my horse away from the hitch rail without getting knocked in the head, I'll leave this town to whatever devil wants to pick its bones!"

"Hear, hear," said another outlaw, giving the group of soldiers a dirty look. "I'm done with this place myself." He looked at the bartender. "I'll just take a tall bottle of whiskey on my way out the door."

As evening shadows stretched long across the dusty streets, and horses and riders rode smaller than their accompanying shadows, Deputy U.S. Marshal Will Summers stood beside his horse, Moby, at the hitch rail, looking down the street toward the saloon. In spite of a rollicking crowd, the place seemed almost peaceful compared to the atmosphere throughout the long hot day.

Now that the troopers had drunk their fill and rode away in one direction, and the outlaws had done the same and rode away in the other, Summers let out a tight breath, knowing how bad the day could have gone. *But it didn't,* he reminded himself.

Aside from a couple of minor incidents like the one earlier at the saloon, the day had moved along well enough. He would take that, he thought. Yes, he would take that every time.

"Looks like the Coyle brothers had better things to do than come visit us here today," Yancy Reed said from the boardwalk behind him. Reed had traded his shotgun for his big Winchester rifle. So had Johnny Two, who stood beside him.

"I can't say I'm sorry they didn't come see us," Summers said.

"You figure because they saw the army in town?" Johnny asked.

"Yep, that's part of it, I think," said Summers. He hung a canteen from his saddle horn and gathered his reins.

Reed chuckled and said, "The outlaws afraid of all the army troops, and the troops and the army brass afraid of the Gatling gun. Too bad this frame of mind ain't going to last a long time."

"I'm afraid you're right," said Summers. He took hold of his saddle horn, but stopped himself when he saw Dr. Adams coming out of his office.

"Hold it, Summers," Dr. Adams called out. "I need to talk to you!" His voice sounded concerned. Summers wrapped Moby's reins back around the hitch rail and waited for the doctor.

"My Lord, am I glad I caught you, Will!" the doctor said when he got close. He looked all around to see who else might be listening. Seeing the street was empty, he added, "I have someone in my office who is waiting to see you!" He gave Summers a seriously concerned look.

"I hope you don't mean who I think you mean," said Summers. He lowered his voice. "Dolan Coyle? I've been expecting him to show up all day."

"Yes, well, now he's here!" said Dr. Adams. "Him and his men have been there waiting for near an hour! If I hadn't seen you, I was afraid he might have stayed all night. He let me come out to get you, because he said he can see me from the office if I tried anything!"

"Okay, Doctor, try to settle down," said Summers. "This is going to be all right. Everybody, stay in sight."

"Want me or Johnny to get up on a rooftop?" Yancy Reed asked. He patted the rifle he held across his belly.

"No," said Summers. "If he says he came here to talk, I'll give him that. Him and Axel haven't been as trigger-happy with us as with some other folks, U.S. Army included."

"I can't believe they all drank at the same saloon," said Reed.

"Well, there's only one saloon here," Johnny Two pointed out.

"Yeah," said Reed, "and nothing brings out good manners like straight-up fear."

"And the need of a good drink," Summers said. He raised his hat a little and lowered it back into place, giving Dolan and any of his men watching a signal that he was on his way. He looked at Reed and Johnny Two. "Now, when we get to the doctor's place, both of you take a seat on the front porch. Nobody needs to know anything about this but us. Let's all look like nothing's going on."

Chapter 21

Out front of Dr. Adams' large white clapboard house, which served as both his office and residence, Summers handed his
rifle to one of the outlaws guarding the
door. He didn't offer his Colt, and no one
asked for it. As he waited for the door to be
opened, Yancy and Johnny Two seated
themselves on the porch swing.

When the door opened, Summers entered.
There were no lamps or lanterns lit. Instead,
the light was soft and shadowy, thanks to
numerous candles, large and small, some
with small reflecting tins and mirrors
mounted on their stands behind them.

At the end of the short hall sat Dolan
Coyle in a tall throne-like chair, his arms
resting on the broad padded arms like some
historical warlord.

"Will Summers," he said. "I believe it's
time to end this conflict between you and
me." His voice sounded stronger than Sum-

mers remembered ever hearing it.

Removing his hat and holding it down at his side, Summers said, "Dolan, I don't know what conflict there is between the two of us. You came here in handcuffs, arrested by a posse that turned out to be illegal. You got wounded and needed a place to get well. Eagles gave you that. I'm a U.S. deputy, and I've tried to make you understand, if you keep putting yourself in front of me, we're going to have to fight, whether we want to or not. But the only thing I want from you and your men is to go away and stay away."

Dolan gave a dark chuckle.

"The *go away* part seemed to work out well," he said within his dim circle of candlelight. "The *stay away* part is where I seem to fall short."

Summers almost smiled, but he caught himself.

"For *what*, Dolan?" Summers said. "Nobody here had anything to do with Claude Parks capturing you! Whatever you think you need here, you better get it this trip. If you don't, you're apt to end up dead here!"

"This is my last trip here, Summers. You can trust me on that. I won't be back." Dolan managed a thin smile. "I think catching a ricochet in my head might have thrown me off some. But I've thought it

303

through." He shook his head. "I'm not coming back —"

They both shut up, stunned, as a string of Gatling gun bullets streaked across the doctor's house. Shattered pictures flew from the walls in sprays and chunks of plaster. Summers leaped forward, grabbed Dolan by his shirt and jerked him from his makeshift throne to the floor. The front door flew open and one of the gunmen flew inside amidst a hail of bullets shredding his back.

"You son of a bitch!" Dolan shouted at Summers as he drew his holstered Colt. Seeing what was coming, Summers grabbed Dolan's hand, gun and all, and pointed it at the ceiling as it went off. He wrenched the gun from Dolan's hand before he could cock it again.

"Let's get out of here," Summers shouted as the Gatling gun started firing again. He shoved Dolan's Colt down behind his gun belt and patted it. "For safekeeping," he said.

Crawling across the floor, through broken glass and pieces of broken furniture, Summers pulled Dolan along with him until they reached a side door that led out to a small barn. The big gun still hammered the front of the doctor's house as the two crawled inside the barn and managed to pull the doctor's buggy horse from its stable.

The horse, scared out of its mind, put up a fight until Summers got it dressed for the trail. With its familiar rigging on its back, the horse bolted out through the yard when Summers opened the door and jumped onto the driver's seat, grabbing Dolan by his shoulder and pulling him in.

"I should kill you!" Dolan shouted as the two jounced away in the doctor's rig.

"I had nothing to do with this!" Summers shouted in reply. "And I think you know it!"

On the front lawn, Johnny Two and Yancy Reed lunged for the flower bed and rolled into it as the Gatling gun started firing again.

"That was Will Summers!" Johnny shouted. "I recognized his voice."

"So did I," said Reed, "and Dolan Coyle, too! They sounded like they were ready to kill each other!"

The gun had fallen silent. People ran from the saloon to get a closer look at the smoking rubble that had been the doctor's house. Reed nodded toward two dead gunmen lying near what was left of the front porch.

"There's where I dropped my rifle," he said. "Come on! Let's get armed and cut out before that big gun starts shooting again! If I know Will, he'll take that buggy to the livery barn and get some horses under them."

"Will Summers and Dolan Coyle running off together is hard to figure. What d'you suppose they're doing, Yancy?" Johnny asked as they ran across the doctor's yard.

"Right now, all they're doing is keeping from getting their head blown off! We're going to grab some horses and ride out with them, wherever they're going! Summers is going to try to get all this shooting away from town before it levels everything here! Whoa there —" He pointed at a line of horses hitched to a big tree at the corner of Dr. Adams' front yard.

"There's some cayuses! We'll take these, in case the barn is empty," Reed said. They hurried over to where the doctor stood leaning against the big white oak.

Dr. Adams waved and called out, "Come and get them. I know what you want. Take them!"

"Much obliged," said Reed. "We need to get to Summers and see what's going on! The cavalry had no business doing this."

"Cavalry, *ha!*" the doctor said. "You ever seen the U.S. Cavalry ride anything looking this bad?" He gestured toward the group of rough unkempt horses hitched to the tree.

"No, Doctor, I never have," said Reed. "What is all this?"

"I'd say it's that *sumbitch* Dolan's *sumbitch* brother, Axel, wanting to do a little ol'-fashioned kinfolk killing. It's just one lunatic killing another. Meanwhile, look at my house!"

Johnny Two just shook his head.

"All right, Dr. Adams," Reed said quietly, "we're going to take a couple of these horses and see if we can help Summers. Whoever's shooting the big gun, he's going to want to get them out of Eagles before the damage gets worse."

Out front of the livery barn, the gun in its new battle position was ready to start firing, but drinkers from the saloon milled in the street directly in the gun's firing line.

"This will show you it's not the U.S. Cavalry operating the Gatling gun. *Watch!*" Adams said.

"Clear the damn street," a voice called out from behind the Gatling gun. When no one moved out of the way, the gun started firing full force with no further warning.

Reed and Johnny Two watched, stunned.

A man went down. He dragged himself out of the street while bullets exploded. A mule fell dead at a hitch rail. Bullets blew out store windows on both sides of the street. The gun operator swung the gun back and forth in wider and wider arcs, filling the air between the barn and what was left of the doctor's house with screaming bullets.

The livery barn was about forty yards from the doctor's house, straight down Eagles' main street. Reed and Johnny Two could now see that the Gatling gun had been set up about ten feet from the barn's large front doors.

Inside the barn, Summers was thinking, *All this, just to kill one man.* He knew he had to get the Coyle brothers and their gang out of here. Take them to a place where they could kill only one another.

Summers and Dolan had leaped out of the doctor's buggy only a moment earlier, and let the frightened horse pull it to a dark rear corner. Summers saw Dolan looking around at the few remaining horses and said, "Take any of them that suits you. They all belong to Johnny Two Red Wolves and me."

At the slightest sound from the rear of the barn, Summers and Dolan both turned and saw that Reed and Johnny had led their horses through the rear door without being seen.

"Don't shoot, Will!" said Johnny. Outside,

the gun crew shouted and made a great commotion setting up ammunition crates beside the gun. One man's voice distinguished itself above the others with a string of curses.

"Wait a minute!" said Dolan. "I recognize that voice! He's one of *my* men! Or he was before now!" He slapped a hand against his empty holster. "Damn it! Somebody give me a gun! I'll kill him right now and be done with it!"

"Forget it, Dolan," said Summers. "You're not going to shoot somebody and bring your whole gang down on us. I expect by now your brother, Axel, has taken over your entire operation."

"Then I'll have to kill him, too," said Dolan, "as soon as you give me back my gun!"

Summers didn't answer. Instead, he looked at Johnny Two and Yancy Reed and said, "Watch him close. I don't know what he's apt to do."

"Why you sumbitch, Will Summers!" said Dolan, almost shouting too loud. "If I hadn't taken you in and taught you a long rider's skills, you would have died on some dark road with a mask on your face!"

Summers ignored him. "If he gets loud again, stuff your pocket handkerchief inside his mouth and tie a bandanna around his face."

Dolan started to spill out an angry reply, but he caught himself and shut up.

"Good," said Summers. He stepped over to the small ammunition crate he had packed to take up to Gunman's Pass. This seemed like a good time to take it.

"How many men are riding with you now, Dolan?" he asked quietly.

Dolan kept his voice quiet as well. "People keep asking me that," he said. "Fact is, I don't know. I've been letting Axel handle everything, especially ever since I got binged here." He touched a fingertip to his wounded forehead. "As it turns out, that was a bad idea."

The talking stopped suddenly as they heard a noise and saw men walk in through the rear door, leading their horses. Reed recognized the two men right away, but he decided to keep quiet about it for now.

Summers raised his Colt and held it out at arm's length.

"Whoa!" one of the men said, both of them stopping in the shadowy light. He raised a hand. "We're not looking for trouble. Just the opposite. We are both men with reputations for serving the law. We've seen signs that there is an urgent need here for our

particular services?"

"Oh, what signs have you seen?" said Yancy Reed, keeping his hat brim lowered in the already dimly lit barn. Johnny Two stood back a couple of steps, his hand holding his rifle cocked and ready. Dolan Coyle sat on an upturned iron bucket. He studied his worn and battered boots.

"What signs have we seen?" the man echoed. "Well, it looks like a ghost town. The doors and windows are all broken and lying in the street. If you need more, when we rode in moments ago, a Gatling gun sat outside, chewing up anything that crossed its path."

The barn was silent.

"Anything else?" said Reed.

The man took a closer look at Reed and said, "Do I know you, sir?"

"Have you been in Eagles before?"

"I have," the man said. "We both have." The two nodded.

The first man continued, "We were going to work for a businessman here as security men. But before we even got to work, we were thrown from atop a building and very nearly killed."

"I'll be darned — and you've come back?" said Reed, giving Summers a glance. "Going to give it another try?"

311

"Once we embark on a job, we don't give up easily," said the other man, not yet realizing that Reed was making fun of them both.

Dolan Coyle looked up and put the conversation to rest.

"You are Dallas Ekland, I believe?"

"Yes, I am," said Ekland. Before he could say more, Dolan's finger swung from him to Sanget. "And you are Carlos Sanget, the man who shot and killed Clifford Swain in Nevada."

"I am," said Sanget. He was all set to boast a little, but Dolan cut in, saying, "How'd you do it? Did you catch Swain asleep? Knocked-out drunk? Shot him in the back?"

Sanget's temper was starting to stir. He'd had enough, and he decided to put a stop to it. Nothing good had yet happened to him in this dung-rolling town. He didn't see it changing.

Here goes, he told himself.

"All three," he said, staring intently in Dolan's eyes. "I got him drunk until he passed out and, while he was asleep, I rolled him onto his belly, and I shot him in the back. Is that the kind of gunman you're looking for? I've heard it suits you just right."

The barn grew deathly quiet for a few hard, tight seconds.

Yancy Reed had lifted a bag of fixings from his shirt pocket. He'd rolled a smoke, watched and listened. He remained silent, an unstruck matchstick in his fingertips. Only when Sanget delivered the part about shooting the sleeping drunk in the back did Reed strike the match with his thumbnail and finish lighting his smoke.

Dolan chuckled.

"Hell, yes, it suits me just fine," Dolan said. He looked at Summers. "You ready to clear out of here, Will? I've got enough work to keep these *security men* busy for a long time." He grinned and added, "You and your pals here, too, if you're ready to make yourselves some *real* money."

Johnny Two had moved in close and un- noticed beside Sanget. Reed had stepped in front of Ekland, and with a smile, yanked Ekland's gun from its holster too quick to be stopped. Ekland saw his own gun an inch from his belly.

"What I want," Summers continued, "is to get you, your gunmen and your Gatling gun crew out of Eagles while most of the town is still standing."

"You can't blame me for what's happen- ing here," said Dolan. "It's those men who turned against me and want Axel to lead the gang." He spat on the dirt floor. "Damn it, Will, I once thought you and I were trail pals!"

Summers saw that Dolan was standing an inch deep in horse droppings, but he let it go for now.

"We were never *pals,* Dolan," he said. "There was a time when we weren't enemies. Hell, we're still not. But that's a long way from being pals." He nodded toward the outside where the gun crew was busily reloading the cooling gun. "But you have pushed us awfully close to the line here."

Dolan started to chuckle and say something flippant, but seeing the flat somber expressions on the faces of Reed and Johnny Two, he said instead, "I never said *thank you* for what you and your deputies did for me. I want to tell you now, the three of you, I *appreciate it.*" He looked from face to face, this time including Sanget and Ekland. The expressions on all the men were the same, except for a slight spark of restrained interest he saw in those two pairs of eyes.

"My freedom is the most important thing to me," he said. "All this outlawry, it's just a way I had to live free."

Free, thought Summers. *That was it.*

It had come to him all at once. The first

petty crime he and Dolan had ever committed was stealing a big cherry pie a woman had set on her window ledge to cool. Taking something for nothing, that was Dolan's definition of *free*. At some point it had ceased to be Will's.

Dolan's fingertips touched the healing wound on his forehead. "How can I say this? I love my *freedom* more than I . . ." He tried to offer an innocent, almost human smile. "I love my freedom more than I love . . ."

He mentally searched for an analogy.

"A piece of *sweet cherry pie*?" suggested Summers. The men gave him a curious look, but Dolan's smile turned more real as it widened slightly.

"My, what a strange way to put it, Will," he said. "But yes, I like that. I love my freedom more than I love sweet cherry pie. You remembered how I love cherry pie?" He lowered his voice between them.

Summers ignored the attempt at intimacy. "That's *your* freedom, Dolan Coyle," he said. "You don't give a damn about anybody else's." He nodded down at Dolan's boots. "Quit the horseshit." Turning to the others he said, "Before the gun cools, let's get ready to get up out of here."

As the men readied their horses, Summers saw Sanget scraping the horse dung from

Dolan's boots with a stick.

"Security man is a job I never heard before today," said Reed.

"Dolan just came up with it," said Summers. "It's a good warning for us to keep him in close check, no matter how he acts or what he says."

"That goes without saying, Will," said Reed.

"I know it does for you two," Summers said. "Maybe I'm saying it for myself." He turned to Johnny Two. "Get up front and lead everybody toward Gunman's Pass. Reed and I will drop back and take care of the Gatling gun."

"Got it," said Johnny Two Red Wolves. He slipped a large boot knife up his loose shirtsleeve, sheath and all.

Just in case.

CHAPTER 22

The six riders were strewn out along the narrow upward trail in the direction of Gunman's Pass, Johnny Two at the head and Yancy Reed at the rear, riding along quietly, shortening and lengthening his distance from the others so that his exact position on the trail was in constant question. He was alternately in and out of sight and the three outlaws took it for granted he was watching their back trail.

When the first testing blasts of the Gatling gun roared, Summers reined in Moby beside Johnny Two and said, "Start watching through the back of your head. We'll hurry."

Johnny Two stared straight ahead as Summers rode Moby back to where Reed had been only seconds earlier.

Be careful, Johnny, he thought to himself, knowing Johnny Two would never stand for such talk as that.

He nudged Moby down off the trail and onto an even narrower rock trail a few steep yards below. Once on the thinner, rockier trail, he tapped Moby with his knees. Even on a trail as bad as this, the big buckskin shot out, and Summers trusted the horse, letting him read the reins in his rider's hand. With Summers' left palm loosely on Moby's withers, they raced along on the high side of the trail.

About sixty yards back, Summers saw Reed atop a boulder looking down on Eagles, with a clear view of the livery barn and the main street reaching out from it. Slowing the big buckskin to a walk, he let its hoofs pick their way up the steep hillside. When Summers rounded the boulder to a walking path, he hitched Moby beside Reed's horse and hurried up the boulder, his rifle against his side.

"They're ready to open fire," said Reed as Summers eased up the boulder face and stooped down beside him. "But look out of Eagles on the main trail." He handed Summers a pair of dusty binoculars.

Seeing the cavalry column that was headed into Eagles from the opposite end of town, Summers muttered, "Okay, we'll still knock out the gun crew. But then we leave here, *fast*! Let the army handle them before they get another crew organized."

"Sounds right to me, Will," said Reed. "It'll get us back to Johnny Two a lot sooner, before they know we've tricked them. I like that."

"So do I," said Summers. "He's still the only one with a gun, but they'll soon get their nerve up." He laid the binoculars aside and levered a round into his rifle chamber. He eyed the gun crew as the men gathered near the big gun.

"Now," Summers said, knowing Reed was ready, "before they cut Eagles to shreds."

Summers set his sights on his first target below and squeezed the trigger. Reed followed suit. Two of the gun crew fell as Summers and Reed each levered another round and took aim. A loader collapsed over the gun, the ammunition belt falling from his hands.

The operator came from behind the gun, scrambling for the ammunition belt. With perfect aim, Reed's next bullet hit him in the center of his back. The ill-fated man threw his shoulder blades back so far it appeared he would touch them together. Suddenly his contorted frame went limp, and he fell facedown against the stacked crates of ammunition belts.

Summers' next shot hit a man who had

been showing the others how to handle the big gun. His blue trousers had a line of darker blue down the leg where the gold uniform stripe had been removed.

A traitor? More than likely, Summers reasoned; yet he had no time to ponder it. He levered another round into the chamber as the instructor hit the ground.

Adios, teacher.

Blood had been slung wildly, splashing itself everywhere. The men trying to take over the operator and loading crew positions had a slippery time making anything fit, or work. Faces that had turned toward Reed and Summers' spot on the boulder now turned away and looked toward the other end of the street.

Reed and Summers looked with them.

"Here comes the cavalry," said Summers.

"I'm glad they could make it." Reed grinned. "Should we pick a few more gunmen off for them?"

"No, let them have this one. We've got to get back on the trail."

Rather than take the same narrow rocky trail Summers had ridden down, the two took a wider trail that led around Johnny, Dolan, and Dolan's two new gunmen, Carlos Sanget and Dallas Ekland. From the hillside, some fifty feet beneath the four riders, Summers and Reed heard no hoofbeats, just strong words being spoken, which told them that Johnny and his charges were stopped on the trail above.

Communicating with hand signals, Summers and Reed stepped down from their saddles and hitched their horses to a young sapling. Then, with their rifles at port arms, they inched their way upward as quietly and quickly as they could.

Johnny was warning Sanget and Ekland to stay back, letting them know in grim terms what would happen if they didn't. On their bellies, Summers and Reed listened, watching through underbrush, their rifles cocked and ready.

Johnny Two was facing Sanget and Ekland from his saddle. The two tried edging their horses closer, but Johnny drew back the rifle hammer with his thumb, barely moving the rifle on his lap. Meanwhile, Dolan Coyle held his horse back, watching every move.

Carlos Sanget gave Johnny an unfriendly grin, but he had stopped advancing. "What's wrong with you, kid?" he said. "Ain't you going to threaten us one more time?"

Johnny Two didn't answer.

"Tell the truth, Johnny *Two Red Wolves,*"

said Sanget, in a mocking tone. "Do we look like the kind of men you can make do what you say?"

Still no reply. That upset Sanget.

"I hate a sumbitch who won't answer," he said. "Makes me want to come down from this saddle and kick your head all over the hillside."

"You better hurry," Dolan put in.

Still no reply from Johnny Two.

"You know if you fire that rifle, everybody in these low hills will hear it," said Sanget.

"*You* won't," Johnny said.

"I'm telling you both to hurry up," said Dolan. "They'll be back any minute!"

"Shut the hell up, Dolan Coyle," said Ekland. "You've got no say in this."

"No *say*?" said Dolan. "If you're going to work for me, I do!"

Sanget and Ekland laughed.

"You idiot! We're not doing this for you," said Ekland. "We're doing this for the ten thousand dollars bounty money Judge Isaac Parker's court is paying. All we got to do is lop your head off and take it into any marshal's office, either in a feed sack or on a post. That money will be all ours, *lickety-split*!"

"Damn it, man!" said Dolan. "We have an agreement. It is *binding*!"

"*Sue us,* Coyle!" said Ekland. Both gunmen laughed heartily.

"I can't believe you'd think we're stupid enough to turn down ten thousand dollars just to scrape your boots."

"I believe it," Will Summers said quietly. He and Reed stood at the edge of the trail, six feet between them. "Now, everybody, take a deep breath and *reassemble* yourselves."

Carlos Sanget couldn't take any more. He shouted and jumped down from his saddle. He ran toward Summers, but stopped abruptly when Summers swung his rifle around and pointed it at his face.

"I'll blow your head off so fast, your hat will fall on your shoulders."

Summers motioned Sanget back with his rifle barrel. Then to Dolan Coyle he said, "I don't know if this will make you happy or sad, Dolan, but the cavalry has taken custody of your Gatling gun."

"The army will never hold on to it," Dolan snarled. "I hate my brother and can't wait to kill him, but he is smarter than the army by the length of a long field. He'll yank that gun right out from under them."

"Either way, we're riding on up to Gunman's Pass. We'll get things sorted out, like who goes where, with who." Summers looked back at Dolan. "I'm not turning you loose until I see that your men, or Axel's, or whoever else's they are, will no longer be a threat to Eagles." He guided his horse back over beside Reed. Under his breath he said to him, "The Gatling gun is going to remain a problem as long as it's still around. I don't know what it is about a Gatling gun, every outlaw wants one soon as they see one."

"I hear you," said Yancy. "What do you want to do?"

"I'm going to ride into Eagles and get rid of it."

"I'm ready when you are."

"No, I want you and Johnny to take these three on up to Gunman's Pass. You'll be there by nightfall. There's an old underground cell beneath a cattle barn. Leave them there with Barton or Javins. I should be back up there by morning."

Reed gave him a dubious look.

"You're sure you won't need any help?" he asked.

"I'm sure," said Summers. "Anyway," he added with a faint grin, "the army's there. What could go wrong?"

When the cavalry column rode into Eagles, instead of facing the fearsome gun and a force of Coyle Gang gunmen, they found the Gatling gun shut down. Bodies of the crew lay around the gun, covered with blood. An unassigned captain, Rance Harmon, who was awaiting transfer on account of his out-of-control drinking, dismounted and looked around with distaste.

"Damn disgusting!" he cursed aloud to anyone listening, a rifle in his right hand. Three spent brass shells lay smoking on the ground. He thrust the rifle at a young private, who caught it against his chest.

Reaching out a shiny black boot, the captain kicked a skinny dog away from the puddle of blood it was licking. The dog let out a sharp yelp and hurried away, its tail tucked between its hind legs and a string of thick dark blood swinging from its mouth. Overhead three vultures stood on the crossbeam of a telegraph pole.

"Will someone please *please* bring me a shotgun!" Harmon shouted. "I want these scavengers killed! They *offend* me."

"Offend you, sir?" asked a sergeant. "How do they — ?"

"Their *existence* offends me!" yelled the captain.

"Here, Captain Harmon, sir." A young private handed him a shotgun.

"Give my sergeant your name, Private," said Captain Harmon. "I want you *com-*

mended for this!" He quickly swung the shotgun up and blew one of the big buzzards off the line. The other birds flew up and away, landing on another line a block away. The wounded scavenger lay on its side, struggling in a bloody circle.

The captain walked over, looked down and put the unfortunate bird out of its misery.

"There," he said, "let that be the end of the *scavenger incident*! Now, bring me those Coyle gunmen. Let's see how they fly with this long shotgun up their shirt." He laughed aloud. Then he settled down and said, "I want somebody to get this Gatling gun working, right now! These no-good outlaw bastards want to see what these guns will do to a human being? By thunder, we'll show them! Won't we, men?"

The soldiers cheered, but most of them only halfheartedly. One of them leaned toward the trooper who'd brought the captain the shotgun and said almost in his ear, "Be careful following Captain Harmon's orders. He's not supposed to be in charge."

"Oh, damn," replied the trooper.

As they observed their captain guardedly, some soldiers led three captured Coyle gunmen, their hands bound behind them, to stand in front of Captain Harmon.

"So now," said Harmon, "are you three my volunteers?"

Volunteers? The three prisoners looked at one another questioningly. So did the two soldiers guarding them.

"Come come, gentlemen!" said the captain to the three prisoners. "I believe most of you, if not all, are deserters. I won't ask. But I *will* ask if you'd prefer I shoot you in the head or volunteer to show us what this Gatling will do to the human body."

The three stared, bewildered, a little unsteady on their feet and reeking of whiskey.

Finally, one of them started laughing drunkenly and stepped forward.

"What the hell, Captain, I'll do it," he said.

"Are you volunteering?" he asked.

The man's drunken laugh returned.

"Hell, I don't care, *buddy!*" he said. "Gatling gun or bullet in the head? Either one'll do. I've listened to you *beller* long enough. I *druther* you shoot me than have to listen to you any longer!" He stood as upright as he could manage. "Go on now, you straight-up *idiot!* Like they always say, make your first shot the best —"

The captain's pistol shot echoed up across the low hills. The drunk fell dead.

"Who's next?" Captain Harmon asked.

"*Uhh,* I reckon that would be me, sir," said one of the two men left standing.

"Why are this man's hands *unbound*?" Captain Harmon asked. Before anyone could answer, he asked the man himself. "Why are your hands *unbound*?"

"Captain," he said, "I'm not going to lie to you. When we were standing in the lines of prisoners over there, when the line faced one way, my pal Edward Moon laying dead here, he would step up close and start untying my hands." He smiled. "When the line turned the other way, I'd untie his —"

"Enough," said the captain. "I see." He looked around and beckoned for a soldier who was carrying a writing board and a lead pencil. "You and your pal, Edward Moon . . . ?" He paused. "Edward Moon, right?"

"Yes, Captain," the soldier said, pointing the pencil at a list of names. "This one's Edward Moon." He pointed at the dead man, then at the man still standing. "This one's James Hall."

"Well, *James Hall,*" the captain said, stepping closer. "I can see that your pal and you are both drunker than skunks, eh?"

"Well, not *him,* anymore," said Hall. "I'm feeling all right. But lately I outdrink everybody. Drink all I want. Wake up with no hangover, nothing. Like magic, almost."

"Why do you suppose that is?" asked the captain, curious.

"I don't know," said Hall. "I believe it was the whiskey my pal was peddling, Tennessee whiskey, hard to find out here."

"Really?" said the captain. He put a hand on Hall's shoulder and pulled him away from the soldiers and prisoners. "Do you have some on you right now? Say, a shot or two? An eye-opener, as they say?"

"No, Captain, not a drop," said the gunman, though he smelled like a brewery. "When you killed my pal Moon, you killed my whiskey source." He looked the captain in the eyes. "But they sell all the whiskey you'd ever want at the Eagles Saloon."

The captain let out a tense breath. His hands were trembling a little. He folded them. It helped some.

"The problem is the army gave me a final warning. If I'm caught drinking again, or even seen near a saloon, it will cost me my commission." He paused and almost sobbed. "That's why I acted the way I did! I need a drink, *bad*!"

"I'm sorry for you, Captain," the gunman said. "You just shot the one man I know who could've helped you." He thought for a moment. "I can slip into the saloon and bring you a bottle. Not the best, of course. But it'll do until we find you some good stuff! Say, a dollar?"

The captain began searching himself for money. "You know I can have you killed, for making such an offer. Or shoot you in the head, like I did your friend, here?"

"I know, Captain, believe me, I know. But being a veteran myself, I'm happy to help a military man." He took the money Harmon held out and slipped it out of sight. "I just had another idea, Captain. The woman who my pal Moon was getting the whiskey from?"

"What about her?" said the captain excitedly, for he was getting shaky.

"I think I know where we can find her. She moved in with a man up there." He nodded toward the top of the hill trail. "I'd know her if I saw her."

"And you think she'll have Tennessee whiskey? And she'll keep her mouth shut about it if I buy some?"

"I only wish I could tell you these things, Captain," Hall said, feeling more and more sober and starting to want a drink himself. "All I can say is, take me to her. We'll see what she can do for us."

CHAPTER 23

Axel Coyle managed to gather a dozen gunmen who had escaped the cavalry. Now that he and his outlaws had lost possession of the Gatling gun, most of the cavalry had ridden on, leaving only a small number of guards to defend the town. In honor of the bodies of their men stacked in Eagles' streets waiting to be hauled away and buried, Axel tipped a bottle toward the town below, then took a swig.

"Good sumbitches, every one of them," he said. He and his outlaws had hitched their horses beneath the same boulder Summers and Reed had used earlier to attack the gun crew before pushing on up to Gunman's Pass.

"There are no more secrets regarding my lunatic brother. He knows I'm out to kill him, and I know he wants to kill me just as bad. I tried to be civilized about it, but he's beyond reason. It would've been better if

I'd lifted a pistol and blew his brains all over the wall of the doctor's house. But I have lived, and I have learned. Now, if you see him, kill him. I will not hesitate to kill any of my gunmen who allow my brother to get away *alive . . .*" His voice fell away as he looked down on the trail just beneath them. "I'll be double damned," he said. "Speak of the devil and he will appear, *sure as hell.*"

Looking down with Axel, Prince Drako said, "You want him, you've got him. I'll get down there and kill him while you watch from here —"

"The hell you will," Axel snapped. "Maybe you didn't see, but Summers, Reed and Johnny Two Red Wolves are riding with him, not to mention a couple of gunmen I sent for."

"You sent for Dallas Ekland and Carlos Sanget?" said Prince Drako.

"I did," said Axel. "Why? Do you know them?"

"I do," said Drako. "They are backstabbing railroad detectives. I wish you had asked me first."

Axel chuckled.

"I know what they are," said Axel. "I was hoping they would kill Dolan for me, and then I'd swoop in and collect the ten-thousand-dollar bounty."

"I would have done it for you," said Drako. "I'll do it for you *still*!"

"Not now, Prince," said Axel. "With these railroad snakes riding with Summers, we might yet get that reward for killing Dolan." He grinned. "Maybe they'll kill Summers and his boys, too."

He looked at the rest of his men.

"All of you fade back and follow us," he said. "If you can round up some more gunmen, do it. We're scattered all over hell's back pasture. And if you can get your hands on that damn Gatling gun, take it back from the soldiers."

"Where will we find you, Axel?" one man asked.

"Do I have to tell you how to do everything?" Axel snapped. "Listen, if you find the Gatling gun, don't worry. Shoot a few rounds, and I'll find *you*!"

"Not if the gun won't work," the man said.

Axel shot him a look.

"If the gun won't work, leave it," he said, trying to sound patient. "Why would I want a *broken* Gatling gun?"

When Summers arrived in Eagles, he went past the livery barn to a small cottage adjoining the blacksmith shop just off the main street. He walked Moby around the

333

back and was hitching him to the rail when he heard the sound of a shotgun cocking, followed by a familiar voice behind him.

"What are you doing with that horse, mister?" growled Orville Stems, the town blacksmith.

Holding carefully still, Summers said, "Orville, it's me, Will Summers. I need your help."

"Oh! All right." Then, "I hope you're in no hurry, Will. I'll be three days getting to you. Army's got me covered up."

Summers turned and faced him. "I won't take your time, Orville. I just need you to answer one question: How do I ruin a Gatling gun without blowing it up?"

"That's easy!" The blacksmith laughed. "You come get me and have me do it for you!"

"Ordinarily, I would," said Summers, "but not this time. I need you to tell me, so I can do it myself."

"All right, Will," Stems said with a crafty little smile. "Is that a little whiff of something *felonious* in the air?"

"I can't say, Orville," said Summers. "But hypothetically, what if I needed to do something to a Gatling gun to keep it from firing?"

Stems gave him a flat stare.

"I suppose you're talking about the Gatling gun that was sitting in the street?"

"What do you mean, *was*?" said Summers. "It's not there now?"

"Just the stand it was sitting on," Stems said. "The army is paying me to clean it up and see why it's jamming so bad. I could have told them straightaway it's because it's clogged with blood. But they don't believe nothin' unless they pay for it." He laughed.

Summers joined him, feeling relieved.

"You came to the right place, Will," Stems said, waving Summers to follow him inside, "because I know all about that gun. This one is an early model, from 1862 or so. Gats have changed a lot since then." As he spoke he pulled a pair of eyeglasses from his shirt pocket and put them on. He reached under a work desk and took out a folded diagram of a Gatling gun. "Look at this," he said, unfolding it.

The two bent over the engineering drawing of the same model that had been shooting up the area.

"I don't know what to say," said Summers.

"Don't say anything, just look." Stems' large finger circled two items on the drawing. "This first piece is a *lock cylinder.* This piece in front of it is a *carner wheel.* Without both of these pieces, the gun won't fire a lick. If I wanted to kill a Gat, I'd take both of those pieces. The army might carry a spare of one of them, but it's highly doubtful they'd have a spare of both." He chuckled. "You won't even have to take it apart. I've done that already."

"Where is it?" Summers asked.

"It's in *your* livery barn, Will," he said. "I'm surprised you didn't trip over it."

"I didn't come in through my barn," Summers said. "I didn't want to be seen."

"That was probably a good idea," said Stems. "Troopers are guarding the gun until I get it cleaned up and put back together on its stand."

"Is the whole town still crawling with Coyle gunmen?" Summers asked.

"Worse than ever," said Stems. "So, you be careful."

"I will."

"In the indoor corral in the back of the barn," Stems went on, "I've got the gun broken down and laid out on a big tarpaulin. Will you recognize the two parts you've seen here?" He pointed out the two parts again on the diagram.

"Yep," said Summers, "I will."

"Then go get it, Will," he said. "It's all yours."

■ ■ ■ ■

As evening shadows drew closer across the street of Eagles and the surrounding low hills, Will Summers left Moby hitched in a small clearing behind the livery barn. Carrying an empty feed sack he slipped under the washout beneath the rear wall of the barn, into the dim circle of light put out by the guard's oil lamp.

Once inside the livery barn he lay flat and silent, listening for any sound from the soldier dozing in a canvas field chair. He heard nothing for the first few minutes, then, finally, came the sound he was waiting for, a quiet snore from the direction of the chair.

He ventured forward on his belly, into the corral where, as Orville had promised, he saw the Gatling gun laid out in pieces on a large tarpaulin.

So far, so good. He crawled closer and, lifting up on his palms a little, he saw the parts. They were laid out just as in the diagram. Taking the feed sack from under his arm, he spread it on the ground beside him. As quietly as he could, he reached up to the lock cylinder, rolled it onto his palms and stuck it down into the sack. It was heavier than he'd expected it to be.

On the other hand, the carner wheel felt lighter than he'd anticipated. With it similarly tucked away, he folded the sack over twice to keep the two items from rattling against each other, and turned and crawled away.

Outside, he stooped and hurried to where he'd left Moby. But rather than going straight to the horse, he stopped thirty feet away and kept a close watch on the area around him for a few minutes. Now that he had the parts in his possession, he wanted to take no chance of being caught.

For several miles, Johnny Two had watched four gunmen following on the trail above them, but now they'd been gone for a good hour. That upper trail would intersect with their trail farther ahead, and Johnny and Reed had decided to wait and confront the gunmen then, if they were still there.

Johnny Two stayed dropped back a few yards behind Reed and the prisoners as they topped the hill in the last rays of dim sunlight. Where they met the upper trail, Johnny stepped down from his saddle and walked his horse in a short circle, examining the many hoofprints on the ground. He was careful to keep his rifle on the three prisoners, even after Reed topped the trail and joined him.

"Learning anything?" Reed asked.

"Not much," said Johnny. Rarely had a trail revealed so little, in fact.

"They didn't like us to know they were following," he said. He pointed his rifle down at the newer prints, the ones atop the countless layers beneath them. "But they didn't know how to keep us from it." The newer prints ran back in the opposite direction, which told him at some point in time whoever was trailing them had turned back.

He stooped with his rifle over his knee and continued examining the prints, not sensing anyone watching them. Experience had taught him that if a trail revealed nothing, it was only because someone didn't want it to. He knew of Apache who could erase any sign by walking their horse backward, then brushing off their path. But how far back would he have to go to see if that was the case? He wasn't going to do it. If those four had been up here following them with bad intent, they would still be here.

Or they would be back.

"And now they're gone?" Yancy Reed asked quietly. He stayed a few yards away, not liking to interrupt while Johnny was clearly working something out in his mind.

After a moment Johnny stood up and they heard another voice say, "*Hola,* riders," from a stand of saplings on the other side of the trail. There stood Tom Barton, the big cream-colored mare at his side.

"*Hola,* Tom Barton," said Reed.

Barton and his horse walked toward them, the mare tagging along by the hackamore lead and bridle he'd made for her.

"Good to see you," said Reed. "We're glad it's you up here. We were being trailed earlier from along this ridgeline."

"Good to see you both," said Barton. "I saw those four riders were following somebody. Figured it was you. So I kept their horses and sent them back to Eagles on foot."

"Coyle gunmen, were they?" asked Reed. "We've got their boss here." He tossed his head toward Dolan. "Some are out to save him, others out to kill him."

"So they said, or tried to say," Barton replied. "I had doubts about them. One looked like he was trying to sober up after a long drinking spree. He was wearing buckskins and a shiny pair of cavalry boots. The buckskins looked brand-new, like they came off of a dry goods store dummy." He shook his head. "Another one looked like an outlaw I'd seen paper on, name of Eddie

Moon, but he insisted his name is James Hall. No longer being in the bounty hunting business, I let it go. Something about every one of these jakes wasn't right. So I took their guns and set them afoot. This Hall fella kept going on about wanting to see Zetra Wilson. I wouldn't let him. One wrong word to Zetra, Javins would kill him," he said.

"Axel Coyle has been hiring any gunman that shows up," said Reed.

"If he shows up here, he'll need them," Barton said flatly. At the smirk on Dolan Coyle's face, he added, "I've got some nice underground cells for you, each with its own privy bucket! And stone walls around them three feet thick."

"Like I said, Tom," said Reed, "these two wanted to kill that one for some bounty money. Now that they see they're not getting it, they've eased down a lot."

"I know how that goes," said Barton. "We'll all be fine here. I'm used to jakes like these guys."

It was full dark as Summers rode up the trail toward Gunman's Pass. He had gone off the trail into some woods long enough to turn over a downed log and scrape a space under it large enough to bury one of the gun parts. A few feet away he buried the other piece under an overturned rock.

When he'd finished, he sat and observed the moonlit night until he was certain he was all alone, then quietly he wiped his hands on the dry ground, stepped up into his saddle and nudged Moby forward. They rode on.

Two miles farther up the hill he heard a rustling in the brush beside the trail, and the faintest sound of a human voice whispering. Without touching Moby's reins or slowing him a step, Summers slid from his saddle and, staying close to Moby's left flank, he kept to the shadows of the moonlit trail.

Keeping his boot steps muffled under the clopping of Moby's hooves, he eased along, watching, listening. Suddenly a dark figure burst onto the trail like some apparition haunting the low hills.

CHAPTER 24

Moving even quicker than the ghostly figure, Summers drew his rifle back and slammed the butt plate into the face obscured by a bandanna. He felt cartilage crunch gruesomely under the impact of the blow, and saw the figure fall limply to the ground.

"My *God,* man! I heard that!" a voice said. "You've killed this poor soul!"

"This 'poor soul' killed himself," said Summers, "when he decided to waylay me and take my horse. If you don't want to join him and hear his version, get out here on your knees and keep your hands up good and high."

"Before you do something stupid that I know you're going to regret," the voice continued to slur — and Summers thought he even detected a belch — "let me inform you that I am Captain Rance Harmon, an *ossifer* in the U.S. Army!" He stepped out

343

onto the trail and knelt.

"Congratulations," Summers replied sharply. "I'll let your commander know that you identified yourself like any gentleman ossifer knows to do."

"I would just as soon the army never knows I was out here tonight. I am leading a very secret operation. For the sake of our nation, no one can know we're out here."

"Then shut up, stay still and keep your hands up," said Summers. "We'll see how far that takes you."

"I assure you, sir —"

Summers cut him off. "Call the rest of your men out here!" He cocked his rifle slow and loud, for good measure.

Within seconds, there were two more dark apparitions on their knees with their hands raised. Summers took a lariat from his saddle horn and strung the rope from man to man, tying their wrists in turn and letting them lower their hands in front of them.

"May I ask where you're taking us, sir?" said the captain more meekly.

"I'm taking you right back to the place you left," said Summers. "There are outlaws all over this trail tonight. I wouldn't want any of you to get hurt."

The captain fell silent, but then decided to also identify his men.

"These two are my soldiers," he said. "Cavalrymen Decker and Hanks. The one out cold, if you have somehow failed to *kill* him, is James Hall. He is our scout, of sorts."

"What were the four of you searching for out here in the night?" Summers asked.

"I'm afraid that will have to remain condi — confidential," Captain Harmon said. "Right, men?"

"Suit yourself," said Summers. "All of you, on your feet."

"What about Hall?" said the soldier named Henry Hanks.

"Get him up on his feet between you," said Summers. "Keep him moving. He'll soon walk it off."

It was in the deep hours of dark early morning when Summers and the rope line of civilian-dressed soldiers, their buckskin-clad officer and one half-conscious unarmed gunman plodded into the front yard of Summers' secluded cabin in Gunman's Pass. The first rays of sunlight were still only a thin silvery glow wreathing the eastern horizon. In the yard, Summers stopped the men at the first low growl of Javins' hound in the darkness.

Not knowing the hound by any name, Summers whispered for the men to stand

345

perfectly still. In a moment the mother hound trotted quietly to Summers, who had stepped down from his saddle and stood waiting for her. In the darkness behind her, close around the cabin, Summers heard the low familiar whining of her pups.

"Good morning, *Mama,*" he whispered to the hound as she sniffed his legs, his boots, his hands. She licked Summers' right hand, then stepped back and called out to the cabin in three loud barks.

Summers continued to wait until he heard the faint sound of a door opening. Not the door of the cabin, but behind him, the door of a small toolshed near a stone wall.

"Morning, Will," came Javins' calm, easy-going voice as the gunman made his way across the yard. The hound left Summers' side and trotted over to Javins, who reached down and rubbed her head with his left hand.

It figures, Summers thought.

"Morning, Mort," he said.

"I talked to Tom Barton earlier. He said you'd dropped by. Wish you would have come to see Zetra and me, had a nice elk dinner with us."

"I didn't want to barge in," said Summers. He motioned at the four men he'd seated in a row on the ground. "As you see, I'm back

346

here on business." He hitched a thumb at the toolshed beside the well. "What do you think of the entrance?"

"I like the idea of somebody facing the front door while I show up right behind them." Javins smiled. "Good thinking."

"I can't take any credit for it," said Summers. "I found the toolshed overgrown with vines, started clearing it, and there it was — four feet wide by six feet tall —"

"— and over forty feet long," Javins finished. "Somebody wanted it awfully bad, to dig a tunnel so big."

"This place is full of surprises," Summers said.

"I know," said Javins. "Zetra and I enjoy being here. This was some kind of old Spanish outpost?"

"That's what I've always thought."

The morning was turning from dark to gray around them. Javins' eyes went across the seated men, then back to Summers. "Tom Barton said he chased away four gunmen on foot earlier. These aren't them, are they?"

"It would not surprise me if they are," said Summers. "Anyway, I want to put these down in the cells, just until things settle some, and I can get to Eagles and sort them out."

"As long as you please, Will. This is your house. Zetra and I are guests here."

"And I hope you're both guests here for a long time," said Summers. "I think it works out for all of us."

At daylight, Axel Coyle and most of his brother's men gathered on the bank of Little Cimarron Creek. Some stayed in their saddles and talked as they watered their horses well, in preparation for what they thought could be a long day ahead. Others dismounted, rolled smokes for themselves and lit them. Even in this crisp early hour of morning, a long-neck whiskey bottle of rye came into sight and rolled off the tips of one man's fingers into the outstretched hand of another.

"I would ask you how many men we have joining us here, Prince," Axel said loudly enough for everyone to hear, "but I think you're still counting from the last time I asked you!"

The men laughed under their breath.

"I saw that one coming a mile away, I *swear* I did!" said a Missouri man named Argyle Ragland, laughing a little louder than the other men.

"You didn't see a *damn* thing coming, Rags," said Axel. "Now shut up before I walk over there and box your jaws for you real good!"

The men's laughter fell away. Eyes turned to Argyle Ragland, who took his time replying. He lowered the rye bottle from his mouth, let out a whiskey hiss, corked the bottle and passed it along. Finally he said, "Here's something else I swear to, Axel Coyle. I swear you're no man if you don't get over here and box my jaws this damned minute!"

The laughter was still gone; so was talk of any kind. Men on horseback and foot alike moved quickly away from between the two men.

"Boys, boys, *boys,* let's hold it right here!" said a newer gunman named Latimer Grimes.

"Mind your own *gawl-damn* business, Grimes, *you turd*!" a man shouted. "Blood's brewed between these two *a long time*! Keep your crooked nose out of it!"

"Boys! I understand you're upset!" said Grimes.

"Upset?" a voice shouted. "Somebody kill this bastard!"

Men shouted, cursed. Someone hurled a chunk of firewood and it hit Grimes' horse. The spooked horse reared high. When its hooves touched back down, men grabbed

349

Grimes, dragged him down from his saddle and stomped up and down on him with both boots, pounding him into the dirt. The terrified horse managed to get out, and away.

This had drawn most of the men away from the trouble between Axel Coyle and Argyle Ragland, but their fight still brewed. "What say you, sumbitch?" Axel called out. "Do I get to kill you or not?"

"Any damned time, Axel," Ragland shouted back through the open space between them. He adjusted his rifle across his lap and cocked it for a quick grab. "I haven't thought much of you —" But before he finished talking, Drako raised his big Colt and shot Ragland through the side of his head.

The loud shot caused another tense silence among the men. Axel stood up in his stirrups and lofted his rifle.

"I know all of you saw it!" he shouted. "He left me no choice. I had to kill him."

"So what?" a voice shouted. "Kill him again, for all we care!" No one mentioned that it was actually Drako who had shot Ragland.

Prince Drako eased his horse around and sidled up to Axel.

"See?" he said. "I told you nobody gives a

350

damn anymore who kills who. Keep everybody carrying a mad-on at somebody, they don't care if you kill that person, so long as you clean up after yourself."

"Speaking of killing, is everybody here riled up enough to do some killing today?"

"Oh, hell yes!" said Drako. "People would love it if we painted these hills red."

At midmorning, Johnny Two walked around to the side of the cabin where Summers sat drinking a fresh mug of coffee. Tom Barton and Yancy Reed were in the front yard sitting on a thick stone knee wall surrounding a large flower bed.

"Yancy said you might want to see this, Will. Axel Coyle is traveling under a new flag — this time a green one." He couldn't keep from smiling.

Summers tossed back the last swallow of coffee in the mug and set it down on a small folding table beside his chair. "Seems like they could get their hands on a white flag and hang on to it."

"I suppose not," said Johnny, as they headed to the front yard.

"What have you got for me out there, Yancy?" asked Summers, taking the binoculars Reed held out to him.

"I've got Axel Coyle," said Reed. "Whatever he's here to do, I don't think surrender has got anything to do with it."

"I'm with you on that," said Summers. "Whatever this is, I get the feeling that all that's left for the Coyle brothers is a bloodbath. That might just be what they've been searching for all along."

"I can shoot him out of his saddle right now before he gets any closer," said Reed.

"Let's not sink to their level, Yancy," Summers said. "Don't forget, we're working for the U.S. government now. I've even got a federal deputy badge in the mail, or so I'm told."

"Sorry, Will," Reed said with a chuckle. "I forgot."

Axel Coyle rode closer, Prince Drako beside him with a rifle propped up from his lap. Close behind them were several other riders, with more strung along the trail farther back.

"Where's the cavalry when we need them?" muttered Reed.

"I'm expecting them anytime," Summers said. He remembered Leonard Spires telling him that news of his offered appointment as a U.S. federal deputy would go out to all the law agencies. *For what that was worth.*

"Will Summers, I come to talk," Axel

called out, stopping his horse about thirty feet away. He waved the green flag back and forth slowly, as if it were a flag of truce, then held it in front of him like a shield.

"Start talking, Axel," Summers said.

"You've got things I want," said Axel. "For one, I want my brother back!"

"Why?" asked Summers. "So you can kill him?"

"That's none your damn business!" said Axel. "He's my brother, and I reckon I can kill him if I like."

"Dolan is a federal prisoner. I'm a *federal deputy*," said Summers. "I'm ordering you and all your men to lay down your weapons and back away, or you'll all be arrested."

Laughter went up from the Coyle Gang.

"Where's your badge, *Federal Deputy* Summers?" Axel asked with a chortle.

Summers wasn't going to explain his badge situation. Instead, he said, "What else do you want?"

Axel grinned. "I want my Gatling gun!"

"I don't *have* your Gatling gun. Why do you want it so bad, anyway?"

"What's wrong with you, Summers? You ask an outlaw what he wants with a Gatling gun?" He grinned. "Are you the kind of man who would ask a lion what he wants with sharp teeth?"

"You're no lion," said Summers.

"No," said Axel, "but by God I'm getting that gun."

"I told you, I don't have it," said Summers.

"You don't *now*," said Axel, "because *there* it is." He pointed back down the trail, and a wagon carrying the mounted Gatling gun rolled slowly into sight.

"What the *hell*, Will?" said Reed in an urgent whisper. Summers had no answer for him.

"Surprised, *huh*?" Axel guffawed. "While I have never served in the military, us Coyles have lots of friends in the ranks!" He laughed again, and Drako joined in. "I want those parts you stole last night while no one was looking."

"I don't have them. I buried them a long way from here."

Every man in the yard, and the gunmen, fell silent. Axel knew everything. *Who told him?* Summers asked himself. A man he'd known for over three years, the blacksmith Orville Stems? The guard in the barn, a stranger feigning sleep while the gun parts were stolen from under his nose? Other faces and names flashed across his mind.

Forget it. You might never know. Summers took a breath and let it out slowly.

"Well, you can take us there in a little while," said Axel. "But there's one more thing."

"What is it?" Summers asked, knowing that whatever it was, Axel was never going to get it, not now, not ever.

Axel leaned forward, resting his forearms across his saddle horn, the flag of truce hanging from his left hand.

"Thank you for asking, U.S. Federal Deputy Will Summers," Axel said mockingly. He motioned toward the cabin, where Mortimer Javins was standing in the doorway, a Colt hanging down his right side, another Colt in a cross-draw holster at his left side, the butt of it partially across his flat belly. Another was shoved down behind his gun belt. And a shotgun leaned against the doorframe. "I heard the Rebel Kid is here. Bring him on out, *introduce* us. Let's see just how fast he is."

Tom Barton stepped forward.

"I'm the Rebel Kid," he said, his hand poised near the holstered Colt on his hip. "Let's see what you've got, Coyle."

"*Huh-uh,* you're Tom Barton," said Axel. "Step back. I'll likely kill you anyway before we're done here, for riding with Claude Parks' posse."

"You're not killing anybody here today,"

Summers said.

Axel raised his voice so every gunman behind him could hear. "If Summers, Barton or either of these other fools open their mouths again, shoot them all down where they stand!"

Summers was ready to draw and bring things to a head. He took a step toward Axel, who could clearly see the cold killing look in Summers' eyes. Axel got ready.

"*I'm* the Rebel Kid," called Mortimer Javins from the open doorway across the yard.

"Well, well, the Rebel Kid!" said Axel Coyle with a dark laugh. "Don't be shy. Come on out here, meet me!" He swung down from his saddle and let the truce flag fall to the ground. "I'm the man what's fixin' to blow your head clean off!" He adjusted his gun belt and spread his boots shoulder-width apart. "It's time I stop acting like I don't know you're here."

"Axel's so scared, he can't shut up," Summers whispered to Reed and Johnny Two.

"For good reason," Johnny whispered back.

Summers looked around the yard, trying to count how many gunmen there were. A shootout between Axel and the Rebel Kid wouldn't be the end to anything. There would be killing for the rest of the day. He was sure of it. Giving them Dolan wouldn't stop it, so he wouldn't even consider that. Sending someone to bring back the missing gun parts wouldn't stop it, either, so that was out. The only plan he could make was to decide where to start shooting after these two finished.

Javins came forward and stood facing Axel, ready to fight.

Eyeing the three guns on the Rebel Kid, Axel stifled a nervous little laugh.

"Why so many shooting irons, Kid?" he asked. "You plan on missing a lot?" He laughed, and so did his men.

"I'm not going to miss any," the Kid said quietly. "I'll need to reload."

The laughter stopped.

"Oh, it's just your ammunition supply?" said Axel. "You *still* don't have enough to kill us all."

"I'll find more laying on the ground," the Kid said in his soft, quiet voice.

From the open doorway, Zetra cried out, "Mort! Watch out, Mort, I've got him!"

She slung a cocked rifle to her shoulder and pulled the trigger. The shot resounded across the yard, and the mounted gunman beside Prince Drako fell from his saddle, a large bloody bullet hole where half his cheek had been a second earlier. Drako, catching a face full of flesh, blood and bone, fell atop the dead gunman.

"Get back, Zetra!" Javins shouted, even as his Colt came up from his right hip and started firing rapidly. As gunmen fired on the front door, Zetra's house coat flew open and off her bare shoulders. Bullets knocked the naked woman back inside the house and the door swung shut behind her.

"No, *Zetra, no!*" shouted Javins. He dropped the empty Colt, jerked the other one holstered across his belly and kept fanning it, moving backward toward the front door. "I'm coming, Zetra!" he shouted. Gunmen fell steadily as the Rebel Kid's bullets ripped through them.

Summers' rifle fire dropped two gunmen from their saddles as a bullet grazed his shoulder. He fell in with Javins, the two fighting toward the cabin. Tom Barton, Yancy Reed and Johnny Two had spread out. They walked forward firing, three determined men with three hot, accurate rifles.

CHAPTER 25

Less than a half mile down the main trail, the column of cavalry troopers heard the sudden outbreak of gunfire coming down from the trail ahead. In seconds, gray gun smoke drifted down on the breeze. At the head of the column, Captain Daniel Turr waved to his trusted scout, Owen Dunes, who had returned to report back on the large number of riders he'd seen.

"My goodness, Owen," said Turr. "You may have prevented us from riding into a trap of sorts, which is easy to do in this bad terrain!"

"Thank you, sir!" said Dunes. "Shall I ride on up and observe further?"

"No," said the captain. "I believe we'll all ride in together." He turned in his saddle.

"Lieutenant Jameson!" he called out. "Prepare the column to ride into the gunfire!" He drew his sword from its sheath and raced forward, the column right behind him, as ahead of them rifle and pistol shots exploded.

In Gunman's Pass, outlaws lay dead and badly wounded in every direction, many of whom Captain Turr and Owen Dunes recognized from previous skirmishes. Gunmen who were still able to ride grabbed their horses and made a run for it as soon as they saw the cavalry galloping into the yard.

"Sergeant Lewis!" shouted Captain Turr. "Take a detail of ten crack riflemen and run those outlaws into the ground!"

"Yes, sir!" the sergeant replied, waving men in around him and taking off after the fleeing outlaws.

With a bullet graze on his upper shoulder and another on his thigh, Will Summers limped over to where the captain set his horse, watching his men round up surrendering gunmen.

"Captain," he said, "I'm U.S. Federal Deputy Will Summers."

"Of course you are, Deputy," said Captain Turr. "I received a wire of introduction only yesterday announcing your recent appointment. Congratulations!" He swept an arm around the bloody scene and said, "Might I ask what all this is about?"

"Sure thing, Captain," said Summers. "But if you don't mind, I want to first make sure my deputies are all right."

"Certainly," said Captain Turr. "I'll be right here when you're ready."

"Thank you, Captain," said Summers. He turned and started toward the cabin, where the Rebel Kid had helped Zetra back into her housecoat and settled her into a large wooden lawn chair.

"Don't bother with us, Will," Javins called out, waving him on. "See to the other three."

Summers limped on, to a spot in the yard where Reed, Johnny Two Red Wolves and Tom Barton were receiving emergency treatment by a field medic.

"How's everybody here?" he asked.

"We're okay," Barton answered for all of them.

"How are you, Will?" Reed asked.

"I'm good." Summers glanced at the graze across his right shoulder.

"I better take a look at that anyway, Deputy," the attendant said.

"Yes, obliged," said Summers. "As soon as you get these three taken care of." He turned and started limping back to the captain. Gray-brown gun smoke still wafted on the air and hung like a flimsy silver veil in the tops of bushes and tall wild grass.

"Will Summers, you law dog sumbitch!" shouted a bitter voice. Axel Coyle stepped

361

out from behind the trunk of a thick white oak. Blood oozed from his lips. "I've got you now!"

Everyone in the yard stopped cold. Men and even horses seemed to freeze in place. A tense silence tried to take over, but Summers refused to allow it.

"Hello, Axel," he said. Even as he spoke, he wondered how well he could use his hand when he had to, and he knew he had to real soon. He wanted to open and close his hand, loosen it some, but he knew that whatever was coming was on its way. He would have to just wait it out, see what it would bring.

"Let's get this done, Summers. No talk, no threats, no pleading —"

Two rounds exploded from Summers' Colt. Both bullets hit Axel squarely in his chest, staggering him backward. Summers tried to cock the Colt again but couldn't get it done. His right arm and hand had gone numb.

Axel, though shot to pieces, managed a bloody dying grin.

He also managed to raise his gun, point it at Summers. He was too close to miss.

"See you in hell, Will Summers —"

The sound of a rifle shot resounded across the yard. A large bullet hole appeared, like some great predatory bird had planted itself in the middle of Axel's forehead. Axel stood for a moment staring with a sad crazy grin, then sank dead on the ground. Summers jerked around and saw Tom Barton levering a fresh round into his rifle. The two gave each other a *job well done* nod. Summers hoped no one saw it take him both hands to get the big Colt back into his holster. As men ran to make sure Axel was dead, the medic waved Summers to him.

"All right, let's see that arm. Don't let that fast draw you just made fool you. Sometimes it will work all right a time or two, but then go out altogether."

"You don't say," said Summers under his breath. He stood in one spot a moment longer, looking around the yard. He saw soldiers leading out the prisoners being held in the underground cells: buckskin-clad Captain Harmon and his three companions, one of whom Summers could swear was Eddie Moon. Behind the Eddie Moon looka-like walked Ekland and Sanget, sharing a sour expression.

"Keep moving, Buffalo Bill," a soldier said to Captain Harmon with a guiding shove.

"He's not talking to you, Summers," said a raspy voice from the bushes. Dolan Coyle stood, Colt cocked in his right hand, a trickle of fresh blood running down his forehead. "Nobody is talking *to you* ever again." With a crazy grin he raised the Colt a few inches.

"Who let you out, Dolan?"

Dolan jiggled the handcuff hanging loose from his left wrist. "Nobody *let* me, Summers, I *let* myself," said Dolan Coyle. "Are you ready to die?"

"No, I'm ready to watch you die," said Summers.

Dolan cackled. Eyes turned toward them. Summers put out a hand, keeping everybody back.

"You always was a game son of a bitch, Summers. I like that about you. I always wondered what we could have done together."

"Dolan, look at me," said Summers. "Are you here to shoot or talk?"

Dolan made his play, his gun unholstered, raised, cocked, ready. Still Summers' shot hit him in the center of his chest. Dolan rocked back on his feet, tried to steady himself, but was failing. His gun pointed to the ground. "Damn it," he wheezed. A strange sad smile came upon his face. "No . . . cherry pie . . . for me," he said. "Come on, hit me. Hit me hard. To end it right —"

Before he finished his request, Summers' Colt bucked in his hand. Dolan landed facedown, his gun slipping loose on the ground.

Summers knew, as he'd known all along, the only good part of a hard gunfight is when it's over. He unbuttoned a button on his shirt and tucked his numb arm inside it. He thought maybe he'd let his arm take time to heal. Hang around his new office in Eagles. Go through some wanted posters, see who was who in the world of crime, maybe —

All right, stop thinking for just one minute, he told himself. He looked around and saw the she-hound walking proudly toward Zetra Wilson and Mortimer Javins, her three pups hurrying along behind her.

Baby Greta waved from the open door.

ABOUT THE AUTHOR

Ralph Cotton has been an ironworker, a second mate on a commercial barge, a teamster, a horse trainer, and a lay minister with the Lutheran Church. He's now a bestselling author who's written more than seventy western novels.

The employees of Thorndike Press hope you have enjoyed this Large Print book. All our Thorndike, Wheeler, and Kennebec Large Print titles are designed for easy reading, and all our books are made to last. Other Thorndike Press Large Print books are available at your library, through selected bookstores, or directly from us.

For information about titles, please call:
    (800) 223-1244

or visit our website at:
    gale.com/thorndike

To share your comments, please write:
    Publisher
    Thorndike Press
    10 Water St., Suite 310
    Waterville, ME 04901